THE
SEVENTH
CHILD

BROOKS STANWOOD

THE LINDEN PRESS / SIMON & SCHUSTER
NEW YORK

*This novel is a work of fiction. Names, characters, places
and incidents are either the product of the author's
imagination or are used fictitiously. Any resemblance to
actual events or locales or persons, living or dead, is
entirely coincidental.*

This is for
E.M.N., W.R.S., S.Z. and A.Z.

RIPTON FALLS, MASS. Pop. 1,271 ('80). Elev. 1,375 ft. 27 mi. Pittsfield, 22 mi. Northampton. Med. Clin. Library. Golf and Tennis Club. Churches: Cong., R.C.

Nestled around one of the finest village greens in New England, this beautifully preserved old town (incorp. 1712) sits comfortably on the far edge of the fabled Berkshire Hills. The falls from which the town takes part of its name are now, alas, a distant memory due to the construction of the Landers Dam in 1951. There are both a nursery school (Evergreen Montessori) and a primary school (to eighth grade) located in town. The regional high school (Mountain Valley) is 5 mi. from town. Winter sports abound and the Cloud Bowl ski area abuts the town. There is never more than a two- or three-minute wait for the lifts (3 T-bars, 1 J-bar, 1 rope). Likewise, summer offers every conceivable sport with the added inclusion of cultural events. (Tanglewood concerts and Jacob's Pillow dance recitals are only a short drive away over idyllic country roads.) The fulcrum of the town's business life is Hilliard and Company, which employs approximately 80% of the town's and the surrounding area's population. Founded in 1807 and still privately owned and controlled, the firm produces quality camping apparel and equipment. The Hilliard family is largely responsible for the restoration of many of the town's buildings and homes. All in all, this town is

a small green gem snuggled in the folds of an historic
and stunning geographical situation.

Air Index: 99
Crime Index: 98
Livability Index: 99

From *Twain's 1981 Guide to Good Living: The 100
Nicest and Safest Towns in America.*
Pub. by Panorama Press, San Francisco. Hardcover
$14.95, Trade Paperback $7.95. ISBN O-449-2433-8

RIPTON FALLS, MASS. Pop. 1,271 ('80). Elev.
1,375 ft. 27 mi. Pittsfield, 22 mi. Northampton. Med.
Clin. Library. Golf and Tennis Club. Churches:
Cong., R.C.

Nestled around one of the finest village greens in
New England, this beautifully preserved old town
(incorp. 1712) sits comfortably on the far edge of the
fabled Berkshire Hills. The falls from which the town
takes part of its name are now, alas, a distant memory
due to the construction of the Landers Dam in 1951.
There are both a nursery school (Evergreen Montessori) and a primary school (to eighth grade) located
in town. The regional high school (Mountain Valley)
is 5 mi. from town. Winter sports abound and the
Cloud Bowl ski area abuts the town. There is never
more than a two- or three-minute wait for the lifts
(3 T-bars, 1 J-bar, 1 rope). Likewise, summer offers
every conceivable sport with the added inclusion of
cultural events. (Tanglewood concerts and Jacob's
Pillow dance recitals are only a short drive away over
idyllic country roads.) The fulcrum of the town's business life is Hilliard and Company, which employs approximately 80% of the town's and the surrounding
area's population. Founded in 1807 and still privately
owned and controlled, the firm produces quality
camping apparel and equipment. The Hilliard family
is largely responsible for the restoration of many of
the town's buildings and homes. All in all, this town is

a small green gem snuggled in the folds of an historic
and stunning geographical situation.

Air Index: 99
Crime Index: 98
Livability Index: 99

From *Twain's 1981 Guide to Good Living: The 100
Nicest and Safest Towns in America.*
Pub. by Panorama Press, San Francisco. Hardcover
$14.95, Trade Paperback $7.95. ISBN O-449-2433-8

　　　　Though the Los Angeles temperature was 78, as just announced on the car radio, the man behind the wheel wore gloves. They were inexpensive white cotton gloves and the man knew that they made him stand out. But he was used to being stared at. Every trip to the outside from the small town in which he had spent his entire life had taught him that people's eyes followed him like pins to a magnet. He was an immense man who moved with a silken grace. His pale eyes were as detached and expressionless as traffic lights. The white gloves added a bizarre touch to his already unusual appearance, suggesting a mime without make-up. He wore them because of a skin condition induced by nervousness. His hands had broken out the week before when he had started the final evaluation. Small red clusters suddenly had embroidered his palms. The next day they had cracked open and a clear fluid seeped from the sores. Then they started to itch. The itching was so fierce at times that the man's nails furrowed raw red lines into the backs of his hands to counter the torment of his palms. He used an ointment, thick as butter, and this helped some. That was the reason for the gloves. If it weren't for them he would leave a glistening trail on everything he touched, like a snail slicking across a sidewalk in summer.

　　But the man wasn't worried about attracting attention. Because he wasn't doing anything wrong. Oh, ultimately he was doing something very wrong. He smiled at the thought of it. But now he was just waiting and watching. Watching for a particular little girl. A girl just turned nine, ordinary in almost every way except that for his purpose she was perfect. Actually, she wasn't completely ordinary, for this young girl had a large birthmark the color of raspberry sherbet on her neck. It was shaped like a leaf.

Before he had rented the car at the airport, he had bought a copy of *The Village Voice*. Not that he wanted to read it. In fact he had never heard of it. He bought it because it was the right size. He could hold it in front of himself as he sat behind the wheel of the car and still see the front of the ballet studio.

The studio was located in Sherman Oaks. A line of jac-arandas stood like sentinels in front. They were just beginning to bloom. Small tight bunches of purple, like grapes, about to explode. The man had never been in Los Angeles before.

The girls started to arrive. A yellow bus pulled up at the front entrance to the studio and girls came running out. Others arrived with their mothers. The man waited.

And then he saw them. The mother was thirty-five and slen-der. She looked much younger, twenty-seven or twenty-eight, but he knew her real age. The man knew a lot about her. Her hair was light and she wore it tied up in a bandanna. She prob-ably had just washed it. She wore tan shorts with a T-shirt that read "HARD-EDGE POWER." She was pretty but didn't smile much. The girl held her hand. She skipped along next to her mother, laughing at the brown-and-white dog tugging on the leash she clutched in her other hand. She still was wearing her school uniform. A pleated forest-green jumper topped by a white blouse. The girl's hair was red. Like a maple tree in au-tumn, the man thought. Like her father, too.

The man looked down at the newspaper. Facing him was a photograph that he had taped onto the paper the night before. It pictured a girl exactly like the girl who was now passing alongside the car. He turned his head in time to see the leaf-shaped birthmark on her neck. Within moments she was in the ballet studio and her mother was walking with the dog back past the car. The woman never noticed the man sitting inside.

The man looked again at the photograph. The match was perfect. He would take a late afternoon flight and be back home the following morning with the good news. The last piece was in place. Everything was ready. He loosened the picture from the Scotch tape that held it and put it in his shirt pocket. He started the car and, carefully observing the speed limit, drove off.

Later, on the San Diego Freeway, heading toward the airport, he tossed the photograph, which he had cut into confetti in his motel room, out the window.

If someone had been able to retrieve and put together all the little pieces, he would hold in his hand a photograph of a painting. It was of a serious-faced young girl with red hair and a birthmark on her neck, wearing a long blue dress in a style that was popular in the late seventeenth century. The girl in the painting had been dead for more than three hundred years.

1

Every time Hal Richardson seriously thought of Los Angeles, he was reminded of a Hopper painting. The streets were always devoid of life and the light from the sun etched the surrounding buildings into bleached skulls in the desert. He once had conveyed this observation to his next-door neighbor, Darryl Phipps. Darryl, a can of Coors trapped like an insect in his enormous fist, blinked his eyes and then said affably, "Hopper? Is he the guy who paints the kids with the big, sad eyes?" Hal had let it drop and proceeded to follow Darryl's earnest discussion about the merits of a Betamax versus a videodisc player.

Hal and his wife, Judy, were not Angeleno converts. Rather, they were part of that small but vocal minority, almost all easterners, who loathed the place. But that wasn't completely true for Hal. He knew he might have liked it a great deal more if other things had worked out better. Things like his job and Judy's two miscarriages. Things guaranteed not to add a rosy hue to the overall picture. So, maybe it wasn't just good old L.A. but . . . events. Boy, were his thoughts on a nice, steep, depressive slalom today.

He had begun his funk about twenty minutes earlier when he had tried to steal out of his office for a longer-than-usual lunch. Thirty-five, bright, attractive, an M.B.A. in Marketing from Wharton, and look what he was doing. And, of course, Foster caught him. Foster, who was as unimaginative as a maze rat and as tight-assed as a Marine recruiter. Foster, his boss.

Hal parked his car around the block from Ma Maison and

walked slowly up the deserted street. It felt to him like a ghost town without the tumbleweed tripping across his path.

He had known what car fixation was when he was a kid. Sixteen or so. It lasted a couple of years. Since then he simply viewed a car as transportation. Which was the kind of idea that if voiced within a hundred miles of L.A. would guarantee the speaker a free pass to the place where they don't allow you to wear a belt.

The first time Hal had met Jeff Fields at Ma Maison for lunch he had made the mistake of pulling up in front to have his car parked. The parking attendant had looked at his '76 Ford, in dire need of a wash and a new front left fender, as if it were leprous. He'd entered the car with the level of disdain that English royalty has taken centuries to attain. Later, Hal had overtipped, which only made it worse.

As Hal walked into the restaurant, he saw Jeff's new gunmetal Ferrari parked near the entrance. He scanned the outer room, which was actually an open enclosure with a bright awning for a roof. He noticed a few very familiar faces—he was sure that one was Gregory Peck—but was not enough of a celebrity spotter to name any others. And then he saw Jeff waving to him.

"I'm going to get you a guide dog. I've been waving like a fool."

As Hal reached out for Jeff's hand, his friend bounced out of his seat and embraced him. Jeff then quickly kissed him on both cheeks. Hal, slightly flustered, tried to reply in kind but only managed a small peck on Jeff's ear. Jeff had become very demonstrative toward his friends since his success at the movie studio, his split from his wife of almost ten years, and his recent course in assertion therapy taught by a bearded analyst who two years before had been living in an ashram in Nepal.

As Jeff's success had mounted at York Pictures, his dress had become more and more casual, and more expensive-looking. Over a night-blue silk shirt he wore a pale-gray V-neck cashmere sweater. Two gold chains as wide as fettucini fell across his neck. Though Jeff had outwardly gone Hollywood with a vengeance, there was still more than a substantial part of him that remained unassuming, direct, generous, and, always to Hal, compassionate. Though his career had rocketed in the past half-dozen years while Hal's had stopped, perhaps even retro-gressed, Jeff still kept in contact, and these lunches, which came every month, became more and more important to Hal.

By the time Hal was midway through his second Bombay martini, he was running through his litany of frustration.

"I had to sneak out of the office to make it here. If Foster actually had seen me getting into my car, he would have hit me again on whether I'd finished the marketing plan. The son of a bitch has no talent, imagination, or guts. Feeds off my work like a jackal. But . . . he's above me. Five years stuck in a dead-end job. I thought for sure something was going to develop from that lead I told you about at N.B.C. They had my résumé for almost six weeks. But once again it was my usual variation on that old tune: 'Nada con Dios.' I'm sorry. I always lay it on you, Jeff."

"Go ahead, babe, I understand. But it's not you. It's the ratings. Things are bad over there. They're just not hiring."

"I wish I could believe you. I'm beginning to think I really am a loser."

"Hey, cut out that crap. You're a great guy. A winner. You've just caught a few bad breaks. A few? Hell, only one. That rotten company you work for is the whole thing. I'd give my right nut to have a wife like Judy. A kid like Annie. The talent that you two have. Look at the good things. You're only a decent job away from happiness."

"If only it were that simple. Like putting your hand on the radio to rid yourself of arthritis. An Oral Roberts you're not."

"Hal, and I'm not going to bullshit you now, I'm only six months at the most from getting the chief operating officer's job. That means that marketing and advertising will come under me. And that means a job for you. You know what we pay. And on top of that you'll love the business. I know there's a lot of bullshit in the game but the action's the thing. And you'll love it."

"Our friendship doesn't depend on your creating a job for me, Jeff."

"I said that not out of friendship but out of smarts. You're good, baby. Real good. Anyone could see it—except you."

They were interrupted by a small man, radiant with energy and devoid of hair, in a perfectly tailored dove-gray suit with a surgically folded handkerchief set just so in his breast pocket.

"My boy," he said to Jeff, "I looked at my desktop this morning and something was very wrong with it. You know what that was? There was no check for ninety thousand dollars from York Pictures made out to me. Make sure that I receive it by messenger before five. See you."

And like magic he was gone, only to materialize at a table across the room.

"You know who that was?" asked Jeff.

"I think so. The agent. We saw him a few weeks ago on TV."

"He told me a beauty yesterday. What does the sadist do to the masochist?"

"I don't know. What?"

"Nothing."

2

"Mr. Foster has been over here half a dozen times looking for you, Mr. Richardson. He's very angry," said Candi Crockett, the young secretary whom he shared with two other guys in the department.

"Don't you mean pissed, Candi?" replied Hal. A surge of recklessness fueled by two martinis and a large brandy flared a wicked smile across his face. "Mr. Foster's natural state is anger. Yes. I'm sure he was pissed. Real pissed. After all, I committed the Gulag banishment sin of exceeding my fucking lunch hour *by* an hour. Let's wake up Lavrenti Beria so he can start decorating my cell in Lubyanka."

Candi stared at him, pupils the size of olives.

"So that's a given, Candi, dear. What else do we have on the griddle this afternoon?"

"I've never seen you this way, Mr. Richardson."

"That's a pity. You've diagnosed my ailment with Mayo Clinic precision. There's a lot of fun been missing from the old carcass. I used to be a guy who laughed a lot. It felt good. It still does."

Candi searched for Hal's call book on her desk.

"There was something else," she said. "Some man called you. Three times. Here it is. Randall Steloff. Executives Unlimited. Said he has to speak to you. Today. He said that he'd meet you wherever you like. He really sounded as if he wanted to see you."

"Sounds that way. Randall Steloff? Executives Limited?"

"Unlimited, Mr. Richardson. Executives Unlimited."

"Well, I don't recognize that either. I bet it's an American Express ruse. My check must have bounced. Damn it."

"He didn't sound like a bill collector."

"The good ones sound like Billy Graham. What the hell. Try him for me, Candi. It's either him or Foster."

"Yes, Mr. Richardson."

Hal leafed through his other phone messages as Candi dialed the number. One from Judy reminding him to deposit two hundred in their checking account to cover a check to Rittenour Motors. Well, there was still time to do that. Another from Dr. Hills's office verifying his appointment tomorrow for his semi-annual cleaning. His teeth involuntarily clenched with the promise of that one. He was convinced those dental technicians trained somewhere near Berchtesgaden.

"I've got Mr. Steloff. On two."

Warily, Hal picked up the phone. "Hello. This is Hal Richardson."

"Hi, Hal. We've never met but I feel that I know you well. Real well."

Hal hated people he didn't know calling him by his first name. But this smarmy bastard didn't sound like a bill collector. No. This number was sure to be either a mutual-fund salesman or a fund raiser from his college.

"I'm a little busy, Mr.—"

"Steloff. Randall Steloff. But everyone who knows me calls me Punch. That comes from—"

"I said that I was busy, Mr. Steloff."

"Oh, I'm sure of that. You have the résumé of a *very* busy man."

"Résumé? What are you talking about?"

"Didn't your secretary tell you? I'm with Executives Unlimited."

Steloff said "Executives Unlimited" as if he were saying "the Vatican."

"It might sound dumb, Mr. Steloff, but I've never heard of Executives Unlimited."

"Then your copy of the last issue of *Fortune* is gathering a little dust, Hal. We were profiled in it. And I must say it was very flattering. We are one of the largest *and* fastest-growing companies specializing in the recruitment of executive manpower in the United States *and* Western Europe."

"You're a headhunter?" asked Hal, the notion that someone might actively pursue him adding to his inebriated state.

"I truly dislike that term, Hal. It reminds me of *Jaws*. I know that it's an accepted part of the argot, but it makes us seem almost . . . cannibalistic."

"I didn't mean it as an insult," Hal said quickly.

"Of course you didn't, Hal. It's just that I'm very sensitive about that unfortunately pejorative expression. But enough of that. I have something very exciting to offer you. Something *exceptional*. Trust me that it will be more than worth your time to meet me for a drink today."

"But how'd you get my résumé?"

"I'll reveal that when we meet. Say five-thirty at the Hotel Bel-Air? You do know where it is?"

"Sure. Off of Sunset. Five-thirty it is. See you then."

"Hold it a second. You've never met me."

"Right."

"I'm fairly tall with light curly hair. And I'm wearing one of my Giorgio Armanis. Khaki green."

"Got it. I'm wearing—"

"Hal, you can't think that I don't know what you look like? Read the article. Executives Unlimited's motto is 'Total Preparation Is Just the Beginning.' *Ciao*."

Hal was still staring at the phone when Candi walked into his cubicle.

"Mr. Foster just called again. I had to tell him you were on the phone."

"What time is it, Candi?"

"It's almost three-thirty, Mr. Richardson."

"And the bank's open until four, isn't it?"

"I'm pretty sure it is. Yes, I'm positive it is."

"Well, then, I just have time to kick a few dollars into our account so that Karl Malden doesn't come around to steal my wallet and ruin my vacation."

"Karl Malden? Isn't he the actor?"

"Tomorrow, Candi. Today has been an extremely pleasant and unusual day. I hope it carries over to tomorrow."

"But Mr. Foster wants to see you immediately."

"That'll have to wait, I'm afraid, Candi. Why don't you tell him I had to rush off for a . . . that's it! A cannibalistic appointment. Until tomorrow."

3

Judy suddenly realized that she had been reading and rereading the recipe without comprehending a word. Damn it, Hal, where are you? "Please don't let him be hurt," she said out loud, turning to make sure that neither Annie nor Mimi were there. Then she remembered. Annie was upstairs having her bath. Judy had told Annie that Daddy had to work late. Mimi, who had been with the Richardsons since arriving from Haiti almost seven years ago and who was more than a housekeeper and more than a friend and—though it was a particularly cloying cliché—like a member of the family, knew that Judy was worried. When Hal was an hour late Judy had called his office and found out that he had left early. Early! By eight she had canvassed all their friends. He wasn't at their doctor's, dentist's, or accountant's either. A.A.A. had no accident report on the car. She swore to herself that she would call the police if Hal wasn't home by nine. It was now nine-twenty.

And then there was a banging at the kitchen door. The one that led to the breezeway. It wasn't banging. It was kicking. Someone was kicking the bottom of the door. Judy opened the door to see a box. A huge box.

"Guide me to the table," said a strangulated voice from behind the box.

It was Hal!

"Hal, are you all right? Where've you been? I've been worried sill—"

"Later. Now, table. Guide me—"

"Of course. This way."

The table legs creaked as Hal set the box down on it.

"That was stupid. I should have asked Darryl to help. One thing he's not short on is muscles. I barely made it."

"What is this? Hal—"

"Back in a minute."

Moments later Hal came through the door with a slightly smaller box that he gingerly placed on the floor.

"Darling, what's going on?"

"Just one more trip. Back in a sec."

He returned with two gaily wrapped narrow boxes in one hand and a bottle of champagne, held by the neck as if in search of a ship to christen, in the other.

"Into the fridge with this, Jude," he said, shoving the bottle at Judy. "Took me three stores until I could find a decent bottle of bubbly. And all they had was domestic. Society is being taken over by the Ripple drinkers of the world. Now, honey, come over here with me and let's take a looky here at this big mother on the table."

Hal slipped his arm around Judy's waist and steered her to the table. He leaned toward her and lightly kissed her ear.

"How do you always smell so good? Maybe we should have the champagne in bed. But first things first. The box."

"You've been drinking, Hal."

"Not in several hours but the night is still young. Boy, does this kid have a way with dialogue."

Judy laughed giddily, relief flooding through her. Hal was almost manic with joy. But why?

"We'll need pliers and probably—no, wait. No need to uncrate this baby since it'll be moving soon too."

"Hal, slow down. What is all this about?"

"Read the box. I mean read the stencil on the side here."

He moved Judy around to the other side of the box and proudly pointed to some black printing.

"Well? Read it."

"Oh, Hal. You're crazy."

"My mental state is far from that. Please read it."

"Pompeii Super-Matic Espresso! Hal, you *are* mad! This machine has got to cost five hundred dollars."

"Twice that. It's the top of the line. With tax it's almost eleven hundred."

"Hal, I love you. I really do. But you know we can't afford this."

"You're right, Jude. Mr. Harold Arthur Richardson, Associate Manager for Marketing of C.T.R. Industries, at thirty-five thousand and five hundred dollars, could not possibly afford to indulge his wife's passion for strong coffee. Or a lot of other things either. But, and it's a very big but, old Hal Richardson, the new Executive Veep and Director of Marketing for Hilliard and Company, of Ripton Falls, Mass-a-chu-setts, can very well afford it. After all, that Mr. Richardson makes seventy—let me repeat that—seventy thousand dollars a year. And let's not forget a raise to seventy-eight the next year. The following year is even better, but why look that far ahead."

Before Judy could speak, Hal grabbed her tight and kissed her, then pulled back from her and laughed. A laugh so full of happiness it bordered on dementia.

"Don't you see, Jude? All the crap is behind us. It almost makes that disgusting phrase 'Today is the first day of the rest of your life' seem true. It happened today."

"Hal, *what* happened?"

"It's just as I said."

"Said what?"

"That I'm the new Executive Vice-President and Director of Marketing at Hilliard and Company, the Rolls-Royce of the camping and outdoor equipment business, at seventy thousand dollars a year. If the number seems too large for you, just think of ten thousand seven-dollar bills. No, that's not right. I mean seven thousand ten-dollar bills. Yes, that's it."

"You've got a new job!"

"You bet I do! I signed a letter of intent, and tomorrow by messenger I receive a contract to look over *and* two first-class tickets from LAX to Hartford and back. The headhunter, and it'll take another drink or two before I'll be able to do him justice, said we could trade them in for cheap night-coach seats and pocket the difference. *Voilà!* That produced some of the extra bucks for your espresso machine plus the dollhouse over there in the other box that Annie has been willing to sell her soul for for the past year plus two knockout Saint Laurent scarves for Mimi. There's even a little extra left for Daddy, who has his eye on a custom-made fly rod, which he'll be able to use soon. Real soon."

"Pinch me."

"I'm going to do a lot more than that, but let's distribute the rest of the booty. Is Annie still up?"

"Are you kidding? Since when does she go to bed without a kiss from Daddy? Besides, she's been waiting all day to give you something. A clay mouse she made. She asked me if I thought it would cheer you up. Her words. I swear. But, Hal, even with the contract on its way and all, don't you have to pass some sort of interview with the people who run the business? This headhunter man is just a scout, isn't he? I never thought they hired. Only recommended."

"Where'd you study painting? Harvard Business School? You're right, of course. But this thing is different. The headhunter came across my résumé when I applied for a job at one of Hilliard's suppliers. He knew the Hilliards were looking for a guy with my qualifications so he passed it on. Apparently they're putting together a whole new executive team. This Hilliard family—I forgot to tell you it's a family-owned and -run business for, if you believe it, more than one hundred and fifty years, only now it seems they want to go public—well, they studied this lad like the Sacred College of cardinals do before they decide to burn the dry straw. They've been discreetly, but with a jeweler's loupe, checking me out all over the place. They've even cut through Foster's shit. God, it felt great getting credit for some of that good stuff of mine. It was pretty lonesome, wasn't it, all those years? Just you and me knowing the real score. The kind of job they've done on me, I was waiting for this guy Steloff to ask me about the copy of *Penthouse* under my side of the bed. It was almost unnerving. But the offer's been made. It's up to me to accept it or not. And I just know it's going to work. Steloff even showed me pictures of the town. Norman Rockwell would have gone weepy-eyed. And it's only about twenty miles from Smith College and three other schools, all with big art departments. This guy even mentioned that piece about you in *Art in America*. I'm telling you, the only person, *thing,* that's wanted me more than they do is you."

"They knew about the magazine story? Oh, Hal, that's fantastic. I can't believe it. Any of it."

"Believe it. We're going back. Snow. Real Christmas trees. Changes of season. Eye contact. The only time people look at each other in L.A. is at red lights."

"Hey, we might even get there in time for the bulbs. Daffodils and tulips. They should be coming up soon."

"And no smog. Or mellow gold-chained people in brown Mercedes seeking to reach their ultimate human potential."

"Jeff wears gold chains."

"He's different. Exceptions don't make the rule. Let's go up and surprise Annie and Mimi."

"Mimi's going to flip. She'll be back near her aunt and cousins in New York."

"Goodbye land of the laid back. Eastward ho! Come on, I want to tackle this dollhouse."

Hal hefted the box containing the dollhouse and headed toward the stairs.

"Don't forget those two boxes for Mimi," he added.

"Got them. And the champagne. For later."

"I love you," said Hal, over his shoulder. "Now get ready to read out the directions slowly. There's a very good chance I could reduce this thing to kindling."

4

Judy leaned closer to the mirror to get a better angle on her eyes, at the same time glancing quickly at her watch. The shower next door was still roaring, but that didn't mean much because Hal was fireman fast. Just then, as if to underline her thought, he throttled the shower off. She'd better hustle. They were due at the Hilliards' at six o'clock for their first social outing in town. Cocktails and dinner for the new families that had joined the company.

In the sudden swell of silence from the bathroom, other sounds filtered up to Judy. The rhythmic creaking of Annie in the porch hammock. The low clatter of Mimi putting the final touches on Annie's dinner. It amazed Judy. May in Massachusetts! And barely a month ago she didn't even know a town by the name of Ripton Falls existed. They'd been here only five days and their worldly goods were still stacked around them in cartons, but already this house on Quarry Road had taken on a life of its own. It felt like home.

She'd never seen four weeks speed by so quickly, and if she'd really stopped and considered beforehand everything that she would have to do in that short time, a staggering list of items, all with red-flag priority, terminal inertia would have set in and they would still be in L.A. Instead they'd flown across the country twice, located and financed the purchase of the kind of house that until now Judy had only dreamed of owning, arranged for their furniture and other belongings to be shipped east, and enrolled Annie in a school obviously so good that if it had been in a big city, kids would have been jockeying in line for it from the time they were three. And they'd cut their California ties with a minimum of fuss.

Hal's job had been a pleasure to quit. He gave Candi a roller-disco outfit and his boss five minutes of time. He'd positively beamed that night after telling Foster to stuff it. He told Judy he had bent one of Foster's pipe cleaners into a sitting dog as he gave notice, and left the stick figure on his blotter as a parting gift.

Extricating herself from her own job had been a little harder for Judy. But not by much. She spent two days a week at each of two community colleges in the area teaching painting in their adult education programs. Fridays she reserved for herself, as if she could accomplish much in one measly day a week. God, it had been frustrating. Almost ten years ago, *Art in America* had called her work "more than an impressive beginning." Several years after that she'd been represented by four canvases in a group show at the Elsie Stern Gallery in SoHo. "New Colorists for the Seventies." The gallery was now defunct, and her own work had begun to seem precariously close to that too. She was convinced she hadn't had a fresh idea in years. She didn't begrudge Annie the time she gave her. She didn't want to be an absentee mother and on weekends insisted on taking over from Mimi. Nor did she blame Hal. It was simply a fact of their life in L.A. that in order to stay solvent they had to be a two-income family. Everyone knew that ninety-nine percent of serious painters didn't make money. Not that teachers were known for bringing home big bucks either, but they were issued a paycheck regularly, and hers made the difference. She'd had qualms about leaving a couple of her better students in the lurch—old Mr. McCarry, for one, showed a decided gift for portraiture—but these hesitations were blasted away immediately by the Ripton Falls real-estate man. When Judy'd seen the houses available there, houses they could actually afford without selling their corneas, nothing and no one could have prevented her from making the move.

The only tough part was making a choice. Every house they saw, not just the one they bought but the five they turned down, was a steal. It had been a shock to discover that in Ripton Falls it was still possible to buy a really terrific house for under a hundred thousand dollars. In L.A. that might have fetched you a garage.

The house they settled on was a Cape. It was one hundred and seventy-five years old. It had wide floorboards, paneling in every room downstairs, and robust hand-hewn beams that cleaved the living-room ceiling. The original features were all there, carefully preserved, and so was all the comfort they could ask for, from the airy dressing room, where Judy now stood, to Annie's sunny bedroom, its walls covered in a gay flowered wallpaper, exactly what Judy would have selected herself if someone else hadn't beaten her to it, to the tastefully up-to-date kitchen wing. There was even an extra room beyond Annie's that could be turned into a nursery if she and Hal got lucky.

The other house they'd debated about right down to the last moment was a handsome Colonial that faced the Village Green, but the Cape won them over by its setting—two acres of cleared land, a small stream, a picturesque overgrown apple orchard, the protective crooked arm of a state forest on two sides, not a neighbor within sight—and by its unique charm. By what Judy could only describe as the "sweetness" of the lines of the house. There was something about the way the bottom of the gently sloped roof almost grazed the top of the windows in the front, like an oversized cap on a small boy, that endeared the house to her.

Now, in the mirror, Judy caught Hal's reflection. "How're you doing?" he asked.

"Give me five more minutes," said Judy, watching him retreat into the bedroom to dress. God, but she adored him, and thank heaven for the Hilliards. Who would have guessed it? From industrial valves to camping gear in less than thirty days. Hal was a real marketing innovator who could sell anything. Now, after all those dreary, defeating years in L.A., it looked as if, at last, he was also going to have some fun for a change. Moccasins, tents, fishing reels, rucksacks. Hilliard's product line resembled the L. L. Bean catalog. And no wonder. Bean was the leader in the outdoor leisure field, but Hilliard's, with its new talent, was revving up to overtake them.

In the couple of late-night instances when Judy had allowed herself to question their good fortune, to wonder if it would all come crashing down around them, she had only to remind herself of Hal's new contract to stifle her emotional queasiness. Even Jeff said it was a damn good one. Hal had asked Jeff to look at it for him, and Judy well remembered the evening he had dropped by to talk it over.

Later, when they had sat down for a drink, Jeff raised his glass to Hal: "Here's to a new member of the fifty percent club."

"Fifty percent?" Judy asked.

"Right. Fifty percent taxes."

They had laughed and drunk to that, and then Jeff had continued. "There's only one thing unusual about the contract, which I'd object to in principle, though the practical application is negligible. The contract is for three years. That's more than pretty good. But there's a special codicil that says you'll be held liable for half the salary paid and moving costs if you leave before the first six months are up. But," Jeff added, shrugging, "there's no problem sticking out that little time at almost anything. I suspect Hilliard's is just an old-fashioned firm that writes very few contracts."

Hal stepped into the dressing room, bringing Judy back to the present. "Let's go," he said.

He looked handsome in a heather-green tweed jacket that

was just right with his fire-red hair, and Judy wondered if she'd
be warm enough in what she was wearing. In L.A. she had
dressed in T-shirts and cutoffs, as if perpetually on the ready
for a game of volleyball. When she wanted to be dressy, she
traded up from shorts to pants and added one-of-a-kind tops
and accessories. Tonight she wore mauve pants with a lighter-
toned sweater—short sleeves, alas, everything she owned was
summery—and on one shoulder she had clipped a dramatic
pale-gray sculptured pin that Hal had bought for her years ago.
Cold or not, she knew she looked good.

She took one last swipe with her hairbrush at her thick dark-
blond hair, then turned around and smiled expectantly at Hal.

"Are you trying to tell me," said Hal with a look of mock
amazement, "that you are actually ready to leave? Then hold it,
ladies and gentlemen, while I consult my watch. That means,
yes, we are only eleven minutes and twenty-four seconds late.
Hey, that's a record for you."

"Cut it out, love. Don't forget, we're country people now,
and country people don't rush."

"I'll say," said Hal, putting his arms around her and kissing
her lightly. "Thank God we don't live in the Outback. I'd never
ever get you out the front door."

•   •

The station wagon did a little shimmy in what their nearest
neighbors on Quarry Road swore was the last mud of the year.
Then with a tubercular cough from somewhere in its rear end,
it slid onto the paved road. The center of Ripton Falls was only
five minutes away. For Judy, this was the beauty of their new
house. It was private, but not too private. If she ran out of
milk, she could easily dash into town for another quart. And if
she chose to sunbathe in the nude on the patio behind the
house, who would be the wiser?

Already coming up on their right was the turnoff for the
business district, and Hilliard and Company headquarters, Annie's school, the Catholic church, and a small arcade of shops
and doctors' offices. Straight ahead was the soul of the town.
The Village Green.

The Green had mesmerized Judy on their first trip here, and
each time she drove by it, it still knocked her out. It was long

and narrow, with a tear-shaped pond at one end, daffodils massed around it, and several ancient maples at the other end. But what surrounded it counted for just as much. Lining one long side were half a dozen handsome, white, black-shuttered Colonials. The most modest of these was the one they'd rejected in favor of the Cape. All were in mint condition, quite evidently the pride of their owners, freshly painted and impeccably landscaped. The last and largest, at the far corner, belonged to the Hilliards. Facing the Colonials across the band of grass were two nearly identical shingled saltboxes, built in the late 1600s by twin brothers and now the premier attraction of the Ripton Falls Historical Society. They and several neighboring houses had been meticulously restored by the Hilliards, who also, she understood, maintained the Green itself in a state of bucolic perfection year around, snow cleared off the ice in the winter, gardens planted and weeded in the summer. Next to the saltboxes came a combined general store and post office, the one commercial establishment on the Green, there only because it always had been, then an imposing colonnaded town hall and several clapboard houses, some with accordionlike extensions to the back, others with faded red barns. It was picture postcard pretty, with one exception, and Judy was looking straight at it.

"You know," said Judy, gesturing at the church, "I want to stop by later this week and introduce myself to the minister. To see about Sunday School for Annie."

"Are you sure there *is* a minister? The place seems a little seedy to me."

"Of course there's a minister," said Judy, a little too quickly. "And I don't think 'seedy' is the right word to use for a church."

"Would you buy run-down?"

Judy tried to laugh. Why was she so defensive? Hal had said nothing against her launching Annie into yet another Sunday School, though she knew he didn't see the sense of it.

From a distance, the church was every bit the New England classic, all white, with a tall, graceful spire and forest-green shutters. It seemed to complement its more worldly neighbors in just the right way. Up close, though, it was another matter. The paint was peeling off in languid curls, the sill beneath the double front doors was pocked with rot, and, as unlikely as it seemed, it appeared that a hole in one of the side windows had been patched over with cardboard no less. The grass around the building was more hay than lawn, and all together the church had such a desolate air about it that Judy might have written it off as abandoned if she hadn't noticed earlier in the week a beat-up orange Volkswagen in the driveway to the parsonage next door. The car wasn't there now.

"I don't get it," said Judy, as much to herself as to Hal.

"Get what?" said Hal, parking in front of the Hilliards'.

"The church. Why it's such a . . . mess."

"It's not your worry, Jude. What *is* important is meeting the people I work with. You're going to like them. So up and at it, baby."

As she slid out of the car, Judy kept her eye on the church on the other side of the Green. Hal was right of course. It wasn't her concern, but the church was so out of keeping with the rest of the Green, so incongruous, that it was hard to ignore.

Didn't they care? The congregation? The townspeople? The Hilliards? Judy felt faintly uneasy even considering the question. Then, shaking her head to clear the church from her mind, she followed Hal up the path to the Hilliards' imposing entrance.

5

The front door opened and there stood a tall, striking-looking woman with inquiring fog-gray eyes and a curtain of hair falling below her shoulders. She assessed her guests for half a beat, and then shaped her face into a welcoming smile.

This had to be Laurie Hilliard. Quite a surprise. During dinner the night before, Hal had described to Judy the people she would be meeting. He was on such a high about Ripton Falls that he couldn't stop talking about his new colleagues, and Judy was sure she knew exactly what each of them looked like.

Laurie, the old man's granddaughter, had just disproved that notion. When she heard that Laurie was in charge of the plant and a work force of more than five hundred, Judy had pictured her as a female Henry Ford, without the three-button suit, of course, but plain, stolid, no-nonsense. All business she might be, but about the rest, Judy couldn't have been more mistaken. The real Laurie was maybe thirty-four or thirty-five and very attractive—especially her eyes, which were large and deep. An unusual mole, shaped exactly like a sea gull's wings, floated just above her left brow. In the role of hostess, she had about her an air of assurance, instantly communicated, though not altogether likable.

As they murmured hellos, Laurie stepped to one side to let them in. She leaned close to the Richardsons as if to share a secret. "Everybody hates to be the first to arrive at a party," she said. "But don't worry. You've been preceded. Now let me take your coats."

Judy slipped off her jacket, shivering slightly in spite of herself, and looked around. They were in a large, pleasingly proportioned entrance hall dominated by a splendid sweep of staircase. Opposite it, through a wide, arched doorway, was the living room. From where she stood, she could see two high windows curtained in elegant pale-green silk reaching to the floor, a handsome Queen Anne highboy between them. Above it an oil portrait of what was probably an early Hilliard ancestor peered toward them.

"What a beautiful place," said Judy.

"Thank you. We think so too," said Laurie. "I grew up here. So did my father. And my grandfather." She paused and pointed to a crystal decanter and glasses on a silver tray. "Won't you have some sherry? Grandfather is a teetotaler, I'm afraid. It took quite a bit of convincing for him to allow even this."

Dutifully they accepted a glass. Not exactly liquid fire, thought Judy, but it might warm her up a bit.

"Come meet the others," said Laurie, herding them ahead of her into the living room.

The others turned out to be a chunky young couple standing uncertainly in the middle of the room. The woman, who barely topped five feet, if that, was sausaged into a rose-colored knit pants suit. Her husband had black hair and a short, burly build rapidly giving way to paunch beneath his jacket. They looked delighted to see the Richardsons.

"Hal and Aldo, you know each other, of course. Judy Richardson, Teresa Lucci . . ." said Laurie. As they started to shake hands, the doorbell rang, and Laurie excused herself.

"It's Terry. Not Teresa. Except for my mom. Right, honey?"

"Yeah, and that last name is Lucci. It rhymes with Gucci, but all I've ever been able to afford is Thom McAn."

"Oh, Aldo, you're so silly."

"Most people don't know how to pronounce it. They can't figure out what kind of name it is," Aldo said, shrugging.

"It's Italian," said Terry, beaming an adoring look at Aldo, the kind that made it clear that she was as thrilled now as she had been on their wedding day that he let her use the name too. She had large, open blue eyes under heavy lids and teeth like Chiclets, and when she smiled she got every part of her face into the act.

Hal raised his glass, and Aldo followed suit.

"What is this sweet stuff anyway?" Aldo asked, wrinkling his nose. "Thunderbird?"

"I'd begun to think nobody else was coming," Terry was saying to Judy. "We were afraid of being late, so we got here exactly at six. When I saw nobody else was here, I says to myself, 'Terry, you made a boo-boo.' "

"The first thing you should know is, never be on time," said Judy laughingly. "Anywhere. But especially not to a party." Then she saw Laurie approaching with two more people in tow.

The man was powerfully built, with strong, regular features, olive skin, and hair as dense and black as a paintbrush. He held his delicate blond wife by the elbow. This must be Emily and T. C. Gaines.

After Laurie had completed the introductions, Hal shook his head in disbelief and announced to the group at large, "I still can't get over having The Chief here."

"What's 'The Chief'?" asked Terry blankly.

"Oh, no," groaned Hal exaggeratedly. "You're as bad as Judy."

"I played college football for Montana, and The Chief is what they called me," said T.C. helpfully.

"This man is being far too modest," interrupted Hal. "First, ladies, he was called The Chief because he was and is a full-blooded . . ."

"You remember too much sports hyperbole, Hal. My mother is only half Penobscot."

"And secondly," said Hal, "he didn't just play football. He was a star. All-American for three years straight at the University of Montana. One of the best damn running backs of the last ten years. As Howard Cosell was fond of saying, 'A man to watch.' A real standout, who would have had a hell of a career if it weren't for that . . . what was it? A knee injury?"

"That was it," said T.C. to Judy and Terry. "One season with the Oilers. And finito. Most people don't remember The Chief business. The sports pages are the first to go under the Kitty Litter."

"Not in our household they aren't," said Hal. "At least when I'm on cleanup crew. You may have guessed that Judy leaves something to be desired as a football fan."

Even though Hal was teasing, Judy felt herself flushing. "What Hal forgets to say is that it's the same for baseball, hockey, basketball—"

"I know, I know," said T.C., who appeared to be genuinely enjoying the attention. "Emily still celebrates when the Super Bowl is over. She believes that ignorance of sports is more than a virtue."

Judy smiled at Emily Gaines, and as she did she saw that more people had joined the group. Laurie stood next to the newcomers, silencing the others with her steady gaze. Quickly she introduced them.

Sy and Lisa Goldin. He was tall and slim, with pale curly hair, smoked aviator glasses, and a trimly cut sports jacket. His wife wore glasses too, monogrammed in the lower left-hand corner with the initials "L.G." rendered in a bold script.

Peggy and Reid Prescott were older. Their hair was flecked with gray, and they had open, amiable expressions that suggested they agreed on just about everything.

How was she going to sort out all these names and faces, Judy wondered. She glanced at Hal, who was tracking Sy Goldin's progress counterclockwise around the group. He leaned over to Judy and said into her ear, "Our treasurer. The money man, remember? He's thinking of writing a novel. Since I'm supposed to be the creative guy in the company, he wants me to 'advise and critique.' His words. Honest."

Sy had stopped to chat with Aldo and Terry and, her eye on them, Judy whispered, "What does Aldo do? I've forgotten."

"He's our William Casey."

"Who?"

"The head of the C.I.A. But I'm just kidding. Aldo heads up plant security, maintenance, that sort of thing."

They were standing on the edge of the circle closest to the front hall, and now they heard Laurie greeting another guest.

"Must be Claire Simmons," said Hal. "The art director. Divorced."

Laurie stepped into the room with a tense, angular woman whose pale-blond hair was worn in a chic short cut and whose silk blouse and skirt had the understated élan of Calvin Klein. She was still apologizing for being late.

"Erin just wouldn't let me go. I finally had to promise her she could watch *Little House on the Prairie,* though I hate to let her look at TV on a school night."

When Judy and Claire began comparing notes on local shopping, Hal corralled T.C. to quiz him on the recent N.F.L. draft. Reid Prescott, manning the sherry decanter for Laurie, circulated through the group refilling empty glasses. "This sherry stuff isn't bad," said Aldo Lucci to no one in particular, downing his glass and immediately trailing after Reid for another. Emily Gaines and the Goldins launched into what promised to be a serious discussion of historic houses in the area, while Peggy Prescott drifted around the edges of the room studying the paintings.

Then Laurie was in their midst again holding out a plate of Ritz crackers, each topped with Kraft American cheese. Gingerly, Judy reached for one. "Lucky for you they don't pay your salary in hors d'oeuvres," she said to Hal when Laurie was out of earshot.

"Here's Grandfather," announced Laurie all at once from the other side of the room.

Suddenly quiet, the group crowded together near the doorway to the front hall. There, leaning on his son Elliott's arm as he slowly came down the staircase, was Cameron Hilliard.

"This is a first for all of us," whispered Hal. "None of us has met him yet. They say he's been sick."

Judy had been told he was eighty-seven, and the deep lines that filigreed his face testified to it. And he was ghostly pale. But if someone had insisted that Judy give an immediate first impression of Cameron Hilliard, she would have said, "He's got it and he doesn't mean to let it go." Beneath his three-piece pin-stripe suit it was obvious that he was reed-thin, but he held himself straight as a general, and the carriage of his head, topped with turf-thick white hair, was just as commanding. Judy knew before he spoke that his voice would be strong and resonant, and it was.

"Ladies and gentlemen," he said, pausing in his descent, "please forgive me for being late to my own party, but this is my first day up. You may have heard that I fell and broke my hip last month. My problem, you see, is not old age, but *break-age.*" He barked a short laugh of appreciation at his small joke, then slapped his legs. "These pins are still a bit shaky, but ready for action. Now, Elliott," he said to the tall, faded man waiting a few steps below him, "let's get down off these stairs so I can say how-do-you-do to all these good people."

As Cameron Hilliard began greeting his guests, Judy watched him with fascination. Though he carried a cane with a carved handle looped over one wrist, he did not once touch it to the ground. Instead pure energy and charm seemed to propel him forward. When finally it was Judy's turn to be introduced, she was not disappointed. Of course he had been briefed on his guests, on Judy no less than the others, but he went well beyond simply asking the right questions. For the few minutes they spoke, about Annie, the house, even about Judy's painting, Judy felt the full force of his personality. He seemed to be totally engaged by her, every ounce of him focused on her alone, and, in a split second of insight, Judy understood the power inherent in such a concentration of will. Clearly Elliott Hilliard did not possess this gift of his father's, and just as clearly, Laurie did. As if to confirm the link, Judy noticed that Cameron Hilliard shared at least one unique characteristic with his strong-willed granddaughter. On the edge of his right temple, almost hidden by his hair, was the same curious gull-shaped mole, smaller and subtler, which was why she had not spotted it from across the room, but nonetheless pronounced, a badge of distinction, or perhaps more accurately, a badge of difference. It was almost as if Cameron Hilliard's genes had skipped over poor Elliott altogether, only to be picked up again, and triumphantly, by the next generation. By Laurie.

Cameron Hilliard completed his rounds, marking the moment with a long, slow drink from a tumbler of ice water handed him by Elliott, then positioned himself in front of the fireplace. He gave an abrupt shake of his head to Elliott—Judy could see by following his line of vision that he was declining to sit in the tall-backed chair by Elliott's side—listened for a moment to a whispered word from Laurie, and cleared his throat. The room grew silent.

"Welcome, my new friends, to Ripton Falls," he began. "Laurie has just advised me that dinner is ready—you are going to love our cook's poached salmon and new peas—but if you'll bear with me I want to first share with you a few thoughts on the occasion of our gathering here this evening. We are an old firm. Also an old family, though not by local standards. There've been Hilliards in this country since the mid-sixteen hundreds, but we settled in Pennsylvania, and that doesn't count in this part of the world. We moved to Ripton Falls early in the eighteen hundreds. The company was founded in 1807 by another family, and a dozen years later, in 1819, the first Hilliard took over. One hundred and sixty-three years ago. And during those years we have grown and prospered.

"Of course, like all business entities, there were valleys interspersed between the peaks. And it was one particular valley that fortuitously positioned this company on its current path. For, you see, Hilliard's was not always in the camping supply business. For much of our early history we made shades and awnings. For windows, porches, and horse-drawn buggies. It was a nice, though rather small, business. Of course, as you would imagine, all those awnings were made from canvas. We would buy large amounts of canvas and store it behind the factory where our garage is located now. Well, one day a particularly uncoordinated apprentice kicked over a pail of paraffin that he was supposed to deliver to our house where it was to be used in canning. The paraffin happened to fall onto an enormous bolt of canvas. Ruining it. Or at least that's what my great-grandfather thought. Only later, after the canvas had been relegated to the loading dock, did he notice that rainwater, instead of seeping through, beaded harmlessly on top. After that it was only a matter of time before he got the formula right to waterproof canvas. This led to a handsome contract from the Army Department for tents, and Hilliard and Company was launched into the camping supply business."

Cameron Hilliard broke off to take a sip from the glass of water on the table beside him.

"And from the first two-man tent onward, it has been a success story. We now offer a complete line of outdoor equipment, from A to Z, arrows to zippered ponchos, and each and every item is the best of its kind. We are the Tiffany of the camping world. And, I might add, at great profit to all of us. We have in recent years tried diversifying. Why we even invested in a business located in that modern Gomorrah—New York," he said, laughing. "All have been failures, or modest successes at best. We've learned to stick to what we know best. We could go on like this for years to come, of that I am certain, but . . . but I feel a longing in my heart, call it the whim of an old man, if you will . . ." Cameron Hilliard smiled in a way that defied anyone to consider it as such. "A longing to broaden our base. I don't give a fig if the check-out girl at the A and P recognizes this old face of mine, but I do want her, and her beau, to recognize the Hilliard name. Because it's the label on their hiking boots, on their backpacks, on their cross-country skis. Or, I should say, will become so. With your help. For this is where you come into the picture.

"We are now in the sixth generation of family ownership, of Hilliards at the helm, and we are proud of it. Here in this house there are three generations of Hilliards: myself; my son, Elliott; my granddaughter, Laurie; and my grandson, Howard, who I see has not yet graced us with his presence."

"Don't you remember, Grandfather," interrupted Laurie quickly, "he had to drive into Northampton to pick up that prescription?"

"Ah, yes," said Cameron. Then without further comment, he continued. "Our family thrives. It has in the past. It will in the future. But to move forward in the ways we envision we realized that we needed something extra. We needed to add to our management family. We needed to enrich our family core with new talent, with new blood. And, my friends, I am happy to say that we believe we have found that in you. With your help, we will expand our business tenfold. We will take the company public *and* retain control of it. We will make Hilliard a household name. My friends, let us toast to our future. Together."

Cameron Hilliard held up his water glass, conveniently refilled, noted Judy, and paused, waiting for the others to join him. "Hear, hear," said Sy Goldin. Cameron Hilliard smiled benevolently and raised his glass to his lips. And then he suddenly stopped.

"Howard, quick, get yourself a libation and join us," he said to the tall, massively built man who had just closed the front door behind him.

"Yes, Grandfather. Of course," Howard Hilliard said in a voice so small and timid that one might think a child hidden somewhere in the room was using this huge man as a ventriloquist's dummy.

Howard moved across the room to where his sister held out a glass of sherry for him. All eyes followed him. Not because of his size, even though T. C. Gaines looked almost adolescent next to him. And not even for his extraordinarily pale eyes. Eyes that seemed as unseeing as the dead stare of a fish washed up on a beach. What held everyone's attention were the white cotton gloves that covered his hands. The sherry glass against the white hand that held it appeared to be made for a doll. Howard clinked his glass against Laurie's and then turned to his right where Judy stood.

"Good to have you with us, Mrs. Richardson," he said as he touched his glass to hers.

"We're glad to be here, Mr. Hilliard."

She tried as hard as she could but her eyes would not hold on his.

"Yes, I know. These gloves are odd-looking, aren't they? You see, I have this nervous condition. It comes on suddenly. I get a terrible rash that itches so much it's almost maddening. I have a salve that helps some. That's why I have to wear these gloves. I guess the strain of helping plan the move for all of you caused my hands to flare up. But now that you're here and settled in I'm sure it'll go away."

Howard smiled shyly and walked over to his grandfather.

6

"Richardson! Get your head out of those figures. I'm supposed to be the C.P.A. around here, not you."

Hal looked up from the morass of the advertising budget he was preparing, penciled numbers dribbling across half a dozen pages as if poured from a height, to see Sy Goldin in the doorway of his office. Sy was dressed with care and thoroughly monogrammed. The C on the tie, the YSL on the belt, and the BB blazer had the effect of a fashion alphabet soup. Hal could still measure in days the time since he had met Sy, but he felt he had known him forever. He liked him immensely.

"Seriously, don't sweat it," continued Sy, dropping into the armchair across from Hal's desk. "After I get through with the budget, it'll positively sing for the Hilliards."

"You mean for Cameron Hilliard. You remember that marketing meeting last week? Though he wasn't there, I got the feeling he's always there."

"I see you've read *Power*. And I agree. Whatever that is, he has it in spades."

"Have you seen him since the little welcoming party two weeks ago?"

"Only the family has. Hilliard's really is a family affair, you know, and Cameron Hilliard is both C.E.O. and El Caudillo. It's his family store all the way. And let me tell you, he knows what he's doing. Our numbers for last month were terrific. Xerox would envy our return on capital. This is one profitable buggy-whip business. Actually, I think Cameron does want to move the company into the twentieth century—if only he can hurdle the nineteenth. Son Elliott told me this morning that his father was anxiously awaiting the budget, which I've been assured I will personally deliver to him."

"I doubt he'll do cartwheels when you put it in front of him. Why should he? Hilliard products are like Hershey bars. They do great without advertising. Why should he change things?"

Sy, who was busy buffing the buckles of his loafers, looked up at Hal and winked.

"Shh. Don't let anybody hear you say that. This company *is* beautifully run. Strictly seventeen jewels. But we're doing our bit too. We're the window dressing that will help like crazy when they finally make their move to go public. And in time, when the old man gets to know us, he'll let us really wheel and deal. But for now, let's enjoy ourselves. Beautiful town, great living, and, don't forget, I'm the numbers man. I see what we're all getting and it's damn good. That's an understatement. We're as rare as pandas. All of us are outstripping inflation. By a lot."

Sy got up, looked conspiratorially over his shoulder, then quietly closed Hal's office door.

"Can you keep a little secret?"

"Sure."

"An accountant is like a priest, Hal. Except the secrets we keep are dirtier. That's because they involve money. So what follows is totally off the record. I had to do a payroll analysis the other day. For the first time, I looked closely at all the salaries in the company. Of course, I was especially interested in our group. I knew my deal was good, but I was happy to see that all of us have been well taken care of. But what knocked me off my chair was what Aldo Lucci is making. Now, it's quite a bit under you and myself."

"Sy, you've got my attention. What is it?"

"Hold on, it's coming. Aldo is, we'll admit, a splendid guy. Sweet, nice, hardworking. But not possessing a skill that is in particularly short supply. At his last job as custodian of P.S. 193 in Brooklyn he was making seventeen grand. And damn happy to get it. And that was thanks to a pretty strong union."

"And now?" asked Hal.

"And now he's the proud possessor of a forty-six-thousand-dollar-a-year salary."

"Holy shit!"

"That's what I thought, but I didn't express it as well. And the weird thing is, this pay scale only applies to the new team. Cesar Chavez would love to organize the rest of this joint. Let's just thank our lucky stars that the Hilliards believe when you have to go outside for people, you really have to pay."

"Amen."

Sy looked at his watch. Hal stood up and leaned slightly over his desk, trying to read the logo. Cartier. It figured.

"Since we're both wealthy men," said Sy, "how about another spectacular lunch at the fashionable Wayside Inn?"

"Who said you weren't creative?"

"You. Yesterday at lunch. We can flip for the check again."

"Whose coin?" asked Hal.

"Mine. It only has one head."

"In that case I'll order sparingly."

7

The Wayside Inn had once been a tobacco barn. It now sat in the middle of an immense gray-pebbled parking lot that resembled in off-hours an Occidental Zen garden. Huge picture windows in the back of the dining room overlooked a lovely valley, newly painted in vivid early-spring nitric greens. It was *the* restaurant in the area. Its popularity was simple: good food in large quantities at reasonable prices. Its business flourished all year. Crowded both at foliage time and in the dead of winter when the lot was filled with skiers' cars, it was a place for all types of people. The jukebox carried everything from disco for the high-school kids to polkas for the farmers, who still planted tobacco under veil-thin white mesh coverings in the loamy soil that backed off the Connecticut River.

Since Hal and Sy were fast establishing themselves as regulars at the Wayside, Miles Corash, the owner, treated them to a warm greeting and led them to a window table at the rear.

"You know, Sy, I was always under the influence of that old saw about standoffish New Englanders. We've been in this town almost no time at all and Miles gives us a great table every day."

"It stems from two things. One is that we drink expensive—Bombay Gin, Chivas Regal, that kind of stuff—and the other is that we tip well."

"Where'd you lose your affection for warm, open small-town folk, you old cynic?"

"After reading Sherwood Anderson. Let's order."

They both chose the special of the day—Irish stew with new potatoes and parsnips. With spartan resolve, they limited themselves to one lunar-dry martini each. Their talk ranged over wood canoes versus their aluminum cousins, the prime rate, Hilliard and Company's debt-free corporate history, restoring old houses, and Laurie Hilliard, whom, Sy confessed, he found incredibly erotic.

"I admit she's cold as ice," he said, "and I don't exactly know how to put it, but I guess I'd call it a quintessential 'shiksa-ness' that drives myself and other Hebraic lads bananas."

"You're a poet, Sy."

"I know it sounds weird, but it's true."

"I think my feelings should be hurt. What about the shiksa-ness of my wife?"

"Hal, you're missing the point. Judy is lovely, but Laurie Hilliard is different. Maybe it's those two hundred years of highly selective inbreeding that give her that distant fire."

"My friend, I see you like your pleasures tough."

As Sy went on at tortuous length and complexity about this "carnal thing" that Laurie had, Hal gazed across the meadow spreading beyond the windows and slowly tuned out. A small herd of inky black Angus was grazing there, precise blots against a green scrim. Hey, fella, it really is real. You're here at the Wayside Inn in Ripton Falls, Massachusetts. Those actually are cattle you're looking at. And those trees at the back of the field are maples that were lassoed by syrup buckets a couple of months ago. You're an exec v.p. in a successful company and making twice what you had been making. And no one's clocking your lunch hour. Life is great and it's real. Real.

"Richardson! You still with me? What's the matter? Not dirty enough for you?"

"Actually the reverse, Sy. You got me replaying an oldie but goodie. You know what I mean?"

"Do I ever. But memories like that are like snapshots. The more you take them out of the drawer to look at them, the fainter they get. Mine are beginning to resemble cave paintings."

T. C. Gaines walked over as they were finishing dessert,

apple cobbler almost lost under a pillow of fresh whipped cream.

"You two are beginning to become an item. Remember, tongues wag geometrically, not arithmetically, in small towns."

"Take it easy," said Sy. "Even a less than rabid sports fan like myself knows what goes on in locker rooms."

"Sit down, T.C. Have some coffee with us," said Hal quickly. He didn't know T.C. well enough yet to judge his threshold for this kind of humor.

"I'd love to but I'm having lunch with Laurie Hilliard and Bob Loomis. He's the plant foreman. We're discussing a new packaging idea I have that would fit in beautifully with that Christmas promotion plan you talked about last week, Hal."

"Where you sitting?" asked Sy, his head swiveling.

"Over by the fireplace. Have you met Loomis yet? He's a real beaut. He gives new meaning to the word 'taciturn.' 'Nope' is an expression of pure passion with the guy."

"I see her," said Sy almost inaudibly.

Laurie noticed the three men looking in her direction. She smiled and waved. Bob Loomis nodded.

"I just remembered what brought me this way. The john! See you guys later."

As Hal and Sy had their coffee, the talk switched to the budget Hal was preparing.

"When you think you'll have it finished?" asked Sy.

"End of the week. But no later than Monday. I admit up front to you as a friend that there's some fat in it. But I figure that whatever I submit will be whittled down, so why not shoot for the works. Like Wernher von Braun's autobiography, *I Aim for Stars, and Sometimes Hit London.*"

They both laughed for a moment, then Sy stood up.

"We better get going. I'm supposed to meet our banker in an hour and I want to review some numbers before I see him."

As they left the restaurant, Hal noticed that T.C. was back at the table with Laurie and Bob Loomis. T.C. was earnestly making a point. None of them seemed to notice Hal and Sy leave.

Sy's blue Toyota wagon was parked near the road. He had taken delivery of it the week before and its new-car smell was still so strong that being inside it was like living in an expensive wallet. The only words Sy spoke when he was in the car were prefaced by either E.P.A. or M.P.G. He was also fixated on seat belts.

"Seat belt, Hal," said Sy as soon as they got into the car.

"Roger, Captain," said Hal automatically.

Sy turned the ignition but nothing happened. He checked to see that the car was in gear and tried again. Nothing.

"I can't believe this. I don't even have a hundred miles on it yet."

"I have a theory that the next Pearl Harbor attack will be much more subtle. One day, suddenly, all our TVs, clock radios, video recorders, cars, and such will all just stop. The takeover from that point will be simple."

"Stop theorizing. Do you know anything about cars?"

"Just enough to belong to the A.A.A. But what the hell, let's lift the hood anyway."

The car's small engine gleamed with newness. Nothing appeared wrong. No wire hung loose. The fan belt was taut.

"Look at it," said Sy. "You could eat off the damn thing but it won't even turn over."

"Is something wrong?"

They both turned and there was Laurie.

"It won't start," said Sy.

"Oh, dear," said Laurie. "That happened to me too just a few weeks after I received my car. They'd forgotten to put water in the battery. You're probably experiencing the same type of stupidity. But all you have to do is call Mike's Garage. It's just down the road a mile or so. Six-two-seven-five. They'll get you going in just a few minutes."

Sy repeated the number to himself as he started walking toward the restaurant to call.

"There's no sense in your waiting too, Hal. I'm heading back your way. Let me give you a lift."

"But Sy'll wonder—"

"He'll figure it out. If he can't, we're all in trouble. Come on. Let's go. I have to meet my grandfather in fifteen minutes."

Hal followed Laurie around to the side of the lot where her car was parked. She drove fast with a minimum of motion.

She drives like a man, thought Hal. It was, of course, a ridiculous and chauvinistic expression, but what he meant by it was that she was a terrific driver. He realized he had almost expected her to drive that way.

"I hope you know that all of you have been extremely lucky with the weather," said Laurie.

"What do you mean?" Hal asked.

Laurie stared straight ahead. She whipped past an oil truck.

"We say that we have five seasons here in New England. The four regular ones plus the mud season. We really didn't have one this year."

"Well, I've spent the past five years in Los Angeles. Compared to earthquakes, brush fires, floods, killer smogs, and the Hillside Strangler, the mud season doesn't seem too bad."

Laurie smiled and turned toward Hal. For a moment she looked intently at him, appraising him as if he were an object up for auction. It made Hal self-consciously turn away. He could sense that she was still looking.

"I hope you're adjusting to our quiet life," she said. She pulled out an open pack of gum and held it out to Hal. "Want some? A bad habit, I know, but better than some. It's sugarless."

Hal, who hadn't chewed gum since he was a kid, took a piece out of politeness. Or was it just because he was uncomfortable?

"Thanks. And as for getting used to life here, we're loving it. Judy and I are both easterners. She's from Philadelphia and I'm from upstate New York. We've always wanted to live in New England. And Annie's having a ball. Somebody told her it was the trout season, and she's already had me out fishing with her three times."

"Annie's your little girl, isn't she? I can't wait to meet her. I love children."

Laurie stopped the car for a moment at the flashing red light that regulated the traffic onto the road to Ripton Falls. She accelerated smoothly, her left hand cradling the bottom of the steering wheel, while she brushed some hair away from her forehead. Hal noticed the strange gull-shaped mole that perched above her eyebrow. It was tiny compared with Annie's birthmark, but distinctive nonetheless. It was exactly the same as her grandfather's except for the placement. Odd how a family marking of this kind rode the genetic train like some small, not to be denied, caboose.

"You're looking at my sign of strength," said Laurie, smiling.

"Your what?" asked Hal.

"This mole, right here," she said, taking one hand off the steering wheel and touching the mark perfectly.

"What did you call it?"

"Sign of strength. Grandfather, of course, always prefaces that with Hilliard. It bothers my brother no end. My father has gotten used to it. You see, neither of them has it. It supposedly designates power. As in will power."

Hal nodded noncommittally. The last thing he wanted from Laurie were confidences, mystical or otherwise.

"It's been exciting for me having all of you join us," Laurie continued. "There's not a lot of intellectual stimulation in Ripton Falls. I try to get to Boston once a month, but that really doesn't do it. Most of the men here are into either the volunteer fire department or snowmobiles. Even though none of you are available, it's still nice to have attractive and intelligent men around."

"Since I don't get many compliments these days, I'll accept that graciously and thankfully."

They both laughed.

"You deserve compliments. You're a very handsome man."

As she slowed the car for the turn into Ripton Falls, Laurie again looked directly at Hal. This time he couldn't pull away from her look.

"I like talking to you, Hal. It would be nice to have a drink with you once in a while. Or are you one of those married men who have to get home at a certain time? You don't seem the type, but one never knows."

Laurie slowed the car as they approached the Village Green. She does more than drive like a man, thought Hal. She was macho enough to hold her own on a construction gang. But remember, buddy, she's both the boss's daughter *and* the boss's granddaughter. Kiss her off gently.

"I have rather a long leash, Laurie. And I would like to have a drink with you anytime. But I think we'd have much more fun if Judy could make it too. I know the two of you, once you'd spent some time together, would really like each other."

Move aside, Dr. Kissinger.

"I talked to Judy at the party. She's very bright. I'm sure you're correct."

Was the tone a degree or two cooler? Damn right it was. Hal

glanced at Laurie out of the corner of his eye. Her face was taut, and she chewed her gum as if it were important.

"I think the Green is sensational," he said eagerly. "I don't know what your grandfather spent restoring it, but it was worth every buck."

Laurie drove slowly down the south side of the Green. She automatically observed the twenty-mile speed limit. They glided past the saltboxes and then the town hall.

"We know it's not Old Deerfield or Williamsburg, but we're proud of it."

The Lasher house, pale-yellow clapboards capped by a no-nonsense mansard roof, slid by. Then came the Humphrey cottage with its sparkling white rope moldings and picket fence. Beyond it were the church and the parsonage. How odd they looked in this perfect setting. Like a rotten tooth in a starlet's smile.

"It's a shame the church can't get it together," said Hal. "I guess it wouldn't look so bad if the rest of the Green didn't look so good."

They drew even with the church now. Laurie rolled her window down. She glanced at the church for a moment and then, like a pitcher discarding a mouthful of tobacco juice, spat out her gum. It was a gesture so full of contempt that Hal didn't, or really couldn't, say another word until she'd pulled up in front of the office.

"Thanks for the lift, Laurie."

"Thanks for the company. See you soon."

She smiled, her face relaxing for the briefest instant, and then drove off.

Hal watched the car head back in the direction of the Green and the Hilliard house. As he turned toward the office building, he realized his palms were wet. There was something about Laurie Hilliard that Hal didn't like at all. And he couldn't for the life of him say exactly what that thing was.

•   •

Later that day, as Hal was straightening his desk before leaving, a very angry Sy walked into his office.

"There's no escaping it."

"Escaping what, Sy?" asked Hal.

"Punks. Juvenile delinquents. The breakdown of law and order."

"What the hell are you talking about?"

"We all came here to avoid the crap that you find in every big city in America, right? Well, there was nothing wrong with my car this afternoon. The only thing wrong was that some young hood thought he'd have a few laughs by disconnecting the coil wire from my distributor. Great joke, huh?"

8

"Annie! I don't want to hear another 'one more minute, Mom.' It's ten-thirty and I'm already running an hour late."

"I'm almost finished, Mom. Just another min."

Annie's voice, high and twig-thin when she was in the same room, came from her upstairs bedroom like some ancient whispered secret.

"Now. And I mean it."

Annie, aged nine, still had a rabid doll fixation. If she wasn't dressing them, she was washing and styling their hair, giving them the full Lizzie Arden treatment.

Judy patted the pocket of her jacket to make sure the car keys were there, then ducked back into the kitchen where Mimi was peeling potatoes to roast with the leg of lamb they were having that evening. Judy had just remembered that the man from Sears had promised to come today.

"I should be back before he gets here, but if he beats me to it, be sure he fixes the drainpipe. As well as the dryer hose. And if Mrs. Simmons calls, tell her we'll get there as soon as we can."

Judy went back to the foot of the staircase. Percy, who was lying under the hall table watching her with large, melting eyes, started thumping the floor with his tail. He was white with brown patches, part springer spaniel, part who knew what, and devoted to Judy. From upstairs there was only silence.

"This is it, Annie. I'm starting the car now, and I want you down here immediately."

"Do I have to go, really?"

"Oh, Annie, we've already talked about that. Enough!"

The number of times Judy found herself repeating Annie's name out loud always rose in proportion to the frustrations she was experiencing, and already, so early in the day, Judy was beginning to feel outmaneuvered, out-Annied. But as soon as she opened the front door, all the fight went out of her. The day not only looked gorgeous, it smelled gorgeous. During the night it had rained hard, and all that wetness had liberated the apple blossoms from their tight little buds. In the orchard, pale pink had taken over, and the tall, rangy lilac bushes at the front corners of the house were straining to catch up. The air was fresh and clean from the storm and softened by the mingled scents of the flowering trees. Judy shut her eyes and breathed in deeply. The sound of a car approaching made her open them almost at once.

It was Terry Lucci. All smiles and calling good morning, she scrambled from the car, holding aloft a tall jar.

"Marinated vegetables," said Terry in response to Judy's question. "And they're for you. Put these together with a few pieces of salami and a little mortadella and you'll have an antipasto like no other."

"Thanks, Terry, that's awfully nice of you."

"Don't thank me, thank my mother-in-law. She made them. She and Aldo's dad got here yesterday. For a two-week visit. At least two weeks." She allowed herself a small good-natured groan, then continued. "Mama L. really is something with her cooking. Aldo calls her *'l'ottava cuoca,'* the eighth cook."

"What?"

"Yeah, 'cause she always cooks enough for the whole Eighth Army. Everything's extra, extra, extra. 'I'll make just a little bit extra' is what she always says. But the army should be so lucky to have her in charge of the mess. She's good."

Terry rolled her eyes appreciatively and then, before Judy could say a word, tapped the jar that Judy was holding in her hand.

"This may look to you like a jar of antipasto-in-the-making, but what it really is—I'm from Brooklyn, and I'm not very fancy about this sort of thing, by choice!—is an invitation to an old-fashioned Italian picnic. At our place. Next Saturday. A week from today, at noon. Just for us new people. All of us . . . born-again Yankees."

"Sounds great," said Judy, smiling at Terry's remark. "I'll have to check with Hal, but I don't see why we can't be there."

"Hal isn't home?"

"He's at the office. If you can believe it. On a day like this when he doesn't have to be. Speaking of which, forgive me, but I've got to get moving myself. I'm taking Annie over to the church to meet Bradford Peters. The minister. To see what programs the church has for kids."

"Well, we're at Saint Ignatius, so it's not our problem, but I hope looks are deceiving. . . ."

Judy laughed halfheartedly.

"You mean the condition of the church? Hal would agree with you. It's my idea to try it out. I'm the one who's the more traditional of the two of us."

"Hal isn't religious?"

"Religious? For Hal to call himself agnostic would be an act of faith."

•   •

Judy stopped the car in front of the church, though the impulse to drive on was equally strong. Annie's frame of mind did not help. Just after Terry had left, Annie had appeared on the front step, cradling her favorite doll. It was a simpering, sugar-sweet number that would have been at home on the front of a Hallmark card. "You woke up Darcy," she said to Judy snippily. When Judy had ordered Annie back upstairs to brush her hair, which stood out from around her head in a disarray reminiscent of Elsa Lanchester's in *The Bride of Frankenstein,* the mood between mother and daughter had escalated to what could best be described as a draw. On the drive over, Annie was stubbornly silent. To Judy's dismay, she could see in the rearview mirror that Annie's anger had found release, as it always seemed to, in her birthmark. The deep-red leaf shape that splashed from her neck up onto her lower jawline had grown so darkly livid in the last five minutes that it seemed to vibrate. Their doctor in California had recommended they delay surgery to remove it until Annie was at least ten. At moments like this, though, Judy was not at all certain she could wait until then.

Now Judy jumped from the car onto the ragged grass in front of the church, Annie by her side. There was no sign of life, either in the church or in the house next to it.

At the front door of the house, she rapped sharply on the glass pane at the side of the door. When nothing stirred, she beckoned to Annie to follow her around to the back. As they rounded the corner, Annie let out a whoop of pleasure. There, hidden from the street, were a high, old-fashioned slide, a set of tall swings, and a climbing bar.

"Run along," said Judy, not waiting to be asked. "Just promise me not to go anywhere else, and come inside in ten minutes." As she watched Annie skip in wild zigzags toward the swings, she felt a rush of almost painful love for her. Sometimes she was so busy being Mommy, playing the heavy, she lost sight of how important Annie was to her and Hal. She was everything.

She looked back at the house, shaking her head in mild surprise at the bulging trash can next to the back stoop. The lid was slightly askew, and Judy could see inside the can the tip of a Smirnoff bottle poking its nose up.

Judy knocked and waited, then just as she was about to knock again the door was opened by a sandy-haired young man in a rumpled blue work shirt and faded chinos. He needed a shave, and the circles beneath his blue eyes were dark as inked thumbprints. He shook himself straighter, like a dog throwing pond water off its coat, but it was obvious he hadn't really done much for his fatigue. The sag in his shoulders came right back. In fact, he looked bone-tired.

"I'm sorry, but I didn't hear you," he said, his voice cracking as if these were the first words he'd spoken aloud that day. "I was going over some papers in my office, and the door was shut. What can I do for you?" He managed a thin smile.

"Sunday School!" he snorted after Judy had introduced herself and explained why she was there. "That's a story in itself. But come in, and let me give you a cup of coffee. And don't call me Mr. Peters. It's Brad. I don't stand on ceremony. As you can see."

He gestured at the kitchen, which looked as though Annie

had been in charge of the cleanup crew. "My apologies for this mess. I can't seem to hang on to a housekeeper. The last one stayed just one month. She was terrific, but then she got some kind of clerical job at the plant at twice the money. I don't blame her for preferring Hilliard's to this."

Judy laughed, then watched Brad Peters spoon some instant coffee into an unappetizing mug whose sides were stained like a high-tide mark. Through the window above the kitchen sink she could see Annie swinging furiously.

"To answer your question," said Brad, when they were seated at the kitchen table, "there is no Sunday School. I tried to start one up, but it's been a total bust. I don't understand it. The people in this town are really very nice, but . . . but I sometimes think I'm the Congregationalists' answer to Dick Cavett. I run a good show, but I don't draw the audience. Last Sunday we had twenty-one people. When it's sunny we're lucky to get a dozen."

"Oh, dear," said Judy. "But, you know, we're not the only new family in town. Hilliard's has hired a whole bunch of new people. I don't know if they're churchgoers, but we are. At least I am. Is there anything my husband and I can do to help?"

"There's nothing much you can do to help *me*," said Brad. "I'm seriously thinking of telling the board that I've had it. That I want to quit. Before I came here I knew the congregation was in trouble. They'd had a hard time holding on to their ministers—I don't know why really—and people seemed to have lost the habit of going to church. Membership was way off. But it goes beyond that now. It's pitiful. They don't need a church here! But come to services this Sunday and boost my score to twenty-three. Or should I say"—he looked up as the back door banged and Annie came slamming into the kitchen— "make it twenty-four."

"Mommy, Mommy," Annie said, "come and see my new trick. I just invented it. I start off hanging with two legs and then I hang from one leg and then I switch and hang from the other leg and then I hang from both legs and then I do a somersault. It's really great."

"It sounds great," said Judy, putting a lot of enthusiasm into her voice, "and I want to see it. In a moment. Now say hello to Mr. Peters, will you?"

Annie, who looked exceedingly pretty with her flushed cheeks and her flyaway hair, messier than ever, abruptly went tongue-tied.

"Hi there," said Brad, energetically filling the empty space with friendly-sounding noises. "I'm very pleased to meet you and I'm especially happy you liked my jungle gym and swing. Do you know something? You're the first person to use them since the snow melted."

"Am I?" said Annie politely.

Listening to this exchange, Judy was struck by what Brad had just said, by the sadness of it—where you find a playground, you find children: where were they then? why did they stay away?—and the effort it was costing him to be agreeable became so obvious that she pushed back her chair and stood up to leave. They had no business forcing him through any more pleasantries. She liked him, but something was wrong, very wrong, and she had no idea what it was. She searched his eyes for an answer, inadvertently catching the flutter of a tic rippling through one of his eyelids.

"Here," he said, pointing toward the other part of the house, "the least I can do is show you out the right way. Through the front door."

He came up with a short laugh this time. As they moved forward, Annie trailing behind them, he continued, "As for Sunday School, why don't you try your luck in Northampton?" He shook his head. "Truly I don't understand it. This part of the world is supposed to be eighty percent Congregational, but by my numbers, it's eighty percent Buddhist. Whenever I do succeed in involving someone new in the church, it's just at that point they get caught up in their job at Hilliard's. And it's no surprise that time and a half at the company is more tempting to them than sermons and hymn singing at the church. I must say it seems as though everybody works for the Hilliards."

"How about asking *them* for help?"

"I tried—they're on the board, of course—but I got nowhere. I ran into Elliott Hilliard at the post office a few months ago. I asked him if I'd be seeing him in church soon. I thought he might set a good example by attending, that sort of thing. He just laughed. That was all. But the message was clear. You know, you're new here and I don't want to taint your feelings for them, but the Hilliards can be very cold and ungiving when they want to be. Tell you the truth, I think they have their eye on buying the church property."

They had reached the front door now, and Judy realized Annie was no longer behind her. She was standing in the hallway through which they had just passed, staring intently at something out of Judy's line of vision. She called to Annie, but the girl didn't budge. She called a second time and then walked back to see what held her daughter's attention. She was in front of a closed door. It was a thin, narrow door, exactly like all the other doors in the house, except that it literally bristled with locks. There were three of them, plus a big, ugly bolt that would have done a paranoid New Yorker proud.

"Mommy," asked Annie, "what are all these locks for?"

Dumbfounded, Judy glanced questioningly at Brad, and as she did, she caught in his eyes a look of such alarm that she turned away.

After a gulf of silence, Brad spoke. His voice was so thick and muffled that it was difficult to understand. "The door rattles a lot at night."

"Annie, we must go," said Judy briskly. She avoided Brad's eyes.

"See you Sunday," Brad called out with false cheer as they retreated down the front path.

Maybe me, but not Hal, thought Judy, almost dragging Annie behind her. Hal figured all clergymen for neurotics. Confused or unstable or both. Bradford Peters would strike him as a perfect case in point. And why not? For here, if Judy had ever seen one, was a man on the edge. A man heading for a breakdown. And fast.

9

As soon as the Richardsons got out of their car, they were met by Aldo holding two tumblers of red wine dark as coal.

"Lucci '80. Bensonhurst's finest. We who are born and bred there call it the Napa Valley of Brooklyn. Aside from a few toenails, absolutely pure grape. But take it slow. This stuff is sneakier than a three-card monte operator."

Annie, who was out of the car almost before it had stopped, disappeared around the back of the house with Gwen Prescott, who was the same age, and one of the Lucci boys. Tracy Goldin, just five, followed them with the devout adoration that a young child possesses for older ones.

The driveway was filled, and two cars were pulled up tight to the walk in front of the house. The Luccis had bought a large, rambling Victorian that was a couple of miles out of town on the road leading to the reservoir. Aldo, a compulsive do-it-yourselfer, already had put his stamp on the place: the downstairs fretwork wore a fresh coat of primer, the front lawn was newly seeded, and a huge pile of smooth gray pebbles, heaped like a burial mound, waited to be spread on the driveway.

"It'll take me a while to get this place in shape, but I'm having fun doing it. This is our first house. Terry and me used to live in the basement apartment in my folks' place. It was nice but a little small. And I'm not kidding about my dad's wine. We used to drink the stuff out of cups when I was a kid. And all of them had a red ring that sulfuric acid couldn't get out."

Behind the house, the adults were divided into two groups. The men surrounded Aldo's father, Nino, who was giving them instruction in the game of boccie. The women were gathered around a trestle table under a newly constructed grape arbor watching Terry and Mama Lucci put the finishing touches on three outsized platters of food for the first course—seafood salad, roast peppers and anchovies, and a confection of paper-thin mushrooms mixed with strips of cheese. The kids were nowhere in sight, though the sounds of their voices filtered toward the Richardsons from behind a dense stand of white-pine trees.

"The kids are at the pond," said Aldo. "Down the hill behind those trees. Carmine's gone crazy over frogs. He's already got two jarfuls in his bedroom. That's the problem with twins. Double trouble. You wouldn't believe what Rick is into. Terry's fit to be tied about the frogs. I told Carmine I'd kick ass if one gets loose in the house. But. . . ."

Aldo shrugged, then switched his attention back to what really interested him. His new domain. He gestured toward the far end of the property. "I'm going to build a screened-in patio over there to sit out in at night. And next to it, I'll put up a stone barbecue. All native stone. I've checked the fields around here and there are plenty."

"Too many," said Hal, laughing, as he thought of the rock which thrust up in ledges and hummocks across his lawn. He'd damn near wrecked the mower on a particularly vicious piece of it last week.

"Yeah, you're right. You feeling strong? I could use some help."

"No thanks," said Hal, raising his hand to fend off the suggestion. He had too much work to do around their own place. At least two seasons' worth of spare time.

"Over there by the boccie court, Terry'll put in some flowers, and here"—Aldo led them over to an old abandoned stone well whose opening was filled now with concrete—"I'm going to chip the top layer of this stuff out, plant ivy in it, and build a little house over it. I've always wanted a covered well. Terry says it's corny, but I told her, 'So what? That's the Sicilian in me. Take it or leave it.'"

"Aldo," interrupted Judy, "excuse me, but I want to see if I can give Terry a hand." She pointed toward the women, who were disappearing into the kitchen.

"Hold on a moment, and I'll walk you over, but first you must see my prize, my beauty." He stopped in front of a spindly little tree whose leaves were as limp as sails on a becalmed sea. He gave it a long, tender look. "My fig tree. Transplanted from Brooklyn. My dad brought it with him. We put her in the ground as soon as they arrived. It's not a backyard unless you have a fig tree."

Hal nodded vigorously, as if this were one of his guiding principles also.

"Ever had figs and prosciutto?" asked Aldo. "Ah. . . ." He kissed his fingertips. "Nectar of the gods."

They had arrived at the back porch and, taking the steps two at a time, Aldo bounded up after Judy.

"You ladies look like you've known each other for twenty years," Hal heard him call to the group in the kitchen. A moment later he came wheeling back down the stairs.

"I want to take a photo of the kids, and the boss tells me I got time. Help me round them up," he said, a new Polaroid camera held like a precious surgical instrument in his hand.

The kids were still at the pond. One of the Lucci twins—they were very fair and looked so much alike that Hal could not begin to tell them apart—was playing a loose and lazy game of Frisbee with an older boy who had a long, thin face and wavy black hair. This was Seth Goldin, and of the two, he was the one who looked Italian. The rest of the kids hovered together at the edge of the pond egging on the other Lucci boy, who was in frenzied pursuit of another amphibian specimen. He was standing knee-high in the water, and his soaking jeans testified to his having been in even deeper.

"Carmine, get the hell out of there!" yelled Aldo as soon as he sighted his son. "What are you, some kind of dummy?"

"Oh, gross," squealed Erin Simmons as the frog Carmine had been chasing slithered away. The girl's thick lemony hair swirled around her shoulders and was so lovely that Hal found himself wondering if Claire Simmons' hair had once been like that too and, if so, why she had cut it so short.

Carmine Lucci, clearly enjoying the attention, started to make a second pass at the frog to the delight of the group. Gwen Prescott doubled over with laughter, her densely freckled face tomato red, and the other girls jumped up and down excitedly. T. C. Gaines, Jr., a ten-year-old ringer for his dad, had an 8-mm. camera focused on the antic Carmine.

"Out!" said Aldo, beginning to get angry. "What do you think you're doing? Testing our Blue Cross coverage? That's a good way to get pneumonia. Go put some dry pants on."

The dripping boy reluctantly got out of the water, brushing past a curtain of cattails. On the other side of the pond, which could not have been more than twenty yards across, an arthritic old dock reached out into the middle of the water. Pastureland skirted the pond on three sides, and from beyond a barbed-wire fence, three Hereford steers eyed what probably had been some ancestors' watering hole.

"The rest of you come too," continued Aldo. "I want to take a picture of all of you together. And anyway, it's almost time to eat."

"Not me and Seth," said Rick Lucci, expertly winging the Frisbee to his partner. Rick's full name was Enrico, Aldo had explained earlier. A year ago he had demanded to be called Rick. Poor Carmine still hadn't come up with a catchy way to shorten his own name.

"Yeah, you and Seth too," said Aldo with finality. "Everybody."

Rick and the others got the message and straggled up the hill and through the trees behind Hal and Aldo. Quickly Aldo lined them up beside the fig tree according to height. First came Tracy Goldin, damp black curls springing away from her head, her small, puckish face enveloped in a huge grin. Next to her was Rick Lucci. The twins were only eight, but their street-wise cockiness made them seem older. They were blond and toothy like their mother. On Rick's other side were Annie and Erin Simmons, whispering and giggling, and then Gwen Prescott, eyeing them jealously. Next came T. C. Gaines, Jr. He was a movie nut and was reputed to have amazed his English teacher by naming every film in which Laurence Olivier had ever appeared. Seth Goldin stood beside T.C. Junior, looking as resentful as his little sister, Tracy, was thrilled to be part of this group. He would be thirteen in August—Sy's first order of business on arriving in Ripton Falls had been to reserve time at a Pittsfield temple for the boy's bar mitzvah—and was doing his best to seem above it all.

"Now smile everybody," said Aldo, and then his hand froze just as he was about to press the button on the Polaroid. "Damn it, Carmine," he hollered in the direction of the house, "where are you?"

The guilty boy shot out of the house immediately, as if all he'd been waiting for was for his father to boil over, and bobbed up at the end of the line next to Seth. Faithful to the symmetry of his vision, Aldo moved him in next to his brother. Finally satisfied, he took his picture and expectantly peeled back the negative. Sixty seconds later he found himself staring at a perfectly composed and focused picture. It was also totally overexposed. His second shot was too dark, and his third, fuzzy. Risking anarchy, he ordered the kids to stand still for one more shot, and when it turned out perfect, he demanded another.

To Hal's surprise, Aldo insisted on giving him one of the good photographs. Hal carefully eased it into the pocket of his shirt, meaning to take it out later to show everybody. But the lunch was such a marvel that Hal, of course, forgot.

●   ●

Course succeeded course, the women hustling back and forth between the outdoor tables and the kitchen, ferrying out new dishes. Nino's home-grown red gave way for a short while to a first cousin's highly credible variation on a Verdicchio, then came on strong again in fresh quantities with the main course. This was baby spring lamb, grilled over an open pit by Aldo. It followed straw-thin pasta, served with two different sauces, which in turn had followed the platters of antipasti, and it was accompanied by heaping dishes of sautéed broccoli rabe and escarole. By the time they finished, almost two hours had passed, and the hot midafternoon sun had slowed down everyone but the kids. All of them, with the exception of T.C. Junior's two-year-old sister, Meredith, who was seesawing on her mother's knee, were seated at a separate table, though "seated" was no longer the operative word. En route to the kitchen, Terry stopped at the table.

"Okay, kids," she said, raising her voice above the commotion, "you're excused until dessert."

In moments they had scattered back through the pines to the pond.

"Hey, how's about us guys being excused too," Aldo called over.

"Sure, honey, though it's not going to take us long to clear."

"Right, but we have time for a quick round of boccie." He turned to the other men. Sy and Hal were lighting up cigars. "Come on, who'll challenge me?"

"I'll take you on," T.C. said.

"Christ, I'm a goner," Aldo said more than half seriously. He led the way to the long, enclosed dirt alley that ran back from the house parallel to one side of the property. Boccie was the Italian version of lawn bowling, and Aldo's boccie court was almost as new as his fig tree.

"Can you believe the heart of those Hilliards?" he said. "They heard I was throwing a little party for us newcomers. 'Aldo,' Elliott says to me, 'go see John in supplies and ask him to requisition some two-by-fours for you, whatever you need, then go get one of the guys from the plant and let his day's work be at your place setting up your court so it'll be ready in time for your picnic.' I built my last boccie court entirely by myself, and it's a job and a half. They even let me use their roller."

Aldo barely had a chance to demonstrate again the correct stance and toss and T.C. time to take his first turn before Terry called everyone back to the tables. There were large dishes of vanilla ice cream topped with thick fudge sauce, and, for those in training, slices of chilled fresh fruit.

Lisa Goldin walked over to the children's table and looked it over. "Where's Tracy?" she asked Seth.

"She's coming, I guess," the boy said, heaping his dish with ice cream.

"Put that spoon down."

The boy glanced up at his mother for the first time.

"You know you're not supposed to leave your sister alone. Ever. What's wrong with you?"

The boy stared at his mother without answering.

"Sy, go down and get her, will you?" she called to the next table. Then she looked down at her son again. "I'll deal with you later."

"I'll go with you, Sy," said Hal. "I need to stretch my legs."

•   •

Hal was the first to see Tracy. She was lying in the water, partway under the dock, her half-turned face pillowed against a rock at the base of the pilings. Her tiny body was still. A stillness that went beyond sleep.

"Oh, my God," he said, hurtling down the hill toward the

small, frail figure. Beside him he heard Sy shouting his daughter's name over and over again.

He reached Tracy before Sy did. He grasped her around the shoulders and lifted her up. Her head fell heavily against his arm and a thread of water slid down from the corner of her open mouth. Quickly he laid her down on the grass. As he bent over her to begin artificial respiration, Sy caught up with him and pushed him away. Seconds later Sy looked up frantically.

"Can you feel her pulse?"

Hal grabbed Tracy's wrist, concentrating hard. Most of the time he couldn't even find his own pulse.

All at once Hal knew that if Tracy was going to make it, they had to get her to a hospital. Fast.

"Sy, this isn't doing any good. We've got to take her to Cooley Dickinson."

Like a manic windup toy, Sy worked over Tracy. Hal's words made no impression on him.

"Sy," said Hal urgently, shaking his friend's shoulder. "Listen to me."

Sy looked up, his eyes wide with panic.

"We're wasting time, Sy. We have to get to Cooley Dickinson. The hospital. In Northampton. Now. You carry Tracy. I'll go ahead. Okay?"

Sy nodded and gathered his daughter up into his arms. Sweat —or was it tears?—ran off the bottom of his glasses onto her unmoving face. He glanced again at Hal.

"I'm okay," he said. "I really am. Run. I'll catch up."

When Hal was certain that his friend was up and moving, he sprinted toward the house. As soon as he saw the others, he blurted out what had happened. Lisa ran to meet Sy, whom they could hear crashing through the underbrush in the small strip of woods between the Luccis' and the pond. Aldo immediately went to his Pontiac and started it. Mama Lucci ran out of the house carrying a large plaid blanket. After a brief conference with Hal, Judy went inside to call ahead to the hospital.

The Goldins wrapped Tracy in the blanket and stretched her out carefully on the back seat, and they were off. Hal, T.C., and Reid Prescott followed in T.C.'s car. By unspoken agreement, the women stayed behind, which was just as well. The kids needed them. As T.C. accelerated, Hal looked back at them. Annie had given way to tears. Erin too. The others stared after the cars, their faces shocked. And over them all rose the loud wail of little Meredith Gaines, a barometer of woe.

At the entrance to the hospital's Emergency Room, a doctor and two nurses were waiting. They whisked Tracy from Sy's arms and placed her on a gurney. While one nurse took her pulse, the doctor clapped an oxygen mask over her face. The second nurse rolled the gurney forward, already on the move even as they each ticked their way through assigned tasks, as efficient and synchronized as a 747 flight crew. They burst through the swinging doors into the hospital, and then through a second set. Before Hal and the others could catch up with them, the three were halfway down a long corridor, its highly polished linoleum floor mirroring their frenzied activity. An orderly behind a desk prevented the Goldins from chasing after Tracy. As they watched the gurney disappear into another arm of the corridor, Hal heard himself murmuring softly, "Please, God, please, God." He realized that what he was doing, for the first time since he had lost his faith as a sixteen-year-old for no reason that he could pinpoint, only that one day it was no longer there, was praying.

•   •

Hal peered at his watch. So little time had passed. Just under five minutes. A nurse had directed them into a waiting room that was filled with beige leatherette chairs and back issues of *People* and *Yankee*. Sy and Lisa were standing motionless in a corner of the room, their heads tight against each other's shoulders, their arms circling each other in a cocoon of shared anguish.

Hal stepped from the room into the corridor, and as he did, he heard a tiny voice cry, "Mommy, Mommy." He almost threw himself back into the waiting room.

"Sy, Lisa, it's Tracy," he yelled.

The Goldins rushed into the hall just as the doctor turned the corner. He was rolling down the sleeves of his white coat, and that even more than his smile told the story.

"Mrs. Goldin? Mr. Goldin? You can go see her now. Just for a few minutes. She's going to be fine."

The doctor stayed behind in the corridor with Hal and the other men, all of them grinning broadly in relief.

"Can they take her home today?" asked Hal.

"No. She'll have to spend the night here. Just routine. She swallowed a lot of water, but that's the least of it." The doctor paused, studied the faces of the men, then his voice dropped.

"You know, it's the damnedest thing. You remember a couple of years ago this life-after-death stuff was all the rage? Well, I've always discounted it as a lot of claptrap, but I may become a believer yet. When you brought this kid in she had no pulse. I thought we had lost her. I think we did lose her. I've been at this a long time, but I think I've just witnessed my first miracle. She was dead, I could swear it, but we brought her back."

10

That Monday, after dinner, Judy had just poured Hal and herself cups of espresso when the front doorbell rang. It was Aldo. He was wearing a short-sleeved maroon satin shirt with his name embroidered in white on the pocket. He held a small white envelope. After exchanging assurances about Tracy Goldin—both families had talked with Lisa, who reported that Tracy was home from the hospital and seemed fine—Aldo thrust the envelope toward Judy.

"Terry asked me to drop this off."

"What is it?" asked Judy, taking the envelope.

"Come in and have some coffee," said Hal.

"Thanks, but I'm already late. We're bowling against Plainfield tonight."

"I don't understand," said Judy, holding aloft an exquisite antique child's necklace. A tiny silver mesh purse was suspended on the short chain. "What's this for? I mean, it's beautiful, but why're you giving it to us?"

"It's not Annie's?"

"No. I've never seen it before in my life."

"You sure? I found it at the end of the dock. Hanging on one of the pilings. I figure Tracy spotted it and reached for it.

Maybe that's how she fell in. You really sure it doesn't belong to Annie?"

"Of course I'm sure. Her Strawberry Shortcake bracelet is the prize of her collection."

"Okay. If you say so," said Aldo doubtfully. "Terry's asked everyone else already, all the mothers, and no one knows anything about it. I figured it had to be Annie's. What did Perry Mason use to say? Process of elimination."

"Look," said Judy, growing a trifle impatient, "Annie's upstairs doing her homework and I'd be delighted to call her downstairs to say no for herself, but it isn't necessary."

"Okay, okay," said Aldo, taking back the necklace. "I suppose it's like the vise I found in my shop the other day. You know, I have a shop down in my cellar, and I was down there doing some framing when I saw something over in the corner. It was a big vise, in almost perfect shape, and it amazed me that I hadn't noticed it before. The people we bought the house from must have left it there. Forgotten it. Just like this, I guess. It's funny the things people overlook."

After Aldo had left and as they were carrying their empty cups to the kitchen, Judy caught Hal's eye.

"You know, Aldo can't be right," she said.

"About what?"

"About the necklace. People don't just 'overlook' jewelry like that. It looks like it could be worth some money. Why would anyone leave it behind?"

"Why did you leave the keys in our car at the Farmers' Market last year?"

11

Annie was sleeping over at Gwen Prescott's. Her first overnight since coming to Ripton Falls. Mimi was visiting her aunt in Brooklyn. So Judy and Hal found themselves alone. Deliciously alone. They already had given Annie a call to find out if she needed a little toughening to combat homesickness. Happily, she didn't. In fact, she was in the middle of a game with Gwen and didn't want to come to the phone. With that news in hand, Hal ceremoniously unjacked all the phones in the house.

The night air was soft so they ate on the screened-in porch. By candlelight. Hal took charge. On Mimi's days off, the kitchen became his province. Judy was a great appreciator of good food, but her creativity did not extend to cooking.

Hal sautéed some perfect veal, the price of which he estimated rivaled that of hard drugs. But this was, after all, a special night. Alone to themselves. A small mound of new carrots, as bright as candy and cooked *al dente,* accompanied the veal. Then came salad. Small curls of Bibb lettuce sprinkled with a dusting of chopped chives from the backyard. The dressing was a swirl of walnut oil and tarragon vinegar and a dash of Dijon mustard. The meal was almost Japanese in its simplicity and presentation.

They had finished a California rosé that was surprisingly good and were halfway through a sand-dry Pouilly-Fumé. Bless the Berkshires and the Hilliards.

"Know something?" said Hal.

"Lots. But what in particular are you interested in?"

"I'm happy. Really happy."

"I'm going to pass up a snappy rejoinder," said Judy, "and just kiss you."

Judy leaned across the table, her arm jostling the candle and producing a rippling shadow across the screen. She kissed Hal.

"Did I ever tell you that I love the way you taste?" said Hal.

"Not quite that way," answered Judy in a whisper.

Hal got up and went to Judy's side. In one easy motion he picked her up.

"I should do this more often," he said. "You're still light as—"

"No comparisons, please. It might interrupt your train of thought."

"Nothing short of a tactical nuclear weapon could keep this courier from completing his mission."

Hal carried Judy up the stairs to their bedroom. A quick tug and the spread was on the floor. They undressed each other with the sensual curiosity of the first time. The sheets were shivery cool and the slice of light that entered from the hall was just right. They were wrapped in the security and privacy of a cave. Outside time and place.

"Has it always been this good?" Hal asked.

"Nothing is this good," Judy moaned back.

They took turns with each other, using every part of their bodies to bring themselves closer and closer to the edge. When they reached it, they clawed their way back to the surface to start again.

Later they showered, soaping each other's back with care. Wearing bathrobes and holding snifters of brandy, they returned to the porch. They stretched out in a large glider that had come with the house. It made a comfortable creaking noise, like an old Liberty ship on a calm sea. The candle had gone out and the only light came from a wedge of moon and an occasional firefly that was more like a distant star.

"Is this whole thing real?" asked Judy after some time.

"It's crazy but it is."

"Even the Village Green? And old man Hilliard? And the dirt roads?"

"All of it. And it's been waiting for us for a long time."

"It's been a long time since we've been able to make love like we did tonight. Since we got here it's been better and better. Why is that?"

Hal sipped his brandy meditatively, feeling its delightful pinch at the tip of his tongue. The nip of the good brandy demon, he thought.

"You know, we were pretty damn unhappy in California. It wasn't just the place, though we both knew it wasn't right for us. Part was my frustration with my job. And the lousy pay. The constant scraping and maneuvering to pay bills. Waking up each day dreading the drive along that clotted highway. Knowing that I was going nowhere with escape-velocity speed. Becoming more sour every day. And then I started to believe that that was my hand. That I didn't deserve better."

"But now we're here. And you have the job you always should have had."

"If only the Hilliards will give me a chance to do some of the things that I know could turn this company on its ear. . . ."

"Hal?"

"What?"

"I want so much for us to have another baby. But here. Promise me we won't wake up tomorrow and find ourselves back in L.A. In a house where an eighty-year-old could punch his way through the walls. Where—"

"Hey! Cut it out. It's not a dream. Believe me."

Judy tucked her head deeper into Hal's shoulder, like a small burrowing animal.

"I want to ask you something."

"What?"

"Do you have another shower in you?"

"Why, for God's sake? We just had one."

"Well, I thought we could do something that might require us to shower again. Something. . . ."

They kissed again, and the night slowly swallowed them in its dark, deep pocket.

12

Judy was feeling very up. She had been in a terrific mood all weekend for lots of reasons, not the least of which was Hal, and here it was Monday, and she was still feeling good. Not just plain good. Great.

That morning she had gotten a firm offer from Smith to teach a painting course twice weekly in its summer arts program. The pay was negligible, but that didn't matter since they didn't need the money anymore. What thrilled her was the unlimited studio time the college gave her for her own work. To celebrate she took the better part of the afternoon off to sketch the older of the two saltboxes on the Green. She had had her eye on it for weeks. She was home again studying the results of her efforts when she heard the beep of a car horn. That would be Claire Simmons. Erin was playing with Annie—as usual, they were in the same class at school and were thick as thieves—and they'd arranged earlier for Claire to pick Erin up on the way home from work. Mimi had promised to take the girls mushroom hunting in the woods and, judging from the quiet of the house, they must still be there.

"Mushrooms? I hope they're not eating them!" said Claire, after Judy explained.

"Don't worry. I have a hard enough time persuading Annie to eat hamburger, let alone anything as arcane as mushrooms. In any case, Mimi knows which are okay."

Judy poured them both tall glasses of iced tea while Claire reported on a chance encounter with Lisa Goldin in the supermarket.

"I was surprised to see her. I thought she'd be home with Tracy. But no such thing. Tracy's back in school."

"Gee, that's terrific."

"Isn't it amazing? She's fine apparently. And not just fine. Better than ever. Lisa thought she was going to have to coddle her, but it's turned out the other way around. She's eating more than she used to, not fussing about going to bed, *and* picking up her room without being asked to."

"I could use a little more of that spirit around here, if you know what I mean," said Judy dryly.

"Me too," said Claire with a laugh. "And, you know, Lisa was funny about that. She said it was almost as if the best thing in the world for a kid was a near drowning. But seriously, Lisa said the only change she's seen is that Tracy's quieter than usual. Much quieter. And whenever they look in on her at night, she always seems to be awake. Not out of bed playing. But awake. Lying there with her eyes open. God, though, think what she went through."

The two women fell silent, and into that stillness stepped Mimi, brandishing a bag of mushrooms.

"The girls are coming right along. Annie wanted to show Erin the tree house."

"Tree house?" asked Claire.

"We discovered it just a few weeks ago," said Judy. "It needs a bit of fixing up, which Hal is going to do, though it's perfectly sound. It can't be more than five feet off the ground, and it has its own little built-in ladder."

"Lucky Annie. I always wanted one when I was a kid. Hey, wait a minute." Claire paused. "What's that noise?"

The sound of crying, now unmistakable, grew louder, and

then the back door slammed open and in burst Erin and Annie. Erin was in tears. It wasn't her sobbing, though, but the way she looked that caused the women to gasp. Her whole upper body was smeared over with something dark, sticky, and alien, but it was her hair that riveted them. Her beautiful blond hair was coated totally, irreparably, by the same terrible viscous substance.

"Are you all right?" cried Claire. "Are you hurt anywhere?"

A muffled "No" was all Erin could manage, and then she collapsed against her mother's side.

Annie broke in excitedly. "We stopped to see the tree house, and Erin wanted to go up the ladder first, and I said yes, because she was the guest, and she had just started up when this awful yukky junk came pouring down. She couldn't get out of the way. There was some big pail up there of this . . . stuff. It just came down like crazy."

"Damn it!" said Judy fiercely. "It must have been Hal. How could he!"

"What do you mean?" said Claire.

"Remember I said he was going to make some repairs on the tree house? He must have been getting his things together for the job, and just left them there, including a pail of . . . tar. I don't know what else it could be *but* tar."

"Tar?" said Claire. "Do you have any idea how to—"

"No, I don't. I read in that hint book that peanut butter gets gum out of hair, but I don't know if it works for tar."

"What're you going to do to my hair?" demanded Erin, suddenly alert. "Is it going to have to be cut?"

"Darling, I hope not, but we have to do something to get this out," said Claire, gently poking at the slick buttons of tar.

"No! I won't let you! You can't."

"Don't worry, we'll see if we can do something else first. But it'll grow back. I promise," said Claire.

This triggered a fresh outburst from Erin. Annie, who was quickly getting into the spirit of the thing, looked as though she might start crying too. She put her arms around her friend and hugged her.

"If you have to have your hair cut, I'll have mine cut too," she said.

Claire hurriedly said goodbye. As Judy watched mother and

daughter drive off, she thought, Yes, Erin's hair will grow in again. But it will take months. Of all people for this to happen to. Erin, whose hair had been a wonder. Thick, glossy, golden. Who would know it now?

●   ●

Hal came home early that evening, soon after the Simmonses' departure. The first thing he did was straighten Judy out about the tree house.

"I haven't gone near that tree house. But when I do, what would I want with tar? Annie's not going to be up there in the middle of a storm. The roof doesn't have to be waterproofed."

The second thing he did was head for the tree house. Minutes later he was back, slamming the front door behind him.

"Goddamn kids!" he said.

Judy, who had flicked on the local evening news for the weather report, lowered the sound and turned angrily to Hal. "Don't blame Annie and Erin. They didn't know what was up there."

The weather girl had rolled down her map of the country and was smiling mindlessly as she pointed to a storm front that was threatening an uninhabited western area the size of the Kalahari.

"Don't be foolish," said Hal. "I'm not talking about Annie and Erin. I'm talking about high-school kids. Who else would pull a dumb stunt like that?"

"What do you mean?"

"I'll tell you what. That bucket of tar was *rigged* to come down. Some young smarty-pants tied a piece of fishing line from the bucket to the top step of the ladder so that any weight on it would tip the bucket over. Very funny. It must have taken some twerp half an hour to figure that one out. I hate to think what's going to be happening around here come Halloween."

13

The marketing meeting was held every Thursday at three in Hal's office. The room was almost twenty feet square and easily accommodated a circular conference table of highly polished oak. Ten director's chairs in bright orange ringed the table.

On the first day, four weeks ago, that Hal showed up for work, his initial piece of business was to meet with an interior decorator from Boston to discuss the "look" for his office. He quickly got the impression that the Hilliards had not put the decorator on a tight budget. Hal kept trying to take a cheaper desk chair here, a slightly smaller couch there. When Sy told him that everyone was getting the royal treatment, he let the decorator call the shots. And he was more than pleased with the results. It was the office he had dreamed he would have some day, without believing for an instant that it would ever come to pass.

The Hilliards' generosity led to a few strange effects. T.C. asked for, and got, a stand-up writing desk that was more than a hundred years old. Claire Simmons had her entire office done in high-tech, all pimpled black rubber and gleaming metal, which made Hal think of award-winning factories outside Milano. But if the new executive team occupied offices ready for a spread in *Interior Design,* the Hilliards themselves worked in settings befitting the welfare department of a Pennsylvania coal town. Rugs that looked like bath mats from single-room-occupancy hotels were scattered on the floors. They sat behind desks that would be politely refused by Goodwill Industries. Their walls were unadorned except for Howard Hilliard's framed notary-public certificate.

All the newcomers, with the exception of Aldo Lucci, attended the marketing meetings. The meetings were chaired by Elliott Hilliard, though he later had to check with his father on every decision. Cameron's shadow dominated the sessions. This frustrated Hal inordinately. Howard, who sat at his father's side, took the minutes. Roland Penney, who had been with the company more than thirty years and headed office administration, also attended. Hal couldn't recall him ever saying anything. Neither did Howard, for that matter.

Elliott started each meeting by covering matters pending from the last.

"My father thinks, after careful consideration of your proposal, Hal, that the plan to sponsor a hiking marathon on the Appalachian Trail is extremely interesting. He'd like to study it further. After all, it's a little too late to implement it this year anyway. As they say, let's put it in a holding pattern."

Hal leaned toward Sy and whispered, "I've heard that so often I'm beginning to feel like an air-traffic controller."

"New business?" continued Elliott in a soft voice, as if he really didn't want to hear any.

"Yes," said Hal. "We have two very exciting items for this meeting. I'd like Claire to present the first."

Claire Simmons took from a portfolio next to her chair several dummy ads mounted on cardboard and passed them around the table.

"We've talked before about an institutional ad campaign to position the company in the public mind and, more importantly, in the investment community as a quality company that's growing in exciting new directions. Now we've come up with a copy line that I think does the job beautifully. It will be the fulcrum for what is essentially a very comprehensive print approach and it will hit our intended audience on the nose. That line is: 'A great future is built on a great tradition.' The ads will feature a photo of one of our early products, or the first plant, for instance. We've worked out a media plan that will take us into *Business Week, Fortune,* and *The Wall Street Journal* but also extends into *Town and Country, The New Yorker, Down East,* and even *Natural History*."

Hal watched Elliott examine one of the dummy ads as if it were a subpoena. He smiled slightly as he slid the ad back across the table to Claire.

Hal reinforced Claire's presentation with a pitch of his own. He likened the proposed ads to a cross between the early Ogilvy campaign for Mercedes and the long-running and highly successful Jack Daniel's series. Sy followed with an analysis of how the new campaign would fit into the overall budget. He strongly approved the reduced rate that Hal would be able to secure by lining up a group of the magazines.

"Fascinating," said Elliott. "I will pass this plan on to my father. I'm sure he will be enthusiastic."

"Of course," said Hal, his sarcasm draped in tissue-thin cordiality.

"Anything else?" asked Elliott.

"Only the best opportunity I've seen in quite a while," said Hal, trying to cast his annoyance behind by coming on strong.

Hal explained that he had received a call from a fraternity brother who was trying to get the address of another brother. Hal didn't have the address, but they had talked for a while anyway, just catching up. This fellow, George Arden, was doing very well for himself. Just made executive producer with A.B.C. Sports. George started to tell Hal about some of the shows he was preparing. And one of them made Hal sit straight up in his chair. Because of the boom in cross-country skiing, A.B.C was planning to televise, with lots of promotion on the network preceding the event, the first All-American distance cross-country skiing event. Hal got the name of the man who handled the selling of time on the show and called him immediately. And, fortune smiling, there were still two spots open. Hal ran quickly through the costs of producing the spots and buying the time. They fit perfectly within the budget that he and Sy had worked up.

"TV buys like this don't come around very often," Hal stressed. "This is a shot to get the Hilliard name in front of exactly the people our products are designed for. Television generally gives you a mass audience. Here we're getting that plus a class audience. People who will buy our products. It's perfect."

T.C. and Reid added their endorsements and Sy pointed out that since this event was not a football game or championship prize fight, but an untested event, though just right for their uses, the rates were really a bargain.

"That's terrific, Hal. I'm sure my father will be just as excited by this proposal as all of you are. But it will, of course, require some scrutiny on his part."

"Elliott," said Hal quickly, "I realize that decisions like this have to be okayed by your father. But this is not something that can be put on the back burner. I know for a fact that another sponsor is dying to get these spots. And you know who that is? Adidas, for Christ's sake. And they're pushing sneakers! They realize that this is a prime audience. These are people who buy expensive sporting goods. People who wear down vests and save up for a new pair of ski boots or a kayak."

"I'll convey the immediacy of this to my father, Hal. Be assured that I will. I'm happy to say that Father is making marvelous progress and should be able to attend these meetings as well as others within the month. But, remember, this is an old firm. Try to understand what we are and where we come from. We are more than happy with all of you. You are as intelligent and imaginative a group as we had hoped you'd be. It just takes a while for two different rhythms to come into synchronization. It will happen. I can assure you of that. Thank you, Hal. And thanks to all of you for the splendid preparation and presentation. I will be speaking with my father later today and, hopefully, I'll have answers back to you within the week."

As Elliott stood, so did Howard and Roland Penney. Like faithful hunting dogs, they followed Elliott out of the office.

"According to my clock we are just moments short of the sun being over the yardarm," said Sy. "I say we retreat to our respective offices, clear all the unfinished work into our briefcases where it can hibernate for the night, and head to the Wayside for a mind-numbing potion."

"Sy," said T.C., smiling broadly, "a man of your insight and wisdom is sorely needed in the Oval Office."

"But what would the Berkshires do without me?"

• •

Ten minutes later, as the group was leaving the building for the parking area in the back, Hal was still bitching.

"If this company ever goes public, and I'm beginning to seriously wonder if it ever will, I propose that its new name be Spinning Wheels, Inc."

"What I can't understand," said Claire, "is why they don't complain about the cost of making these presentations. The typesetting alone on those ads cost almost six hundred dollars."

"Jesus, that's nothing," said Sy. "You ought to see their R and D budget. They've spent almost half a million bucks in

research and development lab fees over the last two years per-
fecting a preservative for their boots. It's amazing. On everything else they throw around dimes as if they were manhole
covers."

The field behind the building had been mowed the day before and the air was still redolent with it. If a smell could have
a color then this one was deep green. Off to the left came the
sound of hammers banging against metal. Aldo was supervising
two maintenance workers in the installation of a chain link
fence that would soon enclose the parking lot.

"Aldo's the only one who's really getting anything done
around here," mused Hal as he waved toward Aldo.

"I was going over some records a couple of days ago," said
Sy, almost to himself, "and the only break-in that's ever occurred here was in 1946. A drifter stole some bacon and coffee
from the small kitchen downstairs. But Aldo must think he's
still protecting P.S. 193 from the Amboy Dukes. I guess if he
wanted to build a moat, the Hilliards would let him."

Laughing, they all got into Hal's car for the drive to the
Wayside Inn.

14

"My backhand was just beginning to come
around. The rain kept you from a major embarrassment," said
Hal as he peered through the windshield wipers that were losing the battle to the start of an early-summer cloudburst.

"I know it's difficult, dear, to have a wife who is better than
you in tennis, but that's the way it is. I've been playing since I
was seven and you're not the only man I can beat."

"Miss Navratilova, truth is not the way to handle this ego-
shattered case. I'd prefer humoring or even outright falsehood.
The people on the other court thought you were giving me a
lesson."

"You weren't that bad."

"Now that's better. Not truthful, but better. I guess I'm resigned to losing to you. But we have to find a court closer to

home than the ones at Smith. It's almost a half hour each way."

"But not over freeways. Just a short hop on a two-lane road that winds in and around some beautiful hills."

"I've got to get you to do some direct-mail writing for us. You sound like a brochure. Remember, we didn't come to the Berkshires to drive more."

"You have to admit it is convenient to mix tennis with shopping the way we did today."

"I won't admit anything until you promise to throw the next game."

Judy laughed as Hal reached across the seat and traced a lazy, erotic circle against her thigh.

"I wish I had my list," said Judy after a moment. "I just know I forgot something."

"That's impossible. The back of this wagon looks like a supply truck for Stalingrad."

And even with the back seat down, the rear of the station wagon underlined Hal's statement. Two plastic-sheathed bales of loam stood up like a giant's building blocks amid bags of groceries from Stop & Shop. On top of this pile was a new rake and more than twenty dollars' worth of dry cleaning.

"You did pick up the striped bass at Schermerhorn's, didn't you?" Judy asked.

"Before I picked you up at Smith. Just like I told you then."

"Okay. I remember. It's just not having my list. I know it in my bones. There's something I haven't done."

"Annie!"

"No, she's at Erin's."

The rain picked up another notch and Hal flicked the wipers to the fast position. The rain was like a gray curtain, and he slowed the car to a crawl as they entered the village.

"I used to love a rain like this when I was a kid," said Judy.

"And that great smell that came after."

"I still like it."

As they passed the parsonage, Judy snapped her fingers.

"Remember what you forgot?" asked Hal.

"No. But I just remembered I want to invite Brad Peters over to dinner. I'll call him when we get home. The Prescotts will be good to have too. I wish we had a woman to invite as a sixth."

"There's always Laurie Hilliard. But she might try Brad's already stretched faith a little too far. Just remember to buy house-brand vodka for the bar. I might be making a good buck, but old Brad could break us if we poured Smirnoff."

"That's not funny, Hal. Brad's a decent fellow. He just cares a little too much. He seemed a lot better the other day when I ran into him at the post office."

"Take it easy, babe. I was just joking."

"Well, I guess I like you 'joking' better than moaning on about not getting a chance to change the world at Hilliard's."

"I know. I've been an absolute bore about that subject. But I must say, I've come to the realization that all my bitching and complaining vanishes when I endorse my check each month."

They were still laughing when Hal pulled the car into the driveway. The sky was continuing to make a major statement, and the visibility once the wiper blades stopped was nil.

"Let's forget the groceries, Jude. Every man for himself. Just run your ass off for the door."

It was only thirty feet between the car and the kitchen door, but more than enough distance for both of them to get soaked. They stood together on the mat inside the kitchen door as a small puddle formed at their feet.

"I love it."

"A good drenching is soul-purifying. But in my case it has the opposite effect," said Hal as he started to roll Judy's shirt up her back.

"Hal, stop it. Look, there's soup cooking on the stove. Mimi might pop in any second."

"Good thinking. Let's retreat with great stealth to our room and strip each other."

"You're crazy."

"No. Just carnally overwrought."

As they started to climb the steps, Judy stopped.

"What's that?" she said.

"What?"

"That."

From upstairs, almost blocked out by the kettledrum beating of the rain, came a thin, almost whispered sound. They both stood still, transfixed for a moment by the strangeness of the effect.

Then Judy started to race up the stairs.

"It's Mimi," she said.

By the time Hal reached Mimi's room, Judy was already kneeling alongside her. Mimi sat at the foot of her bed, keening softly into her cupped hands.

"What's wrong, Mimi?" asked Judy, stroking the back of her neck as if she were a child.

Mimi looked up, her face glistening with tears, and pointed to the bed. Then she started to cry again.

Hal and Judy saw it at the same time. At first they didn't realize what it was. And then they knew.

"Jesus," said Hal under his breath.

On the bed, looking like a clump of wet confetti, were the remains of Mimi's parakeet, Wonder. She had had Wonder when she came to work for them. A compact little bird of almost Day-Glo color that sang constantly and gloriously. Mimi had named him for Stevie Wonder. It wasn't unusual to see the bird perched on Mimi's shoulder when she cooked. She was devoted to the bird, just as she was devoted to her cat, Matelot. Of course! Matelot.

Hal and Judy looked at each other, both finally understanding what had happened.

"It's all right, Mimi," said Hal quickly. "I'm sure Wonder didn't feel anything. Matelot probably thought he was just playing with Wonder. You know he has gotten a little wild since you've been letting him outdoors here. I know—"

"No. It wasn't Matelot. Not Matelot. The missus took him to the vet this morning. No. Something else, something bad took Wonder."

And Judy knew that Mimi was right. *That* was the thing on the list that she had forgotten until right now. To pick up Matelot from the vet's. So it couldn't have been Matelot. She looked again at the little ball of feathers and blood on the coverlet. But what *had* killed Wonder? Judy thought. She held Mimi in her arms as Hal carefully folded the coverlet and took it out of the room.

15

MRS. EDWIN B. CLARK
273 SANDPIPER WAY
HILTON HEAD, S.C. 29928

June 18

My dear Judith,

Things here have been quiet—which is always good, I guess —so I've had a chance to catch up on a lot of chores that I've put off while we had the Kendalls visiting here. We do love them. After all, they're Daddy's and my best friends since we lived in Philadelphia, which is more years ago than I care to remember. They are *active* guests, though, and they kept both Daddy and myself busy!!! But we did have a fine time together. The Kindalls *loved* Hilton Head and looked at some property. It would be nice to have them down here. Here's hoping.

Hearing Ann on the phone the other day made me realize suddenly what a big girl she's become. And so *fast!* I know you won't believe me but she sounds just the way you did at the same age. She's a button. Daddy is still talking to anyone who'll listen to him at the club about Harold. My, is he proud! I even heard Daddy give Ollie Dickenson more than a clue as to Harold's salary. But don't worry, I stopped him in time. It's just that he's busting with reflected glory. Imagine, Executive Vice-President of a company as old and successful as Hilliard's. You can tell that I'm more than a bit swelled with pride myself.

Now don't get angry with me, Judith. I know that your initial reaction will be to pick up the phone and just yell at me. But stop a second. I've written an old classmate of mine, Margaret Love (that was her name when I knew her back in the *Stone Age!!*), who lives in Northampton and is just the sweetest, liveliest, smartest and almost anything else person I've ever known, and told her that you and Harold have moved into the area. Well, she immediately called me and is absolutely anxious to meet you. So, because I know that you're a little shy about these things, I've taken the liberty of arranging a luncheon get-together for you with her on Wednesday, the 24th. Don't try to call her and give her some excuse to call it off. You'll love her. I saw her at our Vassar *40th* (!!!!) last year, and she's as fabulous as ever. She's widowed and now lives with a marvelous man (quite a bit younger, I might add!!!). She was always the wild one. Margaret sells real estate and is known as quite an historian of the Berkshires. I guarantee that you will be entranced by her. Trust your mother. Please. Daddy's back is better and he sends love too. Kisses to Ann. Say hi to Harold.

> Much love,
> Mother

P.S. Margaret has your number and will be calling almost as soon as you get this letter. Give her my best.

16

The day that Judy was scheduled to have lunch with Margaret Love was one on which she didn't have to be in Northampton. She was there two out of five weekdays, sometimes even three, but this date *had* to fall on a day when she had no need whatsoever to be there. It was like L.A. again. A forty-mile round trip for lunch. Le Mans, here I come. And of course Annie woke up with enough imaginary illnesses to make Proust look like Jack LaLanne. She was going through a phase when a day didn't go by without her insisting that her temperature be taken. The ritual was pat. Annie felt her brow like Camille and announced she was "burning up." Nurse Mommy handed her the mercury wand, once a hated enemy, now an everyday necessity. After the requisite minute and one-half, Annie removed the thermometer and daintily passed it to her mother for the reading. Normal. Always. When, oh, when, Judy thought, will we enter the next phase? She dreaded what it would be.

To add to Annie's hypochondria, Mimi had become almost a basket case since Wonder's death. Hal had assured Mimi repeatedly that Wonder probably had been killed by one of the cats that lived in the Malleys' barn. The Malleys were their nearest neighbors and kept a dozen cows in a barn a quarter of a mile up the road. The barn cats, there were at least three, had the feral cunning of jungle predators. Since the window in Mimi's room had been open, Hal regarded his deduction as flawless. Not so Mimi. She now refused to stay in the house alone. The house had "bad things attached," she insisted. In fact, the town was touched too. God bless the primary-school system in Haiti! With great calm and logic, Judy had gotten Mimi to accept Annie as another person. So, the reasoning was almost Cartesian, she was therefore not alone. This morning Judy had left before Mimi could think of a rebuttal.

•   •

Margaret Love lived on a small street that curled above The Clarke School for the Deaf. The street consisted of large Victorian houses that stood alongside one another like huge linemen grouped for a team picture. Margaret Love's house would have thrust itself forward in Beverly Hills, but here, in this traditional New England setting, it seemed even more incongruous.

To begin with, the house was all glass and native stone. It was set back on a large grassy lot shaded by three enormous white pines. On the front lawn was a large black metal sculpture of what appeared to be cuticle scissors. The mailbox at the corner of the drive read: LOVE/MERRILL/STERN. Below that, in the same stylized script: LOVE REALTY. Judy was mentally running through her little prefatory speech that featured rushing home early to her sick daughter, which meant she couldn't stay as long as she really wanted to, when Margaret Love bounded out the front door.

"Judy! I love people who are on time since I've never managed it in my whole life."

"It's a first, I assure you."

As Judy turned after closing the car door, Margaret grabbed her firmly by both arms and looked intently at her.

"You're better-looking than your mother, though the resemblance is unmistakably there. And thank God you don't dress like her. I bet she still wears those very correct Peck and Peck dresses with just the right straw bag and sensible shoes. She's a dear and I love her, but my, oh, my, does she dress like the proper lady I never learned to be."

Judy joined Margaret in laughter as they walked up the front path.

Margaret gave Judy a quick tour of the house, occasionally breaking away to dash into the kitchen to put the finishing touches to lunch. The living room faced the back where a swimming pool reflected the sun like a hand mirror. The pool was painted black inside and resembled an old-fashioned swimming hole. A Jacuzzi, ringed by cedar, and also painted black, was alongside.

"I hate the look of those rectangular aquamarine jobbies you see everywhere. Then again I never liked Esther Williams' movies either."

The living-room walls were made of the same stone that faced the outside. They were softened and brightened by a quartet of marvelous Amish quilts that looked like early Ad Reinhardt paintings.

"You won't believe what these are worth now, but when I started to collect them in the early fifties they were both plentiful and cheap."

Margaret Love was an inveterate collector, and the spare, clean lines of the house's interior showed off her possessions beautifully. One wall in the kitchen was lined with fanciful tin Victorian food molds.

"You can still get in early on these. The prices are not out of sight yet."

Her bedroom, which had a window greenhouse set into one wall, housed her Early American basket collection. Judy never would have believed that old things could live so easily in this very modern setting.

The tour over, they went out to the slate patio in the back for lunch.

"I felt like having a slimming-green lunch. I hope you're not in the mood for knockwurst because this is aeons away from that."

They started with a cold asparagus soup.

"It takes a terribly long time for a bed of asparagus to get its act together, but I think the work and time are worth it."

Little bits of a darker green, like miniature lily pads, freckled the surface of the soup.

"Basil," answered Margaret before Judy could ask. "I'm mad for it. Harvey calls me a pesto maniac. I put it in everything."

Harvey turned out to be Harvey Stern, Margaret's live-in boy friend of almost ten years. He taught architecture at UMass and they had met when Harvey designed the plans for this house.

"Andrew had just died," Margaret said, "and I was an emotional dish towel. I knew I had to recharge the old batteries. I loved the house we had together. I must show it to you sometime. But I realized I needed something new. Something different. My boys, who were just out of college at the time, were very supportive, even though they loved the old house dearly. After all, it was the only house they had known. And as Harvey helped me plan and build this house we—well, we just fell in love. Of course everyone was scandalized at first. Andrew dead less than a year and here I was living with a Jewish architect, with a beard, who was ten years younger than myself. Horrors! But, again, the boys were very supportive. I don't know what Andrew and I did that was right in bringing them up, but I'll take full credit for it. They're marvelous guys.

"Since I felt I needed a fresh beginning I went back to my maiden name. Love. I had never liked the name when I was growing up, but I wanted something light, that people could even make a joke of once in a while. I've even told Harvey that if we go ahead and do the horrible deed of tying the knot, the furthest I'll go is Love-Stern. Harvey says it sounds like a tennis score."

After the soup, Margaret served a Bibb and fennel salad, picked fresh from her garden. Brown flakes of what Judy thought was bacon studded the tender leaves.

"Duck," said Margaret, again anticipating Judy's question. "I fry it and then kick it about a bit in the Cuisinart. I forget where I got the idea. I'm not that original. My strength is in adaptation."

After lunch, she served small cups of green Japanese tea.

"I told you it would be a green lunch. Now tell me all about yourself and Hal and Annie. And lots and lots about your house. I think I know which one it is. Real estate is not just a profession with me. I really love old houses."

As Judy recounted their move from Los Angeles, Hal's new job with Hilliard's, her getting back into painting again, in short, her life, Margaret sat across from her gazing steadily, a small smile playing at the corners of her mouth. Margaret was a marvelous listener, only interrupting for a clarification or some additional detail. Her eyes were the kind of blue found on old china. Though she was tanned from working outdoors in her garden, her skin was remarkably unlined. Her hair was naturally silver-gray and lustrous. She was wearing a simple pair of blue pants offset with a gay rose-colored silk shirt that was open at the neck.

When Judy finished, or, rather, wound down, Margaret questioned her closely about their house.

"I know it. Absolutely. Used to be owned by a family named Pratt. In the family for more than a hundred years. It was quite run-down when the Hilliards bought it. That must be almost twenty years ago."

"We bought our house from a man named Sharp."

"He's just the man who runs the Hilliards' real-estate interests. They own most of Ripton Falls, you know."

"I know that. But I didn't think they had owned our house. Well, anyway, we got a pretty good deal on it."

After Judy told Margaret what they had paid, Margaret more than agreed with her.

"I'll say you made a good deal," said Margaret. "I'm regarded as a softy by the other agents around here, but even I could have gotten at least twenty thousand more for your place."

"Mother says that you're a historian of this area. Is there something special about our house?" asked Judy, thinking about Mimi's fears and almost dreading what Margaret might say.

"Aside from its being a house of record and a real beauty, I'm sorry to say there's nothing. Its history is as dull as dishwater. The Pratts were the town's veterinarians for almost four generations. And they were as exciting as the bovine creatures they ministered to."

"Well," said Judy, exhaling, "that suits me fine. I don't like things that go bump in the night."

"But you do live in a *town* with a deliciously evil past," said Margaret Love, her smile flickering mischievously.

Before continuing, she ceremoniously refilled their cups with more steaming green tea.

"There's almost no documentation of it, it's legend really, but when historical buffs in this area like myself mention Ripton Falls, it's generally in connection with the Ripton Falls children's coven. So little is known because the town didn't want the outside world to hear about what took place. And what took place must have been . . . horrible. The only written reference to it is a fragment of a rhyme that appeared in a newspaper dozens of years later. And there's a painting. The painting is the most fascinating part. But I'm jumping ahead."

"It's funny," said Judy, "but I haven't heard a word about any coven, children's or otherwise."

"Oh, it's very verboten still. Of course, the Hilliards, being the town's big boosters and major exchequers, look upon talk of the legend as they would publicizing an outbreak of syphilis in their family. After all, we know about the Salem witch trials because there *were* trials. Over a protracted period of time. What happened at about the same time in Ripton Falls, *if* it occurred at all, took place in a frenzy.

"It seems there was a group of children, eventually seven all together. The legend refers to them as a coven, but they weren't really. I gather from my superstitious friends that bona fide covens have thirteen members, always adult. These children were all very young. The first sign the townspeople had that evil was in their midst was a dead animal found by a farmer in one of his fields. A calf only a few days old. Its throat had been ripped out and its heart carved neatly from its body. The slaughterings continued, and they were always the same. Young animals—lambs, baby pigs, calves—always killed in the same fashion. This went on for months. The townspeople suspected who was behind it—the children had been seen together more than once—but they couldn't prove it. And then, so the story goes, these seven vile, evil children decided to increase their numbers. By seven. Audaciously they set out to recruit the new seven from the most religious families in town. Two, in fact, were sons of the minister. What happened next is unclear. Whether they were unable to enlist the 'good seven,' as the legend called them, or they were afraid of being betrayed, the evil seven took to their knives again. Early the next morning, the bodies of the seven good children were found in a field. They were arranged in a circle. They had been slaughtered like the animals. Throats ripped and hearts plucked from their chests. Apparently the villagers had no doubt who committed this monstrous act. They set off en masse, trapped the children in a barn, and burned it to the ground. Destroyed it and them. Soon after, a cautionary rhyme sprang up, the kind of thing mothers must have recited to their small children: 'Tarry not near children seven/Lest your soul rise fast to heaven.' And there you have it. Ripton Falls, indeed all of the Berkshires, have been free of covens ever since. I must say I love the fact that this so-called coven was made up of children. Nice twist, don't you think? Though hardly subject matter for a Disney film."

Judy was quiet for some time before she spoke.

"My God, what a tale. I'd better not repeat a word of it to our Haitian housekeeper. She's a lovely woman, but she believes the devil killed her parakeet. Witches and demons are as real to her as Laverne and Shirley. But what about the painting you mentioned?"

"Ah, the painting. It's reputed to have been done from memory after the event. It's supposed to show all seven of the children."

"The coven children?"

"Yes, of course. I assume so. It's the Lizzie Bordens and the Boston Stranglers of the world who catch our fancy, not their victims. Besides, I can't think of any other reason why it went for the price it did."

"You mean it was up for sale recently?"

"About a year ago. It was found in the attic of an old woman in Maine. Before then it only was rumored to exist. When the old lady died, her estate came up for auction in Springfield. Unfortunately, I was with Harvey at a convention in Chicago at the time, so I didn't get a chance to see the painting. The auctioneer, who's a friend of mine, thought it would go for under three thousand. A price determined mainly by its age. The painting itself, according to my friend, was, to put it mildly, uninspiring. But, as so often happens these days, there was a collector at the auction from Japan. A man who really wanted it. The Japanese, you know, are getting into American art now. Not to mention almost everything else."

"What did he pay for it?" asked Judy.

"Well, that's the fascinating thing. He didn't get it. He was outbid by Cameron Hilliard's granddaughter."

"Laurie?"

"Yes, that's her name. Laurie Hilliard. She just hung in there until finally the Japanese man tossed in his hand. At nine thousand dollars! For an unattributed American primitive. Caused quite a bit of excitement in these parts."

"I'll say. Where's the painting now?" asked Judy.

"Probably in a dark vault somewhere far from here," answered Margaret laughingly. "Wouldn't do to exhibit a painting that had something to do with Ripton Falls's dirty, evil past. But why don't you ask the Hilliards? You're almost family. Maybe they'll give you a peek."

"I think I will," said a smiling Judy. "If I paid nine thousand for something I'd be more than happy to show it off."

A buzzer went off in the kitchen and Margaret got up quickly.

"Now why did that ring? Of course! My quiche. Be back in a sec," she said over her shoulder as she disappeared into the kitchen. A few minutes later she returned.

"You'll have to excuse me, Judy. I'm so terribly forgetful. I've been having such a delightful time with you that I've fallen behind on my timetable for dinner. Harvey has invited the head of his department. A very boring man who Harvey says couldn't design a decent lean-to, but academia is as suffused with politics as politics itself. I must pull out all stops tonight and give it my total Julia Child effort. Plus listen avidly to the old windbag's interminable, pointless stories. I must really love Harvey."

Margaret quickly hugged Judy.

"Your mother is a very lucky woman. But now I feel that I'm even luckier. I'll get to see more of you than she does. We will be friends, won't we?"

"Only forever," answered Judy.

Judy returned the embrace and for a moment neither woman moved.

On the way out to the car, Judy asked Margaret if she believed the legend of the children's coven.

"My family reaches too far back in New England for me not to have a certain . . . predisposition toward believing it. But that's all you're going to get out of me. If Harvey heard me say even that, I'd never hear the end of it. He likes to claim that I'm interested in a Jew because I think I'll learn the secret of the golem. I do admit I love scary things. I never miss *Psycho* when it's on the tube. The coven is just another good yarn. Though it would be even better if it were real."

17

"May I speak to Laurie Hilliard, please?"

"Who shall I say is calling?"

Correct grammar no less. Big-city office technique up here in the Berkshires, thought Judy.

"Judy Richardson. Hal Richardson's wife."

"One moment, please."

Judy didn't have time to file even one nail before Laurie came on.

"Hi, Judy. I hope that everything is well. It's funny that you called. I've been meaning to call you for the past few weeks. A while back I was driving past the church on the Green. You know, the run-down one? Well, I saw your daughter swinging out back. I was worried about her. If that equipment is in the same shape the church is, she could have had a bad accident. I thought she was with your housekeeper so I didn't stop."

"Well, thanks for your concern," said Judy a bit coldly. "She was with me that day. I'm sure the swing is safe."

"What can I do for you?" asked Laurie, back to her crisp business self.

"At lunch the other day a friend of mine told me about a fascinating painting that you bought last year at an auction in Springfield."

"May I ask what friend told you that?" asked Laurie, her voice betraying more than annoyance.

"You probably know her. Margaret Love. She lives in Northampton. She sells real estate."

"I know the woman."

"The painting is of some children. It's very old."

"Of course, *The Ripton Falls Children*," said Laurie, quickly. "I'd love to show it to you, but it will have to wait a while. The painting is out on loan. Somewhere in Europe, I think. You see, the more we lend it out to museums the more its appraised value increases. We did spend quite a bit for it, as you may know, and we want to protect our investment. Anyway, it won't be back for at least a year. Got to run, Judy. I'm late for a meeting. Let's talk again soon. 'Bye."

Judy held the phone to her ear for a moment before she realized the line was dead. She placed the phone back on its cradle softly, as if Laurie were still on the other end. For some reason Judy knew deep down that Laurie had not told her the truth.

18

The *Ripton Rondelay* was a six-page mimeographed weekly paper put out by the Ladies Benevolent Association. The suggested yearly subscription was seven dollars. It listed everything that had happened and was scheduled to happen in Ripton Falls. From chimney fires, weekend visitors, and Riptonites recovering from surgery to what was being served for lunch at the local schools. It was next to an advertisement for yard work and mowing that Judy saw an announcement that the Ripton Falls Historical Society would be taking applications for new members at the town hall the following day. The last organization Judy had joined had been the Girl Scouts. And that was only because her mother thought the uniforms were precious and the mix of girls in the group "good for Judy." Judy hated it. But here she was, seriously entertaining the idea of joining the Historical Society, of all things. Part of it was the coven story Margaret Love had told her and part was her fascination with the town. She had never lived as an adult in a place whose historical roots, like a mangrove's, were so visible.

The next day, before going to Northampton, Judy stopped in at the town hall. She had passed the building often but this was her first time inside. The outside, painted every two years, thanks to the largess of the Hilliards, gleamed like an iceberg in the early-morning light. Stepping into the entry hall, Judy immediately saw the sign "Hist. Soc. Reg." taped to a door on the right. Like everything in the town hall, the pale pine floor shone. Judy almost slipped as she walked across its gleaming polyurethane finish. It would be nice, she thought, to get the Hilliards to endow her wardrobe.

Straight ahead was an auditorium with folding chairs neatly stacked against one of the walls like letters waiting to be mailed. At the far end was a generously proportioned stage. Angling away from the walls were large, old black-and-white photographs framed the old-fashioned way in no-nonsense black. Town panoramas and sports teams. The door to the right led into a much smaller room, a meeting room of some kind for it was dominated by a long, curved conference table surrounded by comfortable-looking wooden chairs. These walls too were dense with memorabilia, the most prominent of which was a relief map of the town. The sole occupant of the room raised her head and smiled as Judy came in.

"Good morning," the woman twittered cheerfully.

She appeared to be in her early seventies, though she clearly worked at looking younger. The results were mixed. She had that wonderfully smooth skin that some elderly women are blessed with—Judy always wanted to touch it to see if it was as pillowy soft as it seemed—and bright, sharp eyes behind bifocals. But her cheeks were outrageously pink and her carefully waved hair had been rinsed in a blue dye that resembled nothing so much as the shade that television sets mutate to when their color-control systems go out of whack.

"I'm Judy Richardson, and I want to—"

"Oh, I know who you are, Judy," interrupted the woman. "Remember, this *is* a small town. I'm so pleased to meet you at last. I've always loved your house. I told Hardy years ago that if ever we sold our own house yours would be the one other spot I'd like to own. Tell me, are you enjoying our lovely town?"

"Yes, indeed. In fact, that's why I'm here right now."

"Lordy, lordy," exclaimed the woman. "Forgive me my rudeness. Here I am going on and I haven't even introduced myself. I'm Minna Gannon."

"How do you do, Mrs. Gannon."

"No, no. You must call me Minna. Everyone does. I guess you might say I'm kind of like the town mother. Comes from all those years of Hardy being the foreman over at Hilliard's. He's retired now, of course, but seems like we've always been at the center of things. And I promise you there's not a soul in Ripton Falls that I don't know, born or moved here, and I'm proud of it."

"I don't wonder. It seems like a very special place, and now that we're settled in, we'd like to join the Historical Society."

"Well, isn't that nice of you to take an interest in our doings here. We'd love to have you as members, but there's a one-year residency requirement before you can join."

"Really?" said Judy. What a joke on her.

"But perhaps you could sit in unofficially at the next meeting," said Minna accommodatingly. "That would be December first. Winter is the start of meeting time around here."

"Not until then? That *is* frustrating."

"Yes, I can see that it would be, but that's our custom. We have our annual membership drive every summer and start our meetings six months later."

Judy nodded. She didn't have to be at Smith until eleven and her other errands could wait until another day.

"Since I'm here," she began tentatively, not sure what other local customs she might bump up against, "do you think I might take a look through some of the town records? I'd love to see if I can trace the history of our house."

Minna's face lighted up.

"But of course," she exclaimed. "I can't think why I didn't suggest that myself. The town records are stored in the room next door. Come with me and I'll show you, but, first, did you notice this map of Ripton Falls? Commissioned by Cameron Hilliard and donated to the town. Every last house is represented on it. Think you can find yours?"

As she followed Minna Gannon up to the map, Judy wondered how even for a minute she could have thought that this nice, friendly woman would say no to her request. Minna, of course, had to locate the house on Quarry Road, making Judy feel a little silly, as if she'd flunked one of those I.Q. tests that ladies' magazines are always featuring. Then Minna led her into the adjoining room. Its floor-to-ceiling bookshelves were crammed with fat leather-bound volumes packed tightly together like loaves of bread at a bakery. A sprinkling of sturdy file boxes for loose items ranged along the lower shelves. After pointing out how the material was organized—birth, marriage, and death records here, title deeds there, town-meeting minutes over there—Minna quietly closed the door behind her.

Judy immediately checked out their house. Its first owner of record was one Joshua Warden, a farmer who had come to Ripton Falls from Greenfield as a young man with three cows, one goat, and a small flock of sheep. Thirty years later he died in the house, the father of seven, and there followed almost fifty more years of Warden ownership as the house passed from father to eldest son. Then came the Leedses, the Newburys, and, yes, Margaret, the Pratts of veterinarian fame. The prospect of their own names being entered into the record thrilled Judy.

The march of dates and events, usually unaccompanied by comment from the less garrulous people of these earlier years, pulled her on. The stories the simple facts told were sometimes comical, sometimes moving. In one year an epidemic of influenza wiped out half the children in the town under the age of five. In another a brick works employing eighteen men failed. Over the course of a dozen years, two brothers with adjoining property issued claims and counterclaims to the rights to a thirty-two-foot-long section of a brook dividing their land. That part of the brook was eventually declared town property.

Gradually Judy became aware that none of the material she had been examining reached back into the seventeen hundreds.

"Why, yes," explained Minna, a little surprised by Judy's question. "There was a terrible fire at the town hall in the early eighteen hundreds. It destroyed everything. All our papers. But, of course, how could you know."

"Your primary sources? What an awful loss."

"Oh, it hasn't really seemed that way to us. We've never

found the lack of those records a handicap, since we've been able to piece together the way it was. In fact, it was the Hilliards who made that possible. They were fairly new in town, but already they were thinking of what was best for Ripton Falls. Seems they hired a young man to go around and talk with the town elders soon after the fire. Draw on what these older folks remembered. It's all down in our official town history."

Minna picked up a slim blue volume from the top of the table and held it up toward Judy.

"I'm putting through an order in a few days for new copies of the history. We offset them and order them in batches of ten. Shall I put you down for one? It's fifteen dollars."

Judy gave Minna her order and arranged to pay for her copy later. She had just noticed how late in the morning it was, and she would have to hustle to make her class in time.

"By the way," Minna called after her, "people around here favor traditional art, but we surely hope you'll donate one of your pictures to our next Historical Society auction."

"Sure thing," said Judy, waving goodbye. There was nothing shy about Minna Gannon, she thought with amusement.

As she hurried down the front steps, her eye was caught by a gleaming brass plaque mounted on the corner of the building. "C. 1773."

How odd. What about the fire? Did only one room burn? But Margaret would be able to explain it. And with that thought, Judy turned her attention to the more important matter at hand: how to make it to Northampton in under twenty minutes.

19

"Do me a favor?" asked Hal as they drove home from Greenfield after dinner and the movies.

"Anything, my dear. I'm feeling very generous tonight," Judy replied suggestively.

"Please. Not after manicotti. Especially the Greenfield variety. I feel as though there's a black hole deep within my abdomen."

"Well, what other favor do you desire?" Judy asked.

"Stop reading Pauline Kael. She has to be the one who led us to that Fassbinder movie tonight. Jesus. Warn me next time. I'd rather entertain Qaddafi."

"You're beginning to sound very provincial, love. Maybe a little supper theater would be more on target for you. Say, Van Johnson and Gisele MacKenzie doing *Two for the Seesaw?* I found the movie interesting."

"The term 'interesting,'" said Hal, "is generally used by the intellectually pretentious to mask a lack of understanding."

"There was nothing in that movie that I didn't understand," Judy replied with a slight testiness.

"Okay. I admit my own aesthetic deficiency. But I want to go on record as saying that I understand as much about quarks as I did about that film. Occasionally, however, I do get a great idea. My latest one is that there's a Friendly's about a quarter of a mile down the old road. A nice dish of butter pecan would do my black hole a lot of good."

Judy thought butter pecan a terrible idea, though walnut fudge had the right ring to it, so she ordered two scoops. They followed the ice cream with coffee, since both were world-ranked sleepers whom nothing could deter from reaching deep sleep within minutes of their heads hitting the pillow.

"I did an un-Judy-like thing today," she said, pouring too much white sugar into her coffee. It just made it taste good.

"Let me guess. You ran into Aldo at the Stop and Shop and suddenly decided to repair to the Pine Crest Motel to watch a few X-rated flicks from the circular water beds."

"No, but you seem to know a lot about the place," answered Judy.

"Just reading the *Berkshire Eagle* closely, that's all."

"You're going to laugh. I went to the town hall today. I asked about joining the Historical Society."

"And you're the one who feels uneasy belonging to the A.A.A.," he said after what seemed like a minute.

"Can't a person change?" she said defensively. "It's just that I'm interested in the town."

"'Fess up. It's the coven story Margaret Love told you."

"Partially. But not entirely. I've never lived in a place where history is everywhere you turn."

"When's the next meeting?" Hal asked, signaling the waitress for a refill.

"Not until December. But I would only be able to sit in as an observer. You have to live in Ripton Falls for a year before you can join."

"Sounds reasonable, though a little strict. Anything else?"

Judy told Hal about her talk with Minna Gannon.

"Picasso could have done his entire 'blue period' with just one of her hair rinses. You must catch her. It does seem strange, though, that their records stop short of the seventeen hundreds even though the building is quite a bit older."

"Probably only part of it burned down. New England history, unfortunately, was wrapped in wood. That's what makes old buildings rare. By the way, did I tell you what Sy told me today?"

"What?"

"T.C. received a job offer from a college classmate. He owns one of those hot chip companies."

"Chip companies? You mean like Famous Amos?" asked Judy.

"No, dummy. Silicon chips. Those little computer gadgets that store information. This guy started the company about ten years ago with just five thousand bucks. Now he's worth millions. Well, he offered T.C. a job that tempted him quite a bit. The company's located on the peninsula outside San Francisco and that's near Emily's parents. Also, it's a pretty nice area. But the real temptation was the bucks."

"How much was T.C. offered?"

"That I don't know. But after T.C. had a long talk with old Cameron himself, Sy received a call instructing him to put in a raise for T.C. of ten thousand dollars effective immediately."

"Not bad," said Judy, smiling.

"Not bad is right," Hal replied, raising his coffee cup and clinking it against Judy's. "Here's to *me* getting a decent offer somewhere else. It could get us a swimming pool."

20

At first Annie didn't want to go.

"There'll just be little kids there, Mom."

"Mrs. Goldin has assured me Erin will be there. Also a few kids older than you."

"Erin'll be there?"

"Absolutely."

Thankfully, everything Judy had told Annie about Tracy's birthday party turned out to be true. Erin *was* there and there were older kids attending too. Of course the older children, friends of Seth, wanted no part of Annie and Erin. But that didn't bother the two girls since they were allowed to sit at their table. The big kids' table!

Lisa, a compulsive organizer, had the party arranged with the precision of the Ice Capades. First there were group games, then individual tests of skill. It was set up that every kid won a prize, so tears were kept to a minimum. After the games an Amherst student did magic tricks. While all this was going on, the parents were grouped around their own table happily eating pâté and Brie washed down with white wine.

Judy was surprised to find Laurie Hilliard there. Had she and Lisa become such good friends? As the two made small talk, Judy was struck by how warm and pleasant Laurie was, completely unlike the way she had been on the phone that day a week ago. And she did seem to charm the kids. They all smiled and waved to her.

Sy, who had taken the afternoon off, was continuously on the move, recording the proceedings with his new video camera. Judy never once had encountered either Sy or Lisa when they were not sporting some bright and shiny new possession.

Tracy, the star attraction, seemed strangely uninvolved with the shouting and laughter surrounding her. Judy watched her as closely as she could without staring. Though she hadn't done a portrait since college, she had almost asked Lisa twice if she could paint the little girl. Part of it was the fact that Tracy had come so close to dying. It had changed her. Made her more lovely. There was something about the repose of her face that made her seem so much older. And her eyes, run-of-the-mill field-mouse brown, now seemed luminous. Gone, too, were the twitchings and tics of the child. Throughout the party, when she wasn't participating in a game, she just sat there, calmly watching the show. It's a hell of a way to mature a child, but it was almost as if the child who emerged from that terrible accident had benefited from it.

And then the lights dimmed. The children hushed, knowing what was coming. Sy moved next to Judy. He handed her the video camera.

"I want to come out of the kitchen with Lisa, so will you take over? This thing is easier to use than a regular camera. I've already adjusted the exposure. Just focus here and press this to run it. Keep your finger down. I don't want to miss anything."

Before Judy could tell Sy that she had trouble using a Brownie, he was gone. Shouldering the camera, Judy moved closer to Tracy, who sat at the head of the small kids' table. They all wore shiny pointed party hats, and as Judy sighted the group she thought for a second that they looked like two rows of sharpened pencils. She directed the camera at Tracy. Sy had set up a portable spot near the entranceway aimed at her. The light produced a Rembrandt effect that popped Tracy out of the background.

Judy was focused on Tracy when Sy and Lisa entered carrying the cake. Instead of a regular-sized birthday cake, the Goldins had bought one that would have satisfied a Teamster fund raiser. And instead of small candles, they had used tapers, each as long as a straw and as thick as a thumb. Everybody started singing "Happy Birthday." As the Goldins moved closer to Tracy, the little girl started to cry. At first, tears rolled down her face and a low sound, like the whimper of a forlorn animal, seemed to come from somewhere within her. And then Tracy began to shake. The singing began to trail off as the child's moan raised in pitch and seemed louder than a small child was capable of producing. Judy, mesmerized, stared through the lens, her finger locked on the recording button. Sy quickly placed the cake in front of Tracy. Points of light from the candles jigged across her face. Tracy raised her hands and jerked back. The chair tipped to the rear and she fell. Quickly, Sy scooped her up. Lisa blew out the candles and turned the lights on.

"That's okay, honey," said Sy to Tracy, who clung to him fiercely.

"Just a little too much excitement," one of the parents next to Judy volunteered.

"That's right, dear, it was a little scary, wasn't it," said Sy to the still-shaking child.

And then Judy watched as Laurie went to Tracy's side. Laurie reached down and stroked the little girl's fine, dark hair. Just like an adoring aunt. Tracy looked up and through her tears saw who was touching her. Almost as if a switch had been thrown, the child settled down.

21

Every Sunday over the past month, while Hal plunged into what he termed a "field hand's" breakfast and *The New York Times,* Judy, Mimi, and Annie had started going to church. Judy had become quite fond of Brad Peters and she tried to help him as much as she could. She had recruited a half-dozen parishioners from friends at Smith and even had convinced the Prescotts to attend. Brad seemed a different person from the one she had first met, more at ease with himself, more self-confident, and his sermons, to what now could be called a real congregation, were witty and moving. He was well read and it wasn't unusual for him to deliver a sermon that contained quotes running the gamut from Unamuno and Wittgenstein to Alice Cooper and Yogi Berra. Mimi always had to have the sermon explained at length to her on the drive home. Annie had developed the gift of sitting still and liked the singing.

The idea for Spruce-Up Saturday was Annie's.

"You know, Mom," she said to Judy as they drove past the church one afternoon, "Mr. Peters' church could really use some sprucing up."

"Annie, that's a pretty good idea."

Brad Peters thought so too. Quickly signs were made, friends enlisted, contributions solicited. Hal gave up an afternoon of trout fishing and Aldo generously volunteered his talents—and those of his bowling team. Even the Hilliards responded. Judy was more than a little surprised when Brad showed her a pile of paints, brushes, and other hardware that had just arrived from Anderson's General Store.

"I told him I didn't order this. There must be some mistake. No mistake, Mr. Anderson told me. It was ordered by Cameron Hilliard. Said to charge it to their account."

Spruce-Up Saturday was a beautiful summer's day. A few powder-puff clouds hung motionless against a pale-blue sky.

"It's nice to see that He occasionally listens to me," said Brad Peters to Judy, smiling as he looked up at the postcard sky.

"It's nicer to see the Hilliards finally do something for the church for a change."

By noon there were more than two dozen adults and half as many kids painting, scraping, raking, and, best of all, laughing. The kids were being paid fifty cents an hour and all the soda they could drink. It got results. T.C. Junior was taking turns on the power lawn mower with Rob Schackman, whose father was the town's dentist. The Lucci twins were weeding the flower beds that bordered the front walk.

Though Annie sulked a bit after unsuccessfully lobbying for painting, when she was teamed with Gwen Prescott at washing windows she liked it fine. And even with a soda break every fifteen minutes, they seemed actually to be making progress.

Just past one Margaret Love showed up with her boy friend, Harvey. When Margaret had heard about the cleanup she immediately volunteered to supply lunch. She and Harvey carried tray after cellophane-wrapped tray of sandwiches out of their BMW.

"We've got a real ethnic mix here. Everything from prosciutto to pastrami," said Margaret as she undid the wrappings.

"I vouch for the pastrami," said Harvey. "I had some business in New York yesterday and I got it at the deli that won the *New York* magazine contest last year."

Harvey was a tall, thin man with a shy, almost self-deprecating smile. His full beard was crosshatched with filaments of gray. He never took his eyes off of Margaret and touched her at every opportunity.

While the group stopped for lunch, Margaret and Harvey walked in and about the church with Brad Peters, sharing fine points of its architecture and history. Lunch broke up when Howard and Lauri Hilliard arrived in a company pickup truck filled with plywood sheeting, clapboards, and two-by-fours.

"Hope there's something left for us," said Laurie as she got out of the truck.

"There's plenty," answered Judy, walking up to her. "Margaret made enough sandwiches to feed the town."

Brad Peters came up to them and the three walked to the back of the truck.

"I haven't thanked you yet, Miss Hilliard, for all the hardware. Now this," he said, pointing to the filled truck bed.

"First off, Mr. Peters, it's Laurie. Secondly, all this material comes from a misestimated wine cellar that Father put in last year. And thirdly, we'd very much appreciate your giving us a contribution receipt to help us with Uncle Sam."

"You're still being very kind. And please call me Brad."

Howard Hilliard came silently up to them. He tried to smile, the corners of his mouth briefly tenting upward and then immediately collapsing.

"Brad, this is my brother, Howard. And, Howard, you know Judy Richardson, of course."

Howard nodded to both of them and then shook Brad's hand. His hand completely covered Brad's. His eyes, as transparent as a Weimaraner's, stared at Brad for a moment and then focused abruptly at some point beyond him.

"Mr. Peters, could you please help me?"

It was Rob Schackman. Behind him he pulled the lawn mower.

"It's this darn mower. It keeps stalling out. Now I can't start it at all."

"I'm afraid you've come to the wrong man, Rob. Try Mr. Lucci. He's the fix-it man here today."

"Mind if I try?" said Howard, his voice as soft as a sigh.

The big man bent down and removed the engine cover from

the mower. Within seconds he replaced it. He gave the pull cord a snap and the motor roared to life.

"Howard can repair anything. From clocks to railroad engines. If it has moving parts, he knows what to do with it," said Laurie, smiling up at her brother. "Well, let's get this show on the road."

Laurie grabbed an armload of clapboarding and walked toward the church. Quickly the others came to the truck and began to unload the material. Within a few minutes the truck bed was almost empty. Only a few large planks remained. Laurie, who already had made two trips, started to raise one of the planks onto her shoulder. Judy, heading back, saw the strain of the weight tighten Laurie's face. Before Judy could reach the truck, Laurie had asked T.C. Junior for help. Though the boy was tall for his age, his end of the board was so much lower that the rest of it angled up steeply toward Laurie.

"Put it on your shoulder, dear," Laurie said to him.

The boy lugged the board to his shoulder.

"I think it would be easier if you shifted to the other side," said Laurie sweetly.

As T.C. Junior hefted the board, Judy saw something on it glint in the sunshine. It was a nail protruding wickedly from the end of the board, just inches from the boy's cheek. And then Laurie moved forward before T.C. Junior was ready. He yelled and dropped the plank at the same time. As Judy got to his side, the blood already was streaming down from a long, sweeping cut that ran in an upward arc across his cheek. She cupped his head in her arms and pressed her handkerchief against the flowing wound.

"Oh, I feel terrible. I thought he was ready," said Laurie, looking down and biting her lip.

The others gathered around the boy.

"Dr. Martin keeps Saturday-afternoon hours at the clinic. Let's get the boy over there. A couple of butterfly stitches and he'll be fine," said a man wearing the same type of bowling shirt as Aldo.

Hal and Brad reached down and helped T.C. Junior to his feet. The initial shock and fear had worn off and the boy tried to smile. He bravely walked with the two men toward the doctor's office, which was just four houses off the Green. Judy watched them as they walked away. She thought of that frozen second when the nail lashed into the boy's cheek. And then of the bright line of blood outlining the scar that would come later. She ran her hand unconsciously across her own cheek. She had felt so helpless watching it happen. It was like the moment a glass falls off a table and is poised for what seems time out of time before it crashes to the floor. Thank God, Judy thought, she hadn't been holding the other end of the board. Poor Laurie. She turned to go to Laurie. To tell her that of course it wasn't her fault. To comfort her. But Laurie was not there. The truck was gone.

22

Hal took possession of his first serious toy and the only real indulgence of his adult life late the following week. It was a shiny blue Jeep. What a difference from the other car. The real thing, with four-wheel drive, an auxiliary gas tank, and a canvas top. Hal viewed the car as eminently useful, what with the snow and mud of the Berkshires. Also, they needed a second car, didn't they? Judy teased him a bit, saying that the next manifestation of his new macho image would be a Marlboro tattoo.

Annie gave the car her ultimate compliment: it was neat-o.

That Saturday Hal and Judy piled Annie, Percy, their mutt, and a picnic hamper into the Jeep and headed out to do some back-road exploring. Percy, long ago labeled the world's laziest dog by Hal, had to be dragged off the porch where, according to Judy, he was doing a great imitation of a throw rug in a splash of sun.

They took a road that backed off the plant and snaked into the hills above. Appropriately called Mountain Road, it bisected a huge tract of Hilliard land. Using a U.S. Geological Survey map that showed most of the old town roads and logging trails, they slowly made their way up into the hills. They drove for fifteen minutes along dirt roads that became rougher and less traveled with each successive mile. Fingers of sunlight reached down through the tunnels of trees.

"That looks like an old cellar hole. Let's take a look," said Hal, stopping the Jeep.

A crumbling stone foundation, like a mouthful of bad teeth, peeped out of the weeds in front of the hole. The Richardsons clambered down into the pit. They poked around in the leafy carpet with sticks and Annie found an old shard of pottery. Perfect material for "show and tell" when school started again in the fall. Nearby they found three other cellar holes.

"You know, Annie, this was probably part of Ripton Falls. A hundred years ago, or even less, I bet these woods were all farms. Just close your eyes tight. You can almost imagine the way it was. Fields with cows grazing on them. Stone walls high and neat. Flowers in the front yards."

"Hal, darling?" asked Judy, "how about imagining up a nice clearing where we can spread the blanket and have some lunch?"

They drove on. Some of the roads looked as if they were never used except by the crews that cut the brush for firebreaks. They passed other cellar holes and an abandoned cemetery. For a few miles a stream ran alongside the road. In places on the opposite bank they saw remnants of what had been mills or dams. They turned off on a road that they could not find on the map. Within two miles, just before a steep hill, they spotted a lovely clearing. It was almost square and at least two acres. It was bordered by white pines and scrub trees.

"It's surprising," said Hal as he helped Judy spread the blanket, "that a small field like this would exist in the middle of nowhere. Second-growth trees always take over cleared land that's not worked. It's almost as if somebody maintains it, but that can't be. It must just be something about the quality of the soil here."

Lunch for Hal and Judy was a local cheddar, crusty French bread, Black Forest ham, and fresh raspberries. Annie had peanut butter with the edges cut off the bread. She ate only half her sandwich, which was usual, but all four of her Oreos, also usual.

Annie started to get restless and insisted on taking Percy for a walk. Percy had resumed his snooze on the blanket. He submitted to being leashed and accompanied Annie with the alacrity of a prisoner facing an execution squad.

"Don't go too far," said Judy as Annie dragged Percy toward the other end of the field.

"Okay," she called back. "We'll just explore a bit."

Hal had forgotten the corkscrew. After struggling for several minutes to pry the cork out of the bottle of Chablis, he finally pushed it in. They toasted each other, and life in general, in paper cups.

"It still seems unreal," said Hal.

"Why is it that when one's unhappy everything reeks of reality and permanence, but when a person's happy he looks to the skies as much as a wheat farmer?"

"The French call it *la condition humaine.* But screw that. Good things that come later are always better. Right?"

"Anything you say, coach," Judy said as she reached over and kissed Hal softly on the lips. "You think Hawkeye will be exploring long enough for us two old numbers to . . ."

"I'm not that much of a gambler, hon. I don't want coitus interruptus to come via Annie running over to show us some little frog she's caught. I think it would traumatize us more than her. Not to mention Percy."

"I hope she doesn't wander too far," said Judy, looking off to the spot where Annie had entered the woods.

"Don't fret. Percy could find his way back to this blanket from Key West. A little more wine, madame?"

"Is the combination of white wine and sun always an aphrodisiac one moment and a soporific the next?" asked Judy as she held her cup out for a refill.

"So. Suddenly you've switched from carnality to nap time. You've always been a woman of many colors."

"As a painter I'll take that as a compliment."

"As a painter you should be pretty damned proud of yourself."

"What do you mean?" said Judy, looking up from her wine.

"You know the other day when I picked you up at your studio? Well, I had a good look at the canvas you're working on. It knocked me out."

"You like it?"

"Like it? I think it's the most exciting thing you've done in years."

"Oh, darling, that makes me so happy. I've had a good feeling about it myself, but hearing you say it makes it real."

A Cooper's hawk wheeled lazily on a thermal above them, while a clutch of chattering jays scooted low across the field. They lay back against the grass and let the sun wash over them.

"Did I tell you that T.C. brought his boy by the office yesterday?"

"How did he seem?"

"Fine. He now wears that scar as proudly as a Heidelberg student. The doctor said that by the time he starts shaving it'll be no more than a line. Looking at him got me thinking about Annie. She's just about old enough to have the birthmark removed."

"Well, Dr. Howard did say to wait until she was ten, but I guess there's some margin there."

"I know there is. I went ahead and asked Sy to check out our medical plan. We're in great shape. Everything would be covered except the private room."

"Let's do it then! I'll look up the name of the surgeon Dr. Howard recommended before we left L.A. He's at Mass General. He's supposed to be really tops. It would be perfect if he could do it before school starts."

"Give him a call on Monday. He can probably fit Annie in."

"I will. She'll be so happy. She's actually looking forward to the hospital. She sees it as a big adventure. By the way, has Sy said anything more about Tracy?"

"She's sound as a dollar. No. That expression doesn't make sense anymore. She's also fine. As you know, they had a doctor check her out again after the birthday party and he couldn't find anything wrong with her. He said kids frequently change their behavior patterns after trauma. He feels it's just a matter of time before she'll revert to her old self. And that seems to be what's happening."

"You know," said Judy reflectively, "kids are changing all the time, but usually it's hard to see. Like Annie. She's gotten a lot more mature lately. Much more grown-up, don't you think?"

"I've noticed it. Though at times I see the three-year-old Annie too."

"It makes me wonder if she'll really need Mimi any longer after school starts. Mimi hasn't been the same since that parakeet incident."

"Mommy! Daddy! We found something. It's really neat-o. Come on. You have to see it," cried Annie as Percy, his leash taut as a clothesline, pulled her across the field.

Reluctantly Hal and Judy rose and followed Annie into the woods. Percy started resisting so hard that Hal had to take the leash. The dog just didn't want to go back.

"Come on, lazy," said Hal, "you've got all night to sleep."

Within yards of the field they were in a pine forest. The ground was spongy soft. The pines abruptly ended and they were in brush as high as Annie's head.

"You sure you know where we're going?" Hal asked Annie, who dove ahead like a retriever.

"It's just a little farther."

And then, just as suddenly, they were in another clearing. This one no larger than a suburban backyard. And there at the other end was a barn. It had no roof but otherwise seemed sound.

"How do you like it? It's a lot more, you know, than those old cellar holes," she said, proud of her discovery.

"It sure is, honey. Let's take a look," said Judy, walking toward the barn.

Hal tried to follow Judy, but Percy pulled him the other way, barking frantically.

"Easy, boy. What's wrong? Some animal around here you don't like?"

He reached down to pat the dog, but Percy was beyond that.

"Annie. Something's bothering this mutt. Probably there's been a large animal through here recently. Take him back to the blanket, please."

Annie refused. The barn was her discovery and she wanted to conduct the tour. Hal was prepared to argue when he remembered the extra Oreos Judy had packed. The negotiation was fast. Hal offered two, Annie wanted five. Annie settled for five. Percy pulled Annie quickly back into the brush.

Judy was standing in the middle of the barn when Hal walked in.

"It's a little like Magritte," she said. "With the sky as the roof."

It was a large barn. The joists and supports that crisscrossed above threw shadows that looked like railroad tracks on the hard earth floor. In the center was a perfect circle the size of a pitcher's mound made of carefully fitted stream-polished stones. Suddenly Hal stumbled and fell to the ground.

"Damn it," he said as he rose slowly, wiping his palms against the legs of his Levi's.

"You all right?" asked Judy.

"I guess so. My ankle feels a little sore," Hal answered as he knelt down to examine the hole that had caused him to trip. It was almost as wide as his shoe and at least two feet deep. The inside was lined with cement. As he stood he noticed that there were other identical holes ringing half the circle.

"I wonder what these are for. They're damn dangerous. I could have broken my ankle."

"You'd have to look pretty far to find someone to sue," said Judy, laughing. "But it's amazing what great shape this barn is in. Almost perfect."

"It's far from perfect," said Hal, looking carefully around. "Don't you see that there are quite a few burned timbers and boards spliced into sound lumber? Why would somebody do that?"

"Save a few dollars, I guess. But why no roof?"

"Maybe they ran out of money. Or they only use it in good weather," said Hal, laughing.

When they got back to the clearing, Annie was eating her last Oreo and Percy was asleep.

23

"Damn it, Annie!" Judy shouted from the kitchen. "Would you please lower that phonograph before I strangle you and Billy Joel."

The sound dropped minutely, a difference that perhaps a bat could detect. But then the foot stomping began. Erin was over for a play date and lately both kids had become stuck on Billy Joel's album *Glass Houses*. Now the two micro-boppers were up in Annie's room shaking their little bottoms and singing along.

Erin was the most relaxed she had been in weeks. She had loved her beautiful long hair and was embarrassed by the gamin cut the tar had forced her to have. But if anything, she now looked cuter. She also seemed looser, less worried about her appearance than when it had been precisely tied to the care she and Claire took with her hair. Actually, thought Judy, Erin had gotten over the tar a lot better than Claire had.

Through the din, Judy heard the front-door knocker. Whoever was banging at the door had done an apprenticeship at a medieval castle. Judy started to call out to Mimi when she realized that this was her day off. Judy walked through the living room to the front door and when she opened it she found Howard Hilliard standing there.

"Good morning, Howard. Is everything all right?" asked a surprised Judy.

"Sure. Everything's fine."

Though he stood below the doorstep, Howard's head was still above Judy's.

"Can I do anything for you?" Judy asked.

"It's more a question of something I can do for you," said Howard, handing Judy an envelope. "Sy told me you were planning an operation for Annie. I tried to see Hal, but he was in a meeting. I thought that since I was passing by here on the way to the plant I'd drop off these forms. The earlier you get them filled in, the quicker we can process them. That way you'll get your money back faster. Everybody should think about cash flow these days."

"Why thank you, Howard. That's very nice of you."

"Is she having her tonsils out?" Howard asked, his voice lowered.

"No. She's had them out already."

"I hope it's not serious."

"No. Nothing to worry about. In fact, she's looking forward to it. We're having the birthmark on her neck removed."

Howard looked at Judy for a long time before he spoke.

"As I said, the quicker you get these filled in the quicker you get the money. And as soon as you get a date for the operation, call me. Don't forget."

He hurried down the path and into his car and turned off their driveway onto Quarry Road. Funny. She was sure Howard said he was on his way to the plant, but he was heading in the wrong direction.

24

It was "treat" day. Judy's third since arriving in Ripton Falls. Each month she treated herself to something that she once had ached to buy but had had to let slide. It was never anything really expensive, but she made sure it was the kind of thing that used to represent luxury to her. An orchid plant. An antique silver pin. Today it was going to be an art book: a sumptuous compendium of the best of Robert Rauschenberg. She had wanted it since last Christmas when she'd considered putting it on the gift-idea list she always gave Hal. But instead she only listed "sensibles." Hal dutifully stuck to the list, and Judy received a bathrobe.

As she entered The Quill Bookshop, she checked the time. Almost six. Hal would be meeting her here at six-thirty, and then they were going to try a new restaurant the Goldins had told them about. She noticed a smudge of charcoal on her right hand and reached into her purse for a piece of Kleenex to rub it clean. She had just come from a life-study class at the arts center. Unlimited auditing was another of the perks enjoyed by the summer teaching staff. Though she hadn't worked much in charcoal in the last couple of years, she'd had a terrific session.

She went directly to the Rauschenberg—she'd scouted its location on a previous visit—paid for it and had it wrapped. Then she began to browse through the new art titles, almost taking physical pleasure in their superb richness and color. She was midway through a new Hockney book when she looked up and there was Hal.

As they pushed out through the door of The Quill, Brad

Peters was on his way in. Judy was instantly struck by how happy he looked.

"Hey, you two," he said cheerily. "How about a quick cup of coffee? I'm just going to be in here a minute."

True to his word, he popped back out of the bookstore almost immediately, his purchase under his arm. When they were settled in a coffeehouse several doors down, complete with shadowy lighting, racks of newspapers, and the inevitable sitar music twanging in the background, Brad raised his cup of espresso in a salute to Hal and Judy.

"I have good news," he said, beaming at them. "I've decided to stay in Ripton Falls."

"I'm so glad," said Judy, reaching out to squeeze Brad's hand, and knowing then, if she hadn't quite known it before, that she counted him as a friend and that she cared very much how things went for him.

"The reason why is . . ." He paused, weighing his words. "Well, there are several reasons. The Hilliards' new friendliness, for one. They were so generous that day. When I called later to thank them, I had a wonderful conversation with Cameron Hilliard. He made no promises, but I can't help thinking they're with us now. They support everything else in town. Why not the church? And for another, we have several new members of the congregation. A lot I attribute to your efforts. More people are actually coming. And there's something else very nice in my life too. Somebody special."

Brad tapped the bag with the book in it.

"This is for her, in a way."

A bit sheepishly he pulled the book out. Pierre Franey's *Sixty-Minute Gourmet*.

"I've been seeing a lot of a gal I knew in college. Her name is Carol Albert. I've wanted to ask her to dinner at my place for a long while. Someone told me that with this book even an idiot can pull off a respectable meal. This idiot is now ready to try."

Judy met Brad's eyes and knew they were both remembering that awful moment in his kitchen the day she and Annie had come to ask about Sunday School.

"Judy," he said, picking up on this unspoken thought, "you saw what was happening to me. I'd begun to hear things, *imag-*

ine things. I don't know if it was doing battle Sunday after Sunday in that empty church that did it, but I thought I was losing my mind. And then, all of a sudden, I stopped running scared. I don't know why. I started looking at things—everything!—a little differently, and I liked what I saw. I still do."

"Brad, I couldn't ask you then, but I will now. Why were all those locks on that door? The one Annie stopped in front of."

"My scary door? The door to the cellar? Well, this is going to sound strange, but I began to think something was down in that cellar. There were weird, sudden noises during the day, and at night I'd wake up and the door would be shaking as if it were in a hurricane. I guess I was imagining it. I was spooked. And it got me drinking a bit too much, and that didn't help. But it's all past history. I've turned the corner now, and I couldn't be happier. And, you know, there's a capper to all this."

And then he told them about finding a cache of town documents and records in the attic of the parsonage. Box after box of them. He had gone up there to look for extra bedspreads, throws, end tables, anything to brighten up the house, which, he said, looked dreary enough to double as a set for *Long Day's Journey into Night*. It had been hot and musty, and he had found nothing he could use. Then he noticed the boxes. Rows of them, tucked back under the eaves in a way that made them barely visible. They were layered with a quarter-inch of undisturbed dust.

"It's amazing stuff. Lots of church-related material. Letters from parishioners, and so on, but town business too. Deeds, minutes, disputes with other towns on hunting rights, that sort of thing. And I've never heard anyone even mention that these records existed."

"How far back do they go?" asked Judy quickly.

"Well, I'm not sure yet. I've only gotten to three boxes, but yesterday I ran across a marriage record dated sixteen something."

"Wow! That old?"

"Have you ever heard of Montaillou?" asked Brad, his voice rising. "It's a little French town in the Pyrenees. Its whole way of life during the Middle Ages was reconstructed from records kept at the time. There was a book written on it. Wouldn't it be great if we could do the same thing here? I've begun cataloging, but it's going to take a long, long while. There'll be at least a few thousand entries."

"I've got to tell Margaret about this," said Judy. "And Minna Gannon. She thinks all the early records were destroyed in the fire at the town hall."

"You know," broke in Hal, "computer time is expensive, but I wouldn't be surprised if the Hilliards would be willing to donate time to put these records on the company computer. I'll speak to Elliott about it."

"Wonderful. Now I know you two have to go along, but before you do I have an idea. I just had a birthday, and my sister sent me a magnum of champagne. Dom Perignon, 1974." He paused and smiled before continuing. "I can't think of any better company with whom to open my present than you two and Carol. How about meeting at my place on Friday for champagne, and then we'll go out for dinner?"

"We'd love it," said Judy, after an affirmative nod from Hal. "Maybe by then Hal will have good news for you about the computer time. And I'd love to peek into those boxes."

"Sure thing. But I'm warning you, you may end up looking like a chimney sweep after just a quick trip to the attic," Brad replied, laughing.

25

HILLIARD AND COMPANY
RIPTON FALLS, MASSACHUSETTS 01070

MEMO TO: Elliott Hilliard
FROM: Hal Richardson

Brad Peters, the minister at the Congregational Church, tells me he has found a considerable amount (several thousand items) of early town documents in the parsonage attic. I suggested that he put them on a computer to make the sorting and analysis a whole lot easier. Which leads me to a request:

Would you be willing to authorize time on our computer to do this work? I know of your family's great interest in this town and I think the cost of the computer time would be more than made up by the information on the town's history that results. I look forward to hearing from you on this.

Hal

HR/mk

"Makers of Quality Goods Since 1807"

26

"Bet I can guess whose daddy you are," said the young man who opened the front door at Claire Simmons' house. He smiled and gestured toward Hal's bright-red hair.

Through the wall of glass at the far end of the living room, Hal spotted Annie, flame-colored hair flying, jumping up and down on the deck outside with Tracy Goldin and Erin. He threw her a wave.

The other man introduced himself as Bob Gallagher, Claire's brother. He had a pleasant, open face, Claire's wide mouth and slightly bony nose, and the kind of fair skin that probably peeled all summer long.

"I had to get the hell out of New York," said Gallagher, flopping into a chair. "Four days of ninety-six and over were enough. I felt as though I were swimming laps at night instead of sleeping. Claire went to Hartford to see a friend in the hospital, so here I am, baby-sitting. Got a few minutes? Want an ale?"

After Bob Gallagher fetched two Ballantines from Claire's fridge, they started shooting the breeze about advertising. Bob and a partner, both ex-B.B.D.&O.'ers, had started up a small agency a year earlier and just last week had won a large Italian wine importer's account, a very profitable one now that the whole country was clamoring for Soaves, Chiantis, and Frascatis.

One of the glass doors to the deck slid open and Annie bounced into the room. "Tinkle, Dad" was all she said. She blew her father a kiss and disappeared down the hall. Hal winked at Bob Gallagher. Outside he could hear Erin arguing with Tracy about whose turn it was to hold the jump rope, and then Bob shut the door, cutting off the kids in mid-sentence.

Hal had just started to describe a campaign he was planning for Hilliard's when from outside came a frenzied, high-pitched howling.

"What the hell?" said Gallagher, leaping up.

Then before either man could really comprehend what was about to happen, let alone make a move to prevent it, they saw Erin and Tracy racing across the deck toward the doors, pursued by two huge, glistening Doberman pinschers. There was the chilling sound of breaking glass and the two girls exploded into the living room. Stunned, Hal rushed toward the sobbing, blood-drenched girls. From the corner of his eye he saw the two sleek Dobermans wheel about abruptly and lope calmly away.

•   •

A few hours later, Hal leaned against the wall of the laundry room watching Judy shove the clothes he had just changed from into the washing machine. His shirt was as splattered as a house painter's overalls, only now the bright-crimson smears of color had faded to an innocuous rust.

"There's nothing scarier than blood, unless you operate five times a day," he said. He was still shaken by what he had seen, and as tightly wound as a boxer's fist.

"The crazy thing was that the blood all over Tracy was Erin's. There was nothing wrong with Tracy at all. Not a scratch. It's amazing. Erin'll be okay, too. She actually needed very few stitches. Another fraction of an inch, though, and the doctor said she probably would have bled to death before we could have gotten her there.

"Poor Gallagher. Jesus, what a thing to have happen while you're watching your sister's kid. We really snatched up those kids and ran. I remembered, thank God, that the clinic was still open. It's only a couple of blocks from Claire's. We were like that scene in *Kramer vs. Kramer*. You remember, when the little boy falls in the playground and there's blood all over his face and Dustin Hoffman takes off? We were just like that, running like maniacs, the kids screaming, Annie right behind us, bawling. The doctor wasn't even shook up though. He said that after lawn mowers, glass doors were at the top of the list in household accidents."

Then Hal explained that almost as soon as they had gotten back to Claire's, the glazier arrived to replace the glass. Bob had called him from the doctor's office as soon as he knew Erin was all right. He wanted to be sure the doors were fixed before Claire got back from Hartford.

"Now listen to this. The guy came in and just looked at the mess on the floor for a bit without saying a word. Then he starts sighing and shaking his head, like some old philosopher. And he says, 'It happens every time. I put the decals up to make the glass safe—so you can see it, you know?—and the customers take them off as soon as I leave. They say the decals don't look good. What's the word? Ass-tetics?'

"*Ass-tetics.* That's the way he pronounced it, I swear to God. And you know what? Gallagher and I looked down at the glass and, sure enough, clear as anything, there was the outline of what must have been a big flower decal, scraped off as neatly as you please."

27

"How's my bucolic marketing whiz? Lined up any barnyard lovelies yet?"

It was Jeff Fields on his speaker phone. His voice seemed to be coming from somewhere deep inside a well.

"Hey, Jeff!" said Hal with pleasure. "But first get off that expensive Dixie cup. You sound like Kermit the Frog."

"Sorry," said Jeff, switching off the device. "It's a crazy world of conference calls out here and I always forget to turn the damn thing off. Now, how are my two favorite girls?"

The next fifteen minutes were what Jeff called an "extended schmooze." They hadn't talked in almost a month, and Jeff was riding high. Though he couldn't name any names, he indicated that he was involved in a major acquisition and moving closer to the chief operating officer's slot. But his voice reached higher levels of excitement when he mentioned his new girl friend.

"I think it's really happened," Jeff said, his voice lower and larded with significance.

"You son of a bitch," Hal shouted. "You sound like cupid used a harpoon gun. Who is she?"

"Her name is Jenny Jakes. You might have heard of her. She's an actress."

Jeff went on to explain that Jenny was one of the stars of a hot new show called *Multinational*. The show, set in New York, Los Angeles, London, and Tokyo, was a combination *Dallas* and *The Rothschilds*. Jenny played one of the immensely wealthy children of the head of the American side of the family business. She apparently was required to play most of her scenes in an ever-shrinking bikini that drove the network censor up the wall each week. She was scheduled to appear on the cover of *People* in a few weeks.

"How serious is it, Jeff?"

"Serious enough for us to be living together and looking to buy a house."

Hal started to hum taps.

"Knock it off, you bastard," Jeff said, laughing. "If I thought you'd be springing your gallows humor on me all the time, I'd give second thoughts to the job here that'll be yours before the year is out."

"You still mean that?" asked Hal, surprised. He had said nothing to Jeff about his growing frustrations about ever getting anything done at Hilliard's. He did not even want to admit it to himself.

"I only know how to talk out of one side of my mouth, Hal. When the announcement goes out about me, your name will be the next on the mimeo. I'm coming east with Jenny in a month or so, and I'm blocking out at least two nights with you guys. We'll talk in detail then. I got to run now. I'm late for a meeting with a couple of very heavy agents. I can hear them sharpening their Gucci loafers in my outer office now. Speak to you soon."

Before Hal could go back to the memo he had been writing

when Jeff called, Laurie Hilliard walked in. She held a glass vase filled with tiger lilies. She carefully placed it on Hal's desk.

"They look nice," she said, taking a step back. "But they're for Judy too. So take them home tonight."

"To what do I owe this, Laurie? Aside from the blizzard of paper I've produced, my accomplishments have been pretty few," Hal said, his backup laughter not at all convincing.

"You demand too much of yourself, Hal," Laurie said, sitting down in a chair alongside his desk. She was wearing an amber linen jacket over her shoulders. The top of the slate-gray shirt beneath it was unbuttoned provocatively. It was hard for Hal not to look at the swell of her pale full breasts filling the shirt's opening. She was a very attractive woman and she knew it.

"I've come to you with what I think is some good news. I'm also going to ask you for a favor."

"First give me the good news. I always wanted to open my Christmas presents in May when I was a kid."

"I've convinced my grandfather that I should sit in on the marketing meetings. I think I can help. I've been bending his ear about some of the proposals you've made that I've read about in the minutes, and I think he's beginning to see the light. The young guard here might have a following of only one, but it's a committed and enthusiastic one."

"That's great," Hal answered. "I'm ready to do any favor within reason. Or beyond reason, for that matter."

"That's the attitude I like. I'm trying to line up some work for my best friend's daughter. Her mother and I were so close in college that we wore each other's clothes. Everyone used to mistake us for sisters. That's why I think of Vicky as almost my own child. She's entering her sophomore year of high school and will be staying with us at least through the first semester." Laurie paused and lowered her voice. "Her mother and father are having problems. You'll really like her. She's a terrific kid."

"What kind of work is she looking for?"

"Baby-sitting. Cleaning. That kind of thing."

"Oh, that's a bit of a problem. We have Mimi, you know."

"Aunt Laurie! Aunt Laurie!"

A girl's voice floated into the office from down the hall.

"In here, Vicky. Just a few doors down," Laurie called out.

A moment later, the girl entered Hal's office.

"Vicky, this is Mr. Richardson. Hal, meet Vicky Leland. I was just telling Mr. Richardson, Vicky, that you're anxious to find some work for this summer."

The girl smiled broadly. She moved next to Laurie.

"Absolutely. I'll even mow lawns."

Vicky's hair was darker than Laurie's. She wore it long. She was pretty and surprisingly mature for her age. She could have passed for eighteen easily. Hal looked at Vicky, then back to Laurie. He heard himself make small talk, but he didn't really know what he was saying.

Vicky Leland did not at all resemble Laurie Hilliard, except that they were both very attractive and had gray eyes. Yet there was something strikingly alike about them. It was hard for Hal to pin down what it was. The way they smiled, yes, but more than that. Now as they both gazed expectantly at Hal, he saw it. The way they moved, gestured, even held their heads was identical. They were like thoroughbreds running in stride.

28

"Color expert! I need my color expert. Now, please," Hal shouted from the bedroom.

"Okay. Just a moment," Judy yelled back from the bathroom.

When Judy walked into the bedroom, she saw Hal holding up three ties for her inspection.

"Your color sense has not been improved by the Berkshire air. None of them works."

Judy scanned the ties hanging on the inside of Hal's closet. She glanced back at him once or twice, as if sketching a model, and then selected a green knit with horizontal black stripes. She held it against Hal's shirt to double-check, then tossed it to him.

"You're all set. *Gentlemen's Quarterly* here we come."

"Are you implying something about my image?"

For an answer, she kissed him deeply and then buried her face in his neck.

"You keep that up and we'll never make it," said Hal.

"That wouldn't do at all. We'd miss some good champagne, caviar, and conversation. Not to mention—"

"Not to mention anything else. My watch shows us fifteen minutes late already. Let's make tracks."

They stopped in Annie's room for a good-night kiss, then headed down the stairs. As Hal went out the front door, Judy stopped in the kitchen. She climbed into the car a moment later clutching two lemons in a plastic bag.

"Not the usual birthday gift, I see."

"Brad called me this afternoon to ask if it was all right to serve caviar with a lime instead of a lemon. All Packard's had was the stuff in plastic. I said a lime would be fine if you were living in Barbados. Therefore these," explained Judy, holding up the lemons.

When they arrived at the parsonage, a red car was pulled up at the curb in front. Hal parked behind it. They found a tall woman with short black hair standing by the front door.

"Carol?" asked Judy.

"Yes. You must be Judy. Brad's told me all about you. And you're Hal."

The three exchanged handshakes. Then Carol Albert turned toward the door and started banging on it.

"I've been here at least five minutes. The bell doesn't seem to work. I've had to pound on the door. It's damn thick."

"Maybe he went out to get something at the last minute," Hal said.

"No. His car is parked around back."

Hal stepped away from the front steps and looked up at the house.

"I don't see any lights on."

Carol Albert started to knock on the door again and shout at the same time.

"Brad! Brad!"

Hal and Judy joined her in shouting Brad's name.

When they stopped they were assaulted by the dark silence of the house.

"Let's go around back," Hal suggested.

The light from the street barely etched out the path as they turned the corner of the house. Hal walked up the back porch steps and tried the door.

"It's locked too."

"I'm worried," said Carol in an unsteady voice.

"Let's just take it easy. I'm sure that nothing's the matter. Brad probably dozed off. You two wait here. I'm going to the car for a flashlight."

Hal came back empty-handed.

"They'll never use me for one of those Eveready commercials where your flashlight alerts a plane flying twenty thousand feet up that you've got a problem. Damn thing is so dim it wouldn't attract a moth."

"I think we should call the police," said Judy.

"That's ridiculous, Jude. You don't call the police because someone doesn't answer the door in five minutes."

Hal went up to the back door again. He tried the window next to the door. He couldn't budge it. He went to the window on the other side. It slid open easily. Hal moved the curtain to the side and entered the house. A few moments later he opened the back door.

"None of the lights in the kitchen work. I think the power is off. You two wait here. I'll find Brad. He's probably in the cellar replacing a fuse."

Hal had to open four kitchen drawers and fumble about before he found a book of matches. Lighting one at a time, he made his way into the house. He was on his fourth match when he found the cellar door. He opened it and yelled down.

"Brad! Brad! Your guests have arrived."

The silence, as palpable as cotton batting, enveloped him.

Hal, he thought to himself, you're not afraid to go down there and look for Brad, are you? He lit another match. A cold draft from the cellar quickly put it out. Of course he wasn't afraid. But the chances were better that Brad was upstairs napping. The cellar could wait. He entered the living room. The curtains were drawn, making the room as dark as a closed box. Hal groped his way to the stairs. By the time he reached the top, only half the matches were left in the book.

He had never been in the house before, so he went into the room that opened first off the top of the stairs. He struck a match and entered. For an instant the flare of light dimly outlined the room and then retreated to firefly intensity. The room was empty.

In the next room Hal found that he could see better if he entered the room partway before striking the match. It also conserved the matches.

Both a spare room and Brad's office were unoccupied.

The door to the room at the end of the hall was closed. The doors to the other rooms had been open. Hal raised his hand to knock when a clock downstairs struck the half hour. He almost jumped. Easy, boy, you've been watching too many late-night films. He banged on the door.

"Okay, birthday boy. Get it together. Your party has arrived," he yelled at the door.

The hall was a perfect echo chamber, and his words pinballed about him.

I can't believe it, dummy. You're scared? Afraid of the dark? Come on, Hal. Stop this shit.

He felt his brow. Wet. Same thing for the back of his neck. His shirt clung to his body like a leaf against a rain-spattered window.

This is ridiculous. Brad probably ran out to buy an onion. That's right. He's serving caviar. So if it wasn't an onion then it was an egg. Enough of the culinary crap. Come on. Open the door.

Hal turned the handle. A well-oiled click and the door opened. A slight push and the door swung silently inward. Hal started to call out for Brad but he stopped. He heard something. What was it? Like the creaking of a hammock, only fainter. Hey! You'll be hearing chains dragging across the floor in a minute.

He had stepped only three paces into the room when something hit him on the cheek. He quickly backed up and crouched down. He could hear the massive beat of his heart in every part of his body. The sound was like being under a waterfall. He balled his fists as tight as he could to stop shaking. He waited. As his body's roar diminished a bit he heard the sound again. It was rhythmic now. Like a small boat rocking against a dock.

He knew what he had to do. And he dreaded it. As quietly as he knew how, he folded back the matchbook flap. He rose slowly. Then, as fast as he could, he struck a match and touched it to the remaining ones in the book. Suddenly the room jumped into light. And there, in front of Hal, was a pair of shoes. They were worn by Brad Peters, whose body hung like wet wash from a light fixture in the ceiling.

Brad's head was twisted to one side like a straw. His face was the color of deep water. A look of pure terror stamped his features.

As the flame reached down to touch Hal's fingers, he noticed one more thing. There was a kitchen chair below Brad's feet. But Brad's feet came nowhere near touching it. Like a frozen moment in some horrible ballet, his feet were suspended a foot above the chair.

29

The Ripton Falls police station was a small two-story building faced in imitation brick. The former police chief's brother-in-law had been in the siding business. The building was sandwiched between the dry cleaner's and Ladd Brothers Appliances. There were two holding cells in the back. They last had been used ten months earlier following the Ripton Falls Volunteer Firemen's annual touch-football game with their rivals from the nearby town of Haydenville. "A bad penalty and a little too much Miller's Lite" was what the arresting officer wrote in his charge book. The three men were let go with a warning after drinking six cups of coffee and shaking hands with one another.

"It doesn't fit," said Hal wearily. "We've been through this thing so many times I'm getting punchy. Things were finally going right for the guy. Suicide makes no sense. None at all."

"I'm inclined to agree with you, Mr. Richardson," Chief Fox answered, after carefully lighting his pipe.

Joe Fox was a tall man, as gangly as a teen-ager, with bright eyes that seemed enormous through the thick bifocals he wore. Hal had heard that he had graduated from law school many years before, but had never been able to pass the bar. He had succeeded the last chief of Ripton Falls two years ago when the man had choked to death on a hamburger during a backyard barbecue. Everybody in the town liked Chief Fox. Even the high-school kids.

"Though I think this was a suicide, plain and simple, as I told you and your wife and Miss Albert last night, I can understand why you feel the way you do. There are some inconsistencies here." Fox paused for a moment to wipe his glasses. "But I think everything will be cleared up when we hear from the coroner."

"What do you think he'll find?"

"Liquor. Lots of it. We found two bottles of Remy Martin brandy near the night table alongside the bed. One empty, one worked over pretty good."

"But he wasn't that kind of drinker. Not anymore."

"That's not what Eddie Breslin says."

"Who the hell is he?"

"Collects the garbage here. Told me the Reverend's trash can always sounded like New Year's Eve. Bottles playing tunes on bottles."

"Why wasn't there a note, Chief?"

"The complainers leave notes, Mr. Richardson. The unhappy just go."

"It just doesn't figure, though. A guy who's going to kill himself doesn't call somebody a few hours earlier to ask her to bring along a lemon!"

"That's because he wanted to be sure you'd be there. They want to be found. Always. Want some more tea?"

"No thanks."

They both lapsed into silence. The small sounds became big: the flow of traffic outside, a radio being played next door.

"I can't stop thinking of Brad dangling there. His feet weren't anywhere near the chair."

"We've been through that already, Mr. Richardson. The Bible we found under the table was almost a foot thick. He put it on the chair and stood on it. That in itself says an awful lot."

Hal rubbed his knuckles along the stubble on his cheek. Of course the chief was right. But Hal still found it difficult to believe Brad could do it. He had never known anyone who had committed suicide. Oh, there was the father of a girl he took out in high school, but all he remembered about him was a sour look when he brought his daughter home after eleven o'clock. Was he just being naïve now?

"I'm not a big-city cop, Mr. Richardson," continued the chief. "We don't get much violence here. Not counting auto accidents, I see as much death as a TV repairman. Thank the good Lord for that. But I've seen enough to learn a few things. And though I agree Mr. Peters' suicide does seem a bit 'theatrical,' I know enough not to be misled by my imagination. He wasn't your standard, despondent, lifetime loser who takes the pill ticket to the other side. That's true. But if you step back a bit, it all makes sense."

"One more thing I don't understand, Chief, is why did Brad turn off the power in the house?"

"Sometimes it's a lot easier to enter the darkness from the darkness."

●   ●

Chief Fox called ten minutes after Hal got home.

"Just like I thought, Mr. Richardson."

"What, Chief?"

"The coroner's report. Just got it. The amount of alcohol in the Reverend's bloodstream makes the Love Canal look like the old swimming hole."

30

It was a perfect August afternoon, light and breezy, with the kind of puffy, pure white clouds hanging in the sky that looked as if a six-year-old had painted them in. Judy was on her way to Poletti's Orchard on Route 233 to pick up some peaches for a picnic supper that evening. They were meeting Margaret and Harvey at Tanglewood. Ozawa was conducting. Debussy's *Nocturnes,* followed by Schubert's Symphony Number 9.

As she approached the Green she could see the church steeple pushing up through the heavy screen of maples. It had been a week since Brad Peters had died, and she still found it upsetting to drive past the church. But she was feeling a bit stronger about it today, a little more accepting. What alternative was there, really, but to accept Brad's death as a suicide, as difficult to reconcile as that seemed. She had thought he was fine. But he had fooled her. Fooled them all.

A blue Datsun was parked in front of the parsonage, and the front door to the house was open. On impulse, Judy parked and went up the front steps. Through the open door she saw a young couple coming downstairs. She could see at once that the woman must be Brad's sister. The same strong nose and eyes the color of faded denim. She was pretty and tanned, and looked as if she spent a lot of time on the tennis courts. Her light-brown hair was streaked with yellow from the sun. They introduced themselves as Mac and Nancy Draper and, recognizing Judy's name, thanked her for her condolence note.

"Excuse me, will you," said Nancy Draper to Judy. "I've got to keep on with the packing. Mother's taking this pretty hard, and we want to get back to the Cape."

"It's so sad, so sad," murmured Mac Draper, watching his wife slip back upstairs. "Brad and I were at Yale Divinity together. That's how Nance and I met. No one really wanted to come to Ripton Falls, but it was just like Brad to answer the call. He assisted for a couple of years in Cohasset, outside of Boston, but this was different. This was his own congregation. His first. He liked challenges. He always found a way to overcome obstacles."

"What was wrong with Ripton Falls?"

"Well, for one thing, the congregation's been in a serious decline for some years now."

"Have they arranged for anyone to take Brad's place?"

"The board hasn't decided yet, but I doubt that they will. There's no need for a church here, and the town knows it. Also there's a local family named . . ."

"Hilliard?" supplied Judy.

"Yes, that's it. Hilliard. They've renewed a standing offer for the property. For a lot more money than it's really worth. Evidently they want to turn it into a cultural center for the use of the whole town. It's depressing to see everything that Brad accomplished here . . . disappear, but I can understand the board's reasoning. Tell me, how is Brad's friend? Carol Albert?"

"I talked with her this morning. She's all right, I guess, but it was a terrible shock."

"Such a lovely girl. I'm sure in time she'll find someone else."

Judy shook her head and studied the floor silently for a few moments, and then, since there didn't seem to be anything more to say, began her goodbyes. Then she remembered the attic.

"Are you going to be taking the records Brad found in the attic?"

Mac Draper looked at Judy blankly. She quickly explained, and they walked up the stairs to the second floor. They climbed the ladder to the attic and pushed open the hatch, which yielded only after Mac applied his shoulder to it. Together they squeezed their heads through the entranceway, like seals coming up for air. What Judy saw robbed her of speech. A flood of light poured through two large rosette windows, one at each end of the attic, and glanced and shone off the beautifully polished, totally empty attic floor.

31

Picnic suppers on the lawn at Tanglewood were an institution, and, as with all institutions, there were touches of madness. When the custom first began years ago, sandwiches and thermoses of coffee were the rule. Now the simple act of having a bite to eat before a concert had reached extravagant culinary heights. One blanket over from where the Richardsons, Margaret Love, and Harvey Stern had staked out a spot, a man was expertly preparing sushi from blush-pink fillets of fish that he lifted from a cooler packed with ice. Another man, stationed at a large, shiny carving trolley, was slicing a side of roast beef with the concentration of a chess master. Behind them, under a tall pine, a foursome had seated themselves on folding chairs at an elegant, formally set table. Linen, silver, crystal. There was the pop of a champagne cork, and one of the men rose to fill their glasses.

The approach Margaret took—for of course she was in charge of the food—was altogether simpler: baked ham, three delectably fresh seasonal salads, and Judy's peaches.

"Damn it, Harvey," she said, placing dishes and condiments on the flowered tablecloth she had spread on the ground, "why didn't you remind me to bring that new tarragon mustard I bought yesterday?"

Harvey and the Richardsons laughed affectionately.

As they ate dinner, Harvey and Hal compared notes on Amsterdam. Hal's grand tour of Europe had been courtesy of the U.S. Army. Even so, he had a few pointers for Harvey, who would be attending a design convention there in September. This was the first time since Brad's death that Judy and Margaret had been able to get together, and though Margaret had made a point of wanting to see Judy ("I must talk with you, but not over the phone"), now that they were face-to-face she was oddly subdued.

Slowly the light, as if on a dimmer, began to fade, and with it came a nearly audible collective sigh of contentment as the thousands on the grass settled back to share the last of their wine and wait for the music to begin. The members of the orchestra tuned their instruments, and then all at once a swell of applause rolled from under the music shed and then out across the lawn. Ozawa was at the podium. As the crowd fell silent, Margaret stood up and signaled to Judy to join her in a walk. This was what Judy had been expecting all evening.

"I didn't want to talk in front of the boys," Margaret began when they were on the far edge of the sprawled gathering, "and I couldn't go into any of this on the phone. I don't trust phones. And not because I'm afraid of bugging. That's a fixation of the electronic age. I'm a product of the party line. But this is the point: I'm as disturbed as you about Brad Peters' death. I didn't know him nearly as well as you, but I'm convinced he didn't kill himself."

Judy stared in astonishment at Margaret.

"When you told me about his fantastic find," Margaret continued, "I called him immediately to make a date to see it. I was there that day. Friday. The day he . . . died."

"Oh, my God!"

"Exactly! I went over about two, and I stayed a couple of hours. Until around four, when he kicked me out. He said he had errands to do. He was awfully cute about it. He told me he was meeting you two and a gal he'd known in college. Said he was seeing a lot of her. It was almost as if he'd won the lottery. He was that up. Oh, Judy—"

Margaret stopped to marshal her strength, and when she continued, her voice rose in a thin wail of anguish: "Damn it, Judy, Brad Peters was *happy*."

"Shh," hissed a voice from a nearby clump of blankets.

The two women stared at each other, silently considering the implications of Margaret's words. In the thin light, Judy could see that Margaret's eyes were glistening, and she shivered involuntarily. As the soft, insinuating sound of Debussy filled up the space between them, they turned and moved farther away from the crowd. In the distance a chain of dark hills was silhouetted against the smoky evening sky.

Margaret began to speak again, her voice lowered.

"Let me tell you what happened. As soon as I arrived, Brad took me upstairs to the attic. I wasn't there more than a few minutes before I realized that those documents are, pure and simple, a treasure trove."

"You mean *were*," interrupted Judy.

"What?"

"I stopped there this afternoon, and the attic floor looks like a TV commercial for Mr. Clean. Immaculate. Christiaan Barnard could operate on it."

As Judy explained, Margaret's initial expression of shock visibly gave way to one of certainty.

"I'm not surprised," she said. "Someone didn't want us to see those records. But what they don't know is that Brad gave me some things to look over at home. I could kick myself for what I didn't take—though Mother always said, 'Don't look back'—but I do have this." While she spoke, Margaret searched through the bag slung over her shoulder. "And just by chance. That's the crazy part. Brad grabbed a bunch of papers from one of the boxes. He hadn't even looked at them himself, he said, but they happened to include this." She thrust a sheet of paper at Judy.

"What is it?" asked Judy, trying to make it out in the near darkness. It appeared to be some kind of diagram.

"Come," said Margaret impatiently, and she led Judy to the base of one of the lights that illuminated the corners of the lawn. Moths and mosquitoes ricocheted above them as Judy studied the paper. Within a faintly drawn rectangular shape was a multitude of small marks. A few had names beneath them. Outside the lines was a cluster of marks without names. And then it occurred to Judy what it was: a map of a cemetery.

"Yes," confirmed Margaret excitedly. "It's a Xerox copy. I didn't dare bring the original with me. Look at the date. Under your right thumb."

Before Judy could figure out the date from the faded Roman numerals, Margaret translated: "Seventeen-oh-six."

"I've been meaning to tell you," said Judy, staring hard at the date. "Did you know there was a big fire in the town hall in Ripton Falls sometime around eighteen hundred? It destroyed everything. They have nothing going back this far. Nothing!"

"I've never believed that story, and I believe it even less now that I've seen this," said Margaret. She bent over the map, pulling Judy close. "Look. These, naturally, are graves." She pointed at the marks inside the lines, and Judy now could see as she looked closer that they were little crosses. "Brackett, Gannon, Kellogg. I recognize the names. Cousins. All members of an important old Ripton Falls family. This map must have been drawn for them, since they're the only ones listed on it. And these"—Margaret pointed to the other marks, which turned out to be small x's, her voice trembling with tension—"these marks outside the lines represent graves in *un*consecrated ground. Don't you see? Some time before this map was made, the town buried some people they would not allow in their churchyard. Want to guess who those people were?"

Before Judy could say a word, Margaret triumphantly answered her own question.

"These have to be the graves of the children in the coven! I'm just sure of it. This map proves that the coven existed. And with it, we can find their graves *and* what their names were."

And then, as if Ozawa had been cued, the music rose to a final crescendo. The *Nocturnes* had ended.

32

Judy flicked the car door shut with her foot and, balancing two heavy shopping bags in her arms, struggled up the path to the front door. She was surprised to see Margaret's car parked in front of the house. Just then Margaret herself came around the side of the house, a trowel in her hand, her knees patched by damp circles of fresh, dark earth.

"What're you doing here?" asked Judy.

"Weeding, of course. I'm going to have to give you a short course in gardening the lazy man's way. Your peonies are moribund. I hate to think what Mrs. Pratt would say about how you're treating her darlings. You must mulch, you know. Mulch, and you'll lead a weedless existence. You *and* your flowers."

Margaret paused, and then got to the real reason she was there. "I'm here because I *had* to talk with you. Mimi said you'd be back soon, so I took a chance and drove over. And, you know me, I just couldn't sit and do nothing while I waited."

After Judy had dispatched Mimi to the car for the rest of the groceries, she poured glasses of club soda for herself and Margaret. Then they pulled two lawn chairs to the edge of the old orchard and sat under the brow of an ancient apple tree. If there was any breeze around, Judy had discovered that it usually found its way to this small corner of their property. It was only a little after eleven, but already the air felt like a hot washcloth.

Margaret pushed back a tendril of silvery hair from her forehead, leaving behind a streak of dirt from Judy's garden. She took a long swallow of the cold drink.

"Our conversation at the concert last night about the children's coven got me thinking again about that painting of them," she began. "I remembered what you told me about the telephone call you made to Laurie about it. How . . . unsatisfactory it was."

"That she lied, you mean."

"Yes. Exactly. So I decided to see if *I* could get anywhere with her. I called her this morning. Not too early, since it's Saturday. I told her I was going to be in Amsterdam next month, traveling with my male friend, and I would love to see the painting. Our schedule would be flexible. So long as the painting wasn't in Albania, I could get to it. But, sure enough, she put me off. She said the painting was in Europe—she remembered she'd told *you* that—but listen to what else she said. It now just happens to be in transit and won't be set up again for exhibition until after we get back from Europe. How convenient! You know, it's interesting. When a cool person—in this case, a *cold* person—loses her cool, the unraveling is awesome to behold. As soon as I hung up the phone, I realized there wasn't a chance in the world that the Hilliards would have let that painting out of their possession. There's no doubt about it. It's here in Ripton Falls."

Margaret took a gulp from her glass, as if to fortify herself for what she was planning to say next. "Judy, we have to get to that painting."

At Margaret's words, Judy felt an icy rush of half excitement, half fear.

"How do we manage that?" Judy heard herself ask, as if someone else was speaking for her. "What do we do?"

"Two things. Immediately. First, we have to find out more about the painting. I called a friend of mine who was at the auction. She always saves the catalogs. She looked it up, but unfortunately there was no picture of it, no write-up. I asked her to send me the catalog anyway. You never can tell. Meantime, I'm almost positive I read a review of the auction somewhere—I don't remember where, damn it—by somebody who teaches at Williams. What I'm wondering is whether one of your contacts at Smith could put us in touch with him."

"What's his name?"

"Glicksman. Alan Glicksman."

"Oh, I know him. Or at least I sort of do. From when we were living in New York. He used to cover gallery openings for the *Voice*. I wonder if he'd remember me? I'll call him today. But I won't tell Hal. He actually was annoyed that time I phoned Laurie Hilliard about the painting. He thinks you and I are being silly about the whole thing. And nosy."

"Secondly," continued Margaret, and there was something about the emphasis she gave that simple word that held Judy, "I have come up with an idea so audacious it scares even me."

"What?"

"Two weeks from now, on August twenty-second, Ripton Falls has its annual house tour. One of the best in the area. *And* the Hilliard house is always included. I have an idea that maybe you and I can find a way to see a little more of that house than the Hilliards would like us to."

33

The day was clear and bright. The light was so luminous that even the gritty old factory towns of Adams and North Adams took on a cheerful, inviting aspect. A few minutes out of North Adams, Judy saw the huge stony knuckle of Mount Greylock. She had been this way twice before to see the rich collection of Renoirs and Whistlers at the Clark Art Institute. She had fallen in love with Williamstown immediately. Seven times smaller than Northampton, it reflected the tradition and charm of the college, which was both the hub and the spokes of the town.

Alan Glicksman's directions were precise and easy to follow. She located the building where she was to meet him on the first shot. As she parked the car, she reminded herself not to tell Hal about this visit. Her cover story was that she was driving to Springfield to price washing machines at Lechmere's. She would stick to that.

Judy was five minutes early, so she strolled idly through a small quadrangle. As she walked back toward the meeting point, an errant Frisbee whistled into her calf. The boy who retrieved it was properly apologetic and the tingling stopped within seconds.

When she had telephoned Alan Glicksman, she was happily surprised that he did remember her. He even mentioned a

SoHo group show in '73 where he had seen some of Judy's paintings. After they had set the time and place, Judy asked what he looked like.

"Short, dark, and hairy. My wife thinks I look like a hirsute Aznavour. But, remember, she loves me."

And true to his word, Alan, all five feet five inches of him, complete with a full pirate's beard, stood at the building's entrance talking animatedly to a student.

"The origins of the silhouette were mainly economic. All you needed was paper and scissors. James Sanford Ellsworth started that way before moving to watercolors."

"Alan?" asked Judy, with very little uncertainty in the question.

"Hi, Judy. Be with you in a sec."

Alan turned back to the student and finished his point. He then guided Judy through the campus to a small coffee shop tucked above a bookstore.

"The pastries are quite good here. I insist you try the cannoli. It'll make you believe you're sitting in Ferrara's. I, however, am on a diet created by Dr. Mengele and will have to enjoy it vicariously."

Since the day was hot, they both had tamarindo sodas. While Judy demolished the cannoli, Alan reminisced about New York.

"I remember seeing you at the opening of that group show in SoHo. I also remember they served a punch made of recycled sterno. One of the others in the show, Lenny Miller, was a friend from college. I still see him. Alas, he also teaches. You had three canvases in the show and I remember wanting to buy one. Unfortunately, I had trouble swinging the purchase of a Mounds bar in those days."

"I'm amazed. I can't conceive of anyone remembering those paintings aside from myself."

"The one that particularly sticks in my head was a shaped canvas with a strong green chevron running down from the corner."

"You're incredible," said Judy.

"Even though my soul, after all these years, is in the eighteenth and nineteenth centuries, my eyes are still in the twentieth. I also recall not being able to take them off you. You were, and are, lovely. But before you blush, you should realize that small men are masters of the compliment and I am happily married. Though I stick by my assessment of you and would happily testify to that in a court of law."

They both laughed, though Judy couldn't help blushing.

"I have a feeling that you paint, Alan. True?"

"Except for a yearly Christmas card, which my family and friends tell me is wonderful, nothing. But in a way, you're right. I used to paint. But that was a long time ago. I started to paint when I was twelve. Seriously. At least it was serious in terms of the amount of canvas and paint. My father was a dentist and he was dashed to see that his only son might not pick up the drill. It was before the age of analysis, so my parents reluctantly encouraged me. Living in Brighton Beach infected my imagination with the sea. Though it was only an extension of Coney Island, I would walk the beach and see great battles take place in the shadow of the Ferris wheel. For two years I divided all my spare time between the library, doing research, and the sun porch—my studio. I turned out huge canvases. Never under five feet square. *The Battle of Trafalgar. The Monitor versus the Merrimac. The Battle of Leyte Gulf.* My brain burned with churning seas and exploding shells. I urged my parents to let me continue with what I knew was my life's work. My mother intelligently followed the Jewish axiom of getting a second opinion. Through a friend of a relative, she wrangled an appointment with an instructor at the Art Students League. He lived in Brooklyn Heights, so he consented to come over to our house to view my prodigious efforts. My mother first plied him with sponge cake and coffee. Finally he rose and we led him into my studio. Canvas after canvas I nervously paraded before him. *The Battle of Lepanto. The Sinking of the Armada.* Foam, smoke, and blood. When the parade ended, he sat silently for what seemed like hours. Then he turned to my mother and said, 'I think the boy should seek a career in the Navy.'"

Judy laughed so hard that people at several tables turned to look.

"As you can tell," said Alan, "that's not the first time I've recounted the story. Set piece or not, though, it's absolutely true. For some reason I can still bring a good deal of emotion to it. But enough of Glicksman the Younger. You want to know something about that painting of the children that was sold in Springfield last year. The one they call *The Ripton Falls Children*. That's right, isn't it?"

Judy nodded and then went on to tell Alan of moving into the town and becoming interested in its history. The painting had captured her imagination, and since it was unavailable for viewing, she wanted to find out what she could about it elsewhere.

"Sure, I remember the painting. Aside from having a memory that is both too good and much too unselective, how could I forget a painting that goes at auction for eight times what it's worth?"

Alan sipped his soda and then leaned across the table and whispered to Judy.

"If I order cannoli, promise you won't give me away?"

The cannoli arrived as Alan told her about the auction.

"I was there for three pieces. One I had never seen and wanted to examine. One I was to authenticate for a collector. Teachers have to look for a buck where they can. And the third I wanted to buy. On that I was outbid. When the painting that you're interested in came up, it was fairly late in the auction. I had heard of its apocryphal history before, but since I'm an art historian, not Stephen King, it didn't grab me. I really only looked at the painting closely after the sale. Just before it was taken by the buyer. It was quite mediocre. A primitive without the virtue of freshness and innocence. The figures were awkwardly posed. Against the side of a barn, as I recall. And the palette was uninspired. But despite these things, it did have a quality that stuck with me. I think that was because of all the death symbols in the painting."

"What do you mean by 'death symbols'?" Judy asked Alan.

"Two children were holding flowers that the petals were falling from. That kind of thing."

"What about the faces?" asked Judy.

"They were quite detailed. Unusually so, in fact. One boy had very high cheekbones. I think one of the girls had a . . . sorry, I'm drawing a blank on that. But my impression is of great detail with the faces. There were other specifics that were not usual for the period. Like one girl missing a part of a finger."

"Why do you think the painting went for so much money?"

"I understand the woman who bought it has money and, I gather, lives in your town. So her problem was a combination of the two. But the real reason the work went out of sight was the persistence of a small Japanese man. He had been bidding unsuccessfully all day when this particular painting came up. Since an American was bidding determinedly for it, his own desire to come away with something increased. Foreign money is buying everything these days—art, land, horses, the works."

The waitress came with the check. After Alan paid it, he walked with Judy to her car.

"You've been very helpful, Alan. Hal and I have to have you and Sasha over for dinner soon."

"We'd love to make it," he said as he closed the car door after Judy got in.

"Just one more question. What do you remember most about the painting?"

"The ridiculous price it went for," said Alan, laughing.

•   •

Later that night, as Alan Glicksman touched a match to a mound of charcoal in the outdoor grill they used in the backyard, he suddenly thought again of the girl in the painting with the facial detail he'd forgotten. A bright, wavering drop of fire as dark as blood danced below him in the grill. The redness of the flame tugged at his memory. It had something to do with the girl.

"Alan. Alan," shouted Sasha through the kitchen window. "It's your mother on the phone. She wants to know why we can't make it to Ira's son's bar mitzvah."

"All right. Coming."

He tossed the rest of the match into the fire and turned and walked to the house. As he composed ripostes to his mother's forthcoming attacks on his familial unconcern, the girl in the painting faded from his mind.

34

"And I'll raise back to you," said Sy, his eyelids heavy with meaning, as if examining the Rosetta stone for the first time.

"Well, it looks as if we're in bump city," answered T.C., a trace of a smile ruining his perfect poker-mask face. "I'll just have to raise back to you, Sy."

There was probably the grand sum of twenty dollars in the pot, but the others at the table watched the action with an intensity that befitted petrodollar play at Crockford's. The weekly poker game rotated. This night Reid Prescott was the host. He had dropped out early on this hand and was now in the kitchen preparing what Sy called "the nosh break." Sy had recruited two C.P.A.'s, Harold Lipton and Sam Schulman, who shared an office in Dalton. They were perfect additions: poor players and good losers. Together with Hal they watched the final moments of the hand.

"I'll take that raise," said Sy. "But I don't want to hurt you, Chief. So I'll just call you. I hope you have something stronger than that pair of diesel dyke queens you're showing. Because, sir, I have completed that which is paramount in making a ruler —a straight!"

Sy turned over his hole cards with the flourish of a Benihana chef. A straight, jack high. T.C. regarded Sy's hand for a moment, then smiled broadly.

"You better watch your language, Sy. Because these two ladies don't take kindly to being referred to that way. And the reason they expect some respect is due to those *other* sisters they keep in reserve in this nasty, dark hole."

With a great bellow of laughter, T.C. flipped over two more queens.

"That's unfair," cried Sy. "I was an early supporter of E.R.A. And I always remember to say spokesperson and all that shit."

The laughter was broken by Reid's announcement that the food was ready.

The late-supper repast was also the signal for other business. Sy went to call his wife. He was concerned about Lisa but not forthcoming with any details. Schulman and Lipton made for the bathrooms. T.C. went out to check something or other that was wrong with his new BMW 302.

A panoply of cold cuts ranging from Genoa salami to West-phalian ham was stretched out on the dining-room table. With quiet deliberation Hal and Reid Prescott constructed sand-wiches. They then each grabbed an ale and walked out to the terrace that edged the dining room. The night sky was clear except for a smudge of cloud that was moving slowly across the chin of the full moon.

"How's it going?" asked Hal, after first finishing one of his two sandwiches.

"Good, I guess," Reid answered. "The checks don't bounce and they keep coming. That's good. But this company really doesn't need a full-time lawyer. Oh, if we ever go public, I'll more than earn my keep, but right now it's strictly plantation time."

"Welcome to the club," said Hal between long gulps of ale. "I've resigned myself to the hard fact that it will take time before we're accepted. You can marry a Du Pont, but it takes a while before you're part of the family."

"I'd think that by now they would know how to deal with outsiders a little better than they have. We aren't the first exec-utives the Hilliards have recruited."

"What are you talking about?" asked Hal.

Reid took a bite of his sandwich before continuing.

"Well, I was down in Springfield last week checking on some minor trademark problem when I ran into a guy I hadn't seen in almost ten years. Name of Stevens. Norman Stevens. Knew him in Boston. Got himself a nice little practice in Springfield now. That's where he's from. His field is negligence. Specializes in infant knockovers. We both had a little time on our hands so we decided to have a drink. Norman's club was nearby."

Hal heard the others attacking the groaning board in the din-ing room.

"We had litigated against each other a few times. He's pretty good. After going through the bio bit for a few minutes I told him I was working for Hilliard's. This made him start laughing maniacally. Jesus! He made quite a scene. Finally he pulled himself together. 'So,' he said, 'you're working for The Settlers.' It seems that the Hilliards will settle a suit before the ink dries. He mentioned two he handled five years ago. Of course it piqued my interest. I stopped by the courthouse afterward and looked them up. Lo and behold, they were contractual settlements. You know that clause we all signed about not leaving the company before six months are out? Well, it's strictly dip shit. And the Hilliards folded like rice paper. They settled the contracts for their full amount. All they asked for was a promise not to discuss the terms. So, Hal, as you can see, we are not the first."

"Hey, Hal. Reid. Come on. This loser is itching to become a winner. Get in here and let's start," shouted Sy from the dining room.

35

"Open up, please," said Judy, rapping on Annie's bedroom door. "Now."

Silence.

"Annie, I mean it!"

More silence. Finally the door cracked open just enough to reveal one of Annie's eyes. She stared defiantly out at Judy as if she were under siege. Through the minute wedge, Judy confirmed what she suspected. The room looked exactly as it had before. Since Judy had last spoken to Annie about it, a good solid ten minutes ago, Annie, of course, had *not* been diligently setting things to rights. She had been doing nothing.

"This is ridiculous, Annie," said Judy, beginning to be exasperated. "This is the fourth time I've had to ask you to clean up your room and, believe me, it'll be the last. Get going immediately or forget about seeing Erin and T.C. Junior."

"Not now, Mom," moaned Annie. "I'll do it before dinner. I promise."

"Sorry, Annie, that's not good enough. You're not a baby anymore. You're a young lady, and I expect you to pick up after yourself, just like everybody else. I'll give you five minutes, and that's it."

"But I'm late, and it's the only chance I've ever had to be in a movie."

"Too bad you didn't think of that a half hour ago."

"Thanks a lot, Mother," said Annie, delivering the line as if Judy deserved to be called "Mommie Dearest."

Judy let it pass. Annie was obsessive about having the last word. Judy understood this brand of stubbornness very well. They were both Tauruses.

The movie in question was something cooked up by T.C. Junior. The kid was an authentic movie freak. Whenever Judy saw him he was lugging around some sort of camera. Already he had told his father that when he grew up he intended to be a "hyphenate." To the uninitiated, Judy among them, this translated to mean he wanted to be a writer-director. His hero was Alfred Hitchcock, though his new production—his *second* production, mind you, the notion tickled Judy—sounded anything but Hitchcockian. A parody of a classic detective movie, it was to be called *The Thin Girls*. Annie and Erin instantly had qualified on the grounds of scrawniness. And devotion. Both had major crushes on T.C. Erin cemented the deal by volunteering her mother's double-sized garage as a sound stage.

Precisely five minutes later, Annie invited Judy to inspect her room. It was in perfect order. Judy resisted asking what all the fuss had been about and instead challenged Annie to a race to the car.

When they arrived at the Simmonses' house, no one was in sight. One peal of the doorbell, however, brought Erin to let them in.

Judy had not seen Erin in almost two weeks. She was dressed in pale-blue shorts with a matching halter top. Despite her near-disastrous encounter the month before with the glass doors, she shone with good health. There was something different about her though. At first Judy was puzzled. Then she realized. Erin's hair was shorter than ever. It hugged the contours of her head like a tight-fitting bathing cap.

"I thought you were growing your hair out," said Judy, surprised.

"I was, but I decided I liked it this way after all," said Erin, smiling sweetly. "Mom took me to the beauty parlor for a trim."

"Where *is* your mom?" asked Judy.

"Here I am," said Claire, emerging from the kitchen, looking harried. "Erin and I have been making chocolate-chip cookies. Erin insisted on it. Can you believe it? I have a houseful of snacks. Brownies. Chocolate ice cream. Half a lemon meringue pie I made yesterday. You name it. But, no, Erin got a bee in her bonnet about chocolate-chip cookies. She had to have them. I could have sworn I'd bought some of those damned chocolate bits two days ago, but I couldn't find them anywhere. So of course I had to drive into town to buy some. We've only got one more batch to bake. Then the kids are going to have cookies and lemonade. You want some lemonade?"

"How about coffee instead? If you have instant."

"Great idea. I could use some myself. I don't know about you, but I can't wait for school to begin. Thank goodness it's not far off now."

Before she followed Claire into the kitchen, Judy rested her hand on the top of Annie's head.

"All set, pumpkin?" she asked. "I'll be here ten more minutes, then I'm going. I'll pick you up at six."

" 'Bye, Mom," said Annie, pulling her mother's face down for a kiss. Then she turned to Erin. "Let's see what T.C.'s doing."

"No!" said Erin, her voice loud and sharp. "First come upstairs. I want to show you my new dollhouse dishes. They have a red stripe around the edge, and they're so cute."

"I want to find out about the movie!"

"Oh, T.C. and his dumb movie. I'll bet he doesn't even know how to make one."

"Well, I want to see what's happening," insisted Annie. "I'm going out to the garage."

Before Annie could make a move, Erin grabbed her by the arm and yanked her toward the staircase. Annie lost her balance and fell against Erin.

"What're you doing?" she yelled at Erin. The two girls glared silently at each other.

"Okay," Erin said sourly. "Let's go see T.C."

"And don't pull my arm again. That hurt."

As Judy watched, smiling at one more crisis in the under-ten set, the two girls headed toward the garage, Erin sulkily trailing behind.

Judy had just walked into the kitchen when she heard Annie's shout. She turned as Annie smacked straight into her. Annie's eyes danced with fright.

"Mommy! Mrs. Simmons! Something's happened to T.C."

The two women stared at each other and then ran. As they entered the garage, they were assaulted by the overpowering, enveloping smell of automobile exhaust. T.C. Junior lay collapsed in the middle of the floor.

"Stay back," said Judy to the girls, pushing them into the house.

She took a deep breath and ran to T.C. He was lying on his back, twisted like a broken toy. His skin was the color of soapstone. Coughing and gagging, Judy bent over him. She couldn't tell if he was still breathing. She felt dizzy and was having trouble seeing, as if she were wearing sunglasses at night. She knew she had to get out of there fast or she would faint. She saw Claire struggling with the roll-up door. There was the sudden shriek of metal biting metal, and the door swung up. At the sound, Judy lurched forward blindly, dragging the boy by his shoulders. Somehow she made it outdoors. She let go of T.C. and fell to the ground, hungrily gulping lungfuls of clean air. Then she saw Claire stagger back into the garage again. Only when she heard the car engine go silent did she realize that neither of them had stopped to turn the ignition key.

Her head began to clear, and she focused on T.C. She could see the rise and fall of his chest, faint but steady. Thank God!

"I don't understand, I don't understand," Claire kept repeating.

Judy saw the girls hovering by the interior door to the garage.

"Get some cold water," she called. "And a towel."

She turned again to T.C., gently brushing a wet forelock of

hair away from his eyes. The boy's cheeks were now tinged with pink, and his breathing seemed normal.

"I think he's going to be okay," Judy said to Claire.

"I don't understand," Claire said again, not listening to Judy. Her voice was plaintive. "I'm sure I shut off the engine when I put the car back in the garage. I've never done anything like that before. Never! I don't understand."

As soon as the girls reappeared, Judy sent Erin back into the house for a blanket. She took the basin of water from Annie. Annie's eyes, swollen with fear, begged Judy for assurance.

"T.C.'s going to be okay, I promise you," said Judy, hugging Annie close. "Everything's all right," she heard herself add, even as she thought how close things had been to *not* being all right.

What if they'd arrived ten minutes later, too late to help T.C. Junior? And then a new thought occurred to her. It was a thought so terrifying that she almost screamed out loud in pain. What if Annie had cleaned up her room when she was supposed to and they hadn't been delayed at all? If they hadn't been delayed, Annie would have been in the suffocating garage with T.C. Junior.

36

It had been raining intermittently all morning, and now it was pouring. Margaret, Judy, Hal, and Harvey were in Minna Gannon's house, along with about a dozen other people. Most were strangers to Judy, though she did recognize and nod to Dr. Schackman's wife as well as to an elderly couple whose names she didn't know but whom she had seen sometimes walking by the Green. He, the frailer of the two, usually leaned on his wife's arm. His small, delicate face was dominated by a full, thick mustache that curled upward at the ends, making it seem as if he wore a constant smile.

The drum roll of rain was punctuated by an almost subliminal flash of lightning followed by a crash of thunder.

"Oh, dear," Minna Gannon said anxiously, "this is the first

time in years it's rained on house-tour day. I'm afraid it's going to cut down on attendance."

Judy glanced at Hal. She knew he wished fervently that he was one of the people rained out. He was checking his watch for the third time at least. She'd really had to drag him along. He was only slightly mollified when Harvey agreed to come too.

Harvey had been primed for the tour by Margaret. She had told him that she and Judy were dying to sneak looks at some of the rooms that were not on the official tour. The kitchen, for instance, and Laurie's bedroom. Just female curiosity, she explained. Harvey was happy to aid and abet. When he got the high sign from Margaret, he would stall the tour by asking a scholarly question that would allow the two women time to make a quick foray unobserved. Margaret had not hinted to him what she and Judy were really after.

Minna led the group into the last room in her house that was open to the tour. Once the kitchen and now the living room, it featured a massive walk-in fireplace, paneling on all the walls, and a collection of boldly patterned hooked rugs. Water washed down the outside of the windows.

"Keep an eye on Jane Forgetful here, will you?" Margaret whispered to Judy, tapping herself on the chest. "So far this year, the umbrella body count is four. This charmer"—she raised the umbrella in her hand—"is the last of the lot."

Judy recognized the rose-and-gray colors of Vassar College. Her mother had one too. It must have been a reunion freebie.

"Hang on to it," she hissed back, smiling as she tried to picture Margaret in the role of loyal alumna.

Minna wound up her tour.

"Check your programs, please. The next house for this group is the Hilliards'. Then we will break for lunch. Buffet at the Wayside Inn. I hope all of you have remembered your lunch tickets."

Murmurs of assent mingled with ohs and ahs of dismay as the group was greeted at the open front door by a blast of raw, wet air. And then, umbrellas opened, they dashed across the Green, Margaret and Harvey bumping awkwardly along together under the Vassar colors, Judy and Hal sprinting ahead.

"After the Hilliards', why don't you split," said Judy,

squeezing Hal's hand. "You can make it home in time for the game. Yankees versus Orioles, right?"

"How'd you guess that's what I wanted to do?"

"You're about as hard to read as *TV Guide.*"

Waiting in the entrance hall for them was Elliott, nervous as a high-school freshman dragooned into a leading part in the senior play. Next to him stood his father, Cameron. This was a surprise. He still only rarely went to the office.

Cameron took charge immediately, welcoming the group with handshakes all around. His voice was charged with excitement as he greeted them, many by name. He had as much presence as Judy remembered, perhaps more, his personality like the punch of a fist. Seeing him now, so unexpectedly, brought home to her the reality of what she and Margaret were contemplating. What fools they were. They would never get away with putting anything over on this man. And when they were caught, how could they explain themselves? She, who couldn't even convincingly make excuses in social situations, would never be able to talk her way out of this. Not that anything would really happen to them. But the embarrassment of it filled her with trepidation.

She must stop Margaret from going ahead. The painting wasn't worth the risk. Margaret and Harvey were now standing in a small circle gathered informally around Cameron. She tried anxiously to catch Margaret's eye, but Margaret didn't look her way. Just then Cameron held up his hand for attention, and Judy knew it was too late to stop anything.

"Ladies and gentlemen," he said, "let us begin. For the last few years we have started our tour with a sidelight, though it's no sidelight to us. If any of you are collectors—*fanatical* collectors like Elliott and myself—you will understand and forgive us for wanting to show off our obsessions."

Cameron directed his guests into a large, square cream-colored study that opened off the entrance hall. The walls were lined with shelves of highly polished mahogany, like those in a bookstore catering to the carriage trade. But no books filled these shelves. Rather there were row after row of antique dolls, none, Cameron explained, dating from later than the nineteenth century. They were made of everything from corncobs, twigs, and pipes to rags, handkerchiefs, and bottles. They stared down from their perches, survivors of childhoods that had long since passed into the dust.

"This darling is a favorite of mine," said Cameron, lifting a pert calico-dressed cloth doll down from a shelf. "When a cloth doll's face faded or no longer entranced its young owner, she simply would ask her mother to sew on another." He gently lifted a corner of fabric by the doll's mouth, revealing underneath it the faint outlines of another doll visage. "You might call this the Colonial version of today's face-lift," he continued with a chuckle. "Though this particular doll can't compete in multiple personalities with that woman Sybil who was written about several years ago, we have confirmed that there are five earlier faces beneath this one."

After showing them several extremely rare scrimshaw dolls, Cameron Hilliard stopped and paused by what looked like a closet door.

"And now, my friends, just as every collection of jewels has its diadem, my collection has its *pièce de résistance*. Come with me."

Cameron opened the door and led them into a surprisingly big interior room. Judy immediately felt a wave of cold air as she entered behind Cameron. He flipped a switch, and a line of pinpoint spots picked out six large dolls, each the size of a healthy young child. They were seated on chairs arranged in a half circle, as if waiting to play charades.

"Forgive the cold, but my children's fragility demands it. The air conditioner hums in this room all day, every day."

Judy stared in fascination at the dolls, all thought of her and Margaret's plan erased by the spell of the figures before her. She listened closely as Cameron described them with the ardor of a starving man recalling a sumptuous meal from his youth.

"Most 'formal' or 'show' dolls had faces made of china or papier-mâché bisque. But a material less substantial was also used with great frequency. Wax. And that is why so few examples of this particular type exist today. Of course, the wax faces you see before you are not as malleable as the wax that's found in tapers, but they are delicate enough that very few examples of this lost art exist today. And when you couple that with the unusual size of these beauties, you can see why I take the care that I do with them."

As Judy studied the dolls' faces, she heard Margaret voice a question that was poised on her own lips.

"Their eyes, Mr. Hilliard. They're quite remarkable. They almost seem real."

Judy heard the others add their incredulous assent.

"Aren't they? The finest glass of their time. Painted by brushes that contained only a single sable's hair."

"They seem to shine from inside," said a man next to Judy.

"Totally modern," said Cameron, laughing. "An artful trick of the lighting designer who positioned the spots. But enough of my fixation. We must end our visit, lest we risk raising the temperature in the room. And it is now time for Elliott to parade you past his own treasures."

Dutifully the group followed Elliott down a long hallway into a spacious room. Here the shelves were glass. Like icy steps they climbed to the ceiling. And on them, gleaming like a bride's array of wedding presents, was a wide assortment of shaving brushes, mugs, and scissors. There were hundreds of combs made of everything from tin to ivory. Other shelves held strange-looking metal implements, some resembling instruments that might be found in a doctor's bag. Arranged on a table in one corner of the room was a display of straight razors, their blades open and laid in an arc like a lady's fan.

"What you see before you is, outside of one or two museums, the finest collection of Early American barbershop equipment in the world."

Like his father, he guided them through a date-and-name-studded tour of his prized possessions. Each time he lifted an instrument he made sure to hold it by a buttery piece of chamois. He then replaced the piece in the exact spot that it had originally rested.

"I imagine some of you are wondering what motivates a person to assemble a collection devoted to the humble profession of the barber. But like all hobbies that seem to consume the hobbyist, the answer is not a simple one. It would be amusing to say that a fascination with *The Barber of Seville* led me to acquire what you see around you. Or a desire to take up scissors and comb. But, alas, no. It was rather, I think, my interest in the history of this country, particularly New England, and the role that the barber played in it. For, in addition to our usual perception of this laborer, he often also served in the varied capacities of doctor, dentist, and surgeon to his village neighbors."

And Elliott went on and on, voluble for once, until Cameron entered the room to resume the tour.

"Thank God for Cameron," Hal whispered to Judy as they followed him out of the room. "I was coming awful close to using one or two of those razors from his collection on old Elliott himself."

"Quiet, you ninny," Judy whispered back, stifling her laughter.

As Cameron invited his guests to follow him to the drawing room, Judy remembered what she and Margaret were about to do. Margaret was ahead of her now. Judy stared at the back of Margaret's head with such intensity, willing her to turn around, that when Margaret actually did so, Judy nearly jumped. If Margaret noticed Judy's distress, she gave no indication. Instead she cocked her head quickly toward a small passageway off the hall through which they were passing. Then Judy saw Margaret rest her hand briefly on Harvey's shoulder. With a sinking sensation, Judy knew the moment had come.

As his audience spread out before him on the threshold of the drawing room, Cameron rapidly warmed to his subject. He pointed to some of the choicest items: the Aubusson rug, the round Chinese teak table, the Hepplewhite side chairs. These, he said, were mere ornaments compared to the house itself. The house was the work of an anonymous disciple of the celebrated Colonial architect Samuel McIntire.

"And this," Cameron said, resting his hand on the marvelously carved mantel of the fireplace, "this we believe to be the work of the master himself, McIntire!"

"Excuse me, sir," said Harvey, "but I always understood that McIntire worked exclusively in the communities north of Boston. How then do you explain . . ."

Judy and Margaret slipped from the room, retracing their steps to the passageway. The first door they tried was locked—Judy felt a stab of relief—but the second opened easily. They switched on the light and saw a flight of stairs reaching down to a neat, clean cellar with a well-swept cement floor and white-washed walls. Woefully conscious of the brightness of the scene before her—where could they hide if they had to?—Judy hurried after Margaret. In the first room to the left were a furnace and a hot-water heater, humming efficiently. In the next, a wine cellar. In the main area, precisely ordered and sectioned off, were gardening implements, numbered storm windows, glistening jars of canned vegetables and fruits, power and wood-working tools. One entire corner was enclosed in chain link fencing, further divided into smaller parts.

"What's this for?" asked Judy.

"Dogs? Maybe they used to keep them."

Just then came the sound of someone moving overhead. The footsteps stopped by the door to the cellar. Had they been heard? Judy held her breath, her heart thudding, and then the sounds faded. They had to get out of here.

"Come on," she said, one foot on the stairs. "The painting's not here."

"Wait," said Margaret, opening one last door, then calling to Judy.

In a closet the size of a small room was a rack jammed with antique children's clothing. The dresses and shoes were charmingly quaint. The fabrics were lush: silks, satins, velvets. Many of the colors were surprisingly bright. Against the back wall was a row of antique children's beds.

"I wonder what these are for?" asked Margaret.

"Another Hilliard collection?"

The question hung in the air. Then the two women hastily closed the door and retreated up the stairs. As they eased open the cellar door, Judy heard Harvey say, "But that's impossible." Cameron snorted out something about the Connecticut Valley and the migration of talent. It was clear that he felt he had settled the issue. He directed the group back into the entrance hall for a presentation of its handsome staircase and English wallpaper. He glared at Harvey, but Harvey was now resolutely silent, once again the compliant tourist. Two, maybe three, minutes had passed since Harvey had opened the discussion. It had been just enough time for them.

As the group prepared to move upstairs to view the family room and the master bedroom, Margaret tugged Judy's sleeve.

"Got the guts to try the other bedrooms?" Margaret whispered.

"Absolutely. I'm beginning to enjoy this. It's bringing out the second-story man in me," answered Judy, not meaning a word of it.

She and Margaret joined the others as they trooped into a sweepingly proportioned bedroom. But almost at once Judy tensed. She saw Margaret signal Harvey and knew that Margaret meant to act immediately. As Cameron began ticking off the high points of the room—the ornately carved mantel, the Chippendale mirror above it, the Directoire bed, the mahogany chest—Harvey's hand shot up.

"With all due respect," began Harvey at his ingratiating worst, "is that mirror an authentic Chippendale or is it just in the Chippendale *manner?*"

Without waiting for Cameron's reply, which was bound to be testy, Judy and Margaret slipped back through the halls and into the next room. The room belonged to one of the men and was simple and unadorned. The closet, a model of organization, brimmed with suits, shoes, ties, belts. And nothing more. The room next to it was dominated by a lovely four-poster bed with a flowered canopy and spread. Laurie's room.

"Damn," said Judy, discovering that the door to the closet was locked.

"Wait a minute," said Margaret, standing on tiptoe and sliding her fingers along the ledge above the door. "Everybody hides keys in places like this. My God, there *is* a key."

Margaret turned the key and opened the door. It was a walk-in cedar closet. Quickly they spotted a large framed painting, placed so that it was facing the wall. Instinctively, they knew at once it was the painting of the children. Gingerly, Margaret turned it around. They both froze. There were the children of the coven. Seven small figures. Just as Alan Glicksman had said, they were posed stiffly against a backdrop of weathered barn siding. But some terrible fury had visited the canvas. A force bred of a hatred so strong that neither Margaret nor Judy could speak. For the faces of the children no longer existed. Gouged away in ugly slashes, not an eyebrow, turn of nose, or curve of neck remained. All were obliterated. Beyond recognition.

For a long moment neither woman could move, held like deer caught by a car's headlights, held by the horror of the destruction. Then, moving as one with exaggerated care, they turned the painting back to the way it had been, locked the closet door, and replaced the key. Silently, they opened the bedroom door and rejoined the others, now in the front parlor. All was as they had found it. All, that is, except for one thing. There, left behind, in the corner by the closet door, was Margaret's rose-and-gray striped umbrella. A few last drops of rainwater slid down it, pooling onto the floor like tiny pearls of blood.

37

It was a Hammer Studios film minus Christopher Lee. Judy could see the script directions: "Exterior: Two women search for abandoned grave sites in Berkshire Hills. Weather: Rotten." It wasn't raining—yet—but it might as well have been.

Judy had to laugh. A few days ago everyone was complaining about how hot it was, and now it felt like London in the depths of winter. She thought briefly of the year she had spent at the Slade when the chill even indoors was sometimes so profound she would paint with her gloves on. A vicious gust of wind rocked Margaret's little car and jolted Judy back to the present. No doubt of it. This was the windiest, rawest, dankest, nastiest day they had had all summer. If the storm clouds dropped any lower they would surely trigger in her an attack of claustrophobia. God bless New England weather. It could not be underestimated. Or forecast.

Margaret drove past the parsonage and parked beyond it on the edge of the road. The church and the parsonage were both closed now and so woebegone—heartbreaking, really—that neither woman said a word. Behind the church was a small cemetery circled on two sides by an old stone wall and on the third by a spiky line of birches. As they rounded the corner of the church, Margaret remembered that she had left the cemetery map on the front seat of her car.

While she waited for Margaret, Judy walked to the edge of

the cemetery. She hung back, almost afraid to enter. She looked out over the gravestones. Some had been there for centuries. The stones were thin, dark, and tilted like playing cards held by an invisible hand. Most of the graves, though, appeared to be fairly recent. Draped against one thick, new gray stone was an Army wreath that looked as if it had been stamped out of the same olive drab as a G.I. Joe doll. Next to several others were bouquets of plastic flowers. Blue gardenias dominated. By one grave was a jelly glass filled with pale roses so fresh that not a petal had fallen.

In this small congregation, thought Judy sadly, the living had given up. Only the dead still made demands.

"Here I am," said Margaret, waving the map. "Now let's see where we are."

Unrolling the map, Margaret advanced into the cemetery. She strode directly to a cluster of older stones, bent to read the inscriptions, then consulted the map. She frowned and hurried to another stone to compare names.

"Damnation!" she exclaimed this time. "I should have guessed."

"Guessed what?" asked Judy.

"This isn't the right cemetery."

"Oh, that's too bad," said Judy, privately relieved.

Just standing here among all these graves made her nervous, and she was freezing. She was about to suggest they drive to the Wayside Inn for a bowl of soup when Margaret continued.

"It's got to be the *old* cemetery. By the old town. I think I remember how to get there."

"Old town?"

"You mean you've never heard of it? Minna Gannon is getting as tight-mouthed as the Hilliards. Or senile. I'm amazed, but I'll explain in a minute. In the car. It's too cold to talk out here."

As they turned off into a small, narrow road that knifed its way through dense second-growth timber, Margaret described how the town of Ripton Falls had been moved to where it was now from its original site on the highest hill in the area. That elevation had been chosen as a precaution against Indian attack.

"But after a while," said Margaret, "the location didn't make sense anymore. They wanted to be in the valley near the good farmland and water power. So, some time in the first half of the eighteenth century, they just picked themselves up and moved. Like Newfane, Vermont. I think that's the name of the other town that did it.

"Only a few of the original Ripton buildings are left. The two saltboxes on the Green and a Cape on the other side. A beauty. There was one thing they couldn't bring with them, though. Their dead. The relatives they had buried in their cemetery. It must have been tough leaving them, but they could ride into the hills to visit. It wasn't as if the town had been flooded out, like the places that used to be where the reservoir is now."

A sharp dip in the road halted Margaret's recitation. A few miles earlier, the road surface had turned to dirt, and now it was becoming progressively rockier and more rutted as they worked their way into the hills. Above them, the canopy of foliage and granite clouds enveloped them in eerie midday darkness. Margaret switched on her beams, puncturing holes in the gloom.

All at once the road they were on fed into another, forcing a choice of directions. Margaret swung the car to the left. As the headlights caught and illuminated the passing landscape, something in the configuration of trees and stone walls nudged at Judy's memory. And then she remembered. Of course.

"I think we went by here one day when we were picnicking," said Judy.

"Well, I wish *I* had been up here recently. It's been at least ten years, maybe more, since I came this way to do some rubbings. And none of this looks very familiar."

After driving several more miles, Margaret abruptly stopped the car. There it was. The old cemetery. Judy peered at it through a ragged screen of brush and trees and then got out of the car and followed Margaret toward it. They edged their way through wild blackberry, fruit the size of gum balls, and a thicket of white pines, the lower branches snapping off like chalk as they passed.

This time the stones were all wafer-thin and the writing on them faint with age. Judy deciphered the inscription on a stone immediately in front of her. At the top was a hand, one finger pointing skyward, as if giving a direction to a passerby. Beneath it were the words:

GONE HOME

Josiah Rice
1659–1706

One corner of the cemetery was overrun by a phalanx of goldenrod. Several stones barely peeked above it.

Map in hand, Margaret moved from stone to stone, crowing in triumph as she matched up names. Then she stooped down, suddenly quiet, before a small stone. She beckoned to Judy.

"So many children used to die young, I guess parents expected it," she said, "but still it breaks my heart to read this kind of thing. Look at this. 'Here lies the body/Of Abigail Banks/Who died October 30th/1682 in/Her 10th year/Called from Darkness/To Eternal Light.' "

"Oh, God," said Judy, thinking at once of Annie, "I couldn't take it."

The sky grew darker. Margaret jumped up and strode ahead again, checking the names on more stones.

"I don't believe it," she called back to Judy after only a few moments. "Here's another kid who died on the exact same date. October thirtieth, 1682. Jonathan Sterling. 'What Evil hath taken from us/Our Lord hath returneth unto Himself.' Judy, do you know what I think?"

"Yes," said Judy softly.

"Right! These are two of the *good* children. The ones killed by the coven. It makes sense. They would be buried here, too. Come on, let's find the rest."

The two women moved off in opposite directions and within minutes they had accounted for the five other children who had died on that terrible night so long ago. The last one was a girl named Lydia Kellogg. She had been five years old.

"Those monsters!" cried Margaret. "They really did it. We've got to find out who they were. I have my bearings now and according to this map, those . . . creatures should be buried right over there."

As Margaret pointed toward a tumble-down section of the

stone wall, there was a loud crack of thunder. The two women scrambled over the wall and stepped into a mass of tangled vine on the other side. They stared in frustration at the dense thicket of growth beneath their feet and then began to tug at it furiously. Finally they wrenched it apart enough to reach into it. Margaret breathed in sharply as her hand felt the cold surface of a stone. Though huge raindrops now pelted down on them like marbles, the women uncovered four more stones almost immediately. They were just where the map had promised, and after a long search, they found a sixth, broken like a chipped tooth. They couldn't find the seventh in the overgrowth and steady rain.

It was exactly as Margaret had believed it would be. But with one difference. The rain slid down the surface of the stones as smoothly as it would have over windowpanes, for the stones were utterly blank. Not one of them carried an inscription. Neither a date nor a name.

For a long moment the two women just listened to the hollow drumbeat of the rain. There was no need for either one to speak, for the blank stones told the whole horrible story more forcefully than words could. The story of a people so outraged by those they buried that they refused to identify them. So outraged that they chose instead to rip their names forever from the earth.

38

"Let's see. I'll take a quarter pound of sesame-seed crunch. And half a pound of chocolate-honey brownies. Wait a sec! Make that half a pound of crunch and up the brownies to a pound."

"Don't forget the Colorado Cowboy cookies, George."

"No one likes them except you."

"Would you guys pull it together. I'm beginning to lose my high," said another voice.

Munchies was running true to form, thought Hal, laughing to

himself. The candy shop was the size of a large telephone booth and always packed. Mostly with college kids, whose sweet tooths had been sharpened on the likes of Acapulco gold and Maui wowee. Its small counter shimmered with glass jars ranked one on top of another layer-cake fashion. In them, neatly labeled in easy-reader printing, were chip, icebox, and rolled cookies, variations on variations of brownies, and a roll call of candies from jelly beans, mints, licorice whips, and sour balls to English toffee, French hard candies, and Swiss chocolate. In a gap in the wall of glass jars stood the shop's proprietor, feet planted apart like a boy inside a snow fort that he knows is the best on the block. He was a short, unflappable man named Ozzie, and he reached for, weighed, and bagged his wares with the calm precision of a surgeon.

The line moved rapidly. Ozzie saw to that. Hal was able now to squeeze inside the shop. He was here to buy surprise treats for Annie and Mimi. They would be getting out of the movie theater in—he glanced at his watch—less than five minutes. Although at least a dozen kids were still wedged into the store, only three were actually ahead of him in line: two Smithies in faded bib overalls and the kid whose high was slipping away.

Hal bought a quarter pound of red-hots for Annie and a tin of *citron pastillines* for Mimi. He tossed the bags onto the front seat of the car, then walked up the street toward the Academy of Music. The car had been a bitch to park. It could stay where it was for the moment.

The movie was breaking as he crossed the street. *Young Frankenstein.* An oldie but goodie of Mel Brooks's. Annie and Mimi loved him equally. They didn't have to have his jokes explained to them, and Annie, bless her nine-year-old heart, found his bathroom humor hilarious.

Annie immediately clamored for an ice-cream cone.

"I've got something else in the car for you, honey, but first I want to stop here," said Hal, steering them into a hardware store two doors down. He needed to price lawn mowers. His had had a near-fatal encounter with an apple-tree root last week. A quick glance at the price tags made him change his mind about Agway's repair estimate on the old one.

They headed back to the car, Annie skipping along in the

lead. When Mimi and Annie were settled in the back seat, Hal scooped up the candy bags.

"This one's for you, honey," he said to Annie.

"You're the best daddy in the world," Annie shouted, peeping into the bag and throwing her arms around Hal's neck.

"And, Mimi," continued Hal, disentangling himself from his daughter and handing back the second bag, "I know there's more than one sweet tooth in the family. Now, ladies, sit back. We're on our way."

Hal had just shifted into reverse when a piercing shriek rang out. Mimi! He whirled around toward her. Her face was twisted into a kabuki mask of fright. She stared rigidly at the crumpled candy bag on the middle of the car seat. What the hell was going on? Before he could ask, a large, ugly black spider scuttled out of the bag and onto the seat of the car. Its body was as big as a half-dollar, each furry leg the size of a man's pinkie. Hal watched in fascination as the creature hesitated, darted up the back of the seat, then froze. Then Mimi screamed again, snapping him to his senses. He ordered Annie and Mimi out of the car, slipped off his shoe, and, bracing for the moment of contact, slammed the heel against the spider. He whipped his handkerchief out, swept the bloody pulp off the seat, and chucked the mess, handkerchief and all, into a trash can on the corner.

"E-yew. Dis-*gust*-ing," said Annie.

"All right, everybody. This is the captain," said Hal brightly. "Resume your seats. The stowaway has been dispatched."

Annie responded immediately to his little joke. She ran over to the car and peered eagerly into it with the excitement of someone fortunate enough to be at the site of a nonfatal disaster. Mimi, however, didn't budge. She stood rooted to the sidewalk, arms wrapped tight around herself, head down, snuffling and gasping into her chest. For the first time Hal realized she might be in shock. He went over and put his arm around her shoulder, then led her to the car.

"See," he said, speaking slowly, as if she were the child. "There's nothing here. It's gone. Dead. If you want you can come sit in front with me."

Mimi climbed in beside Hal. She was snuffling still, but she seemed to have gotten hold of herself. She even fastened her seat belt, something, Hal knew, she had no faith in. And then, just as Hal was congratulating himself on finessing a crisis, it started. The snuffling became a moan, the moan built to a sob, and within seconds, before Hal had even left the downtown area, Mimi was wailing, tears drenching her face like a thunder shower.

"Look, Mimi, I agree," said Hal soothingly. "It *was* awful. I was scared by it too. But it's dead. It's gone."

"No," Mimi's voice broke. "It's not gone."

"What're you talking about?"

"Something evil brought it to me."

"Oh, come on," said Hal. "*I* brought that thing here. Straight from Munchies. You know what a zoo that place is. God knows what those freaky kids in there are slipping each other. I'm amazed something like this hasn't happened before."

"No. Evil brought it here," Mimi repeated, ignoring Hal. "From my island. From Haiti."

"Oh, Mimi," said Hal softly, scarcely believing what he was hearing. "That's ridiculous. There are spiders like that all over the world."

Mimi shook her head and collapsed again into tears.

Hal caught Annie's eyes in the rearview mirror. They were wide with alarm. He reached back and squeezed her hand, then, his expression grim, concentrated his full attention on the road. The sooner he got Mimi—and Annie!—home, the better.

•   •

When they arrived, Mimi went directly to her room and locked the door. Judy could hear her crying and pleaded with her to open the door. She refused.

After Hal, Judy, and Annie had eaten a hasty dinner, picnicking in front of the living-room television in a futile effort to distract themselves, Judy approached Mimi's door again. This time Mimi let Judy in. Over and over she insisted that the spider had been sent to "do" her. It didn't matter that it was dead. Its evil had invaded her. She was sick. She was going to die.

Judy vehemently denied this last possibility, but Mimi did in fact look ill. She lay back against her bed, eyes feverishly shining. Later, after Hal and Judy conferred, Hal made the call to Brooklyn. To Mimi's aunt.

"Take the whole week off if you want, Mimi," said Judy, gently wiping Mimi's forehead dry. "I'll find ways to keep Annie busy. The important thing is for you to get a good rest."

• •

In bed that night, Judy asked Hal if the spider had been as horrible as Mimi said.

"It wasn't like something out of a grade-B movie, if that's what you mean. It was big and nasty, but it was just a spider. It looked like chewing gum after I squashed it."

"She made such a fuss about it," said Judy, "just like with the parakeet. I know she can't help it, but I'm beginning to worry about how all this affects Annie."

Early the next morning Hal drove Mimi to Northampton and put her on a bus for New York.

39

"Dr. Mitchell, please."

"I'm sorry, but he's not in. May I help you? I'm his nurse."

"Oh, your voice sounds different, Miss Curtis. This is Judy Richardson."

"Of course. How are you? My voice *is* different. I've been away on vacation for the last two weeks and I developed an allergy to some flower or weed there."

"Where's there?"

"Falmouth. On the Cape. I'm still stuffed up from it. I've never sneezed so much in my entire life. Dr. Mitchell called in a prescription for me, but that just made me into a marathon napper. Some vacation!" Nurse Curtis laughed.

"It sounds just awful. Poor you. Did you get a tan?"

"The damned medication made me fall asleep on the beach. I look like the 'before' in a Solarcaine ad."

They both laughed.

"I was just calling to go over a few details about checking Annie into the hospital next Thursday."

"Why? Is something wrong?"

"No. For the operation Dr. Mitchell is going to perform on Annie. To remove the birthmark."

"But you canceled that last week."

"What?"

"Miss Morse, who filled in for me, took the message. Wait a second, here it is. 'Mrs. Richardson called. Terribly sorry but had to cancel op. for next week. Will resched. op. in fall.'"

"There must be some mistake. I never canceled. I promise you."

"Wait a minute. It must have been Mrs. *Richards* who called. She's another one of our patients. I'm surprised at Miss Morse, but that's what must have happened."

"Well, let's reschedule then."

"Unfortunately the earliest date I can give you is at least eight weeks from now."

"Why so far off?"

"Well, when you canceled, or we *thought* you canceled, Dr. Mitchell filled in his operating schedule on that day, so Thursday is completely booked. Then he's off on vacation. He and Mrs. Mitchell are going to Kyoto. From there they go to China. And he's completely booked after he returns. China. Now that's one trip I'd love to make. I hear they eat everything that walks and grows. No chance for allergies there."

Nurse Curtis was still laughing when Judy replaced the receiver.

40

Mimi was due back on the 6 P.M. bus. Judy and Annie watched as the passengers got off. No Mimi. Back at the house, Judy called Mimi's aunt. She had spoken to the woman only once before to check out the suitability of a birthday gift for Mimi. The conversation was over almost before it began. Mimi was sick. Sore throat. Fever. She'd call back in a few days. The line went dead before Judy could say thank you.

Two days later the letter arrived. Special delivery. It was addressed to "The Richardson Family." Judy opened it quickly and read the precisely printed contents.

Dear Mr. and Mrs. Richardson,

I am writing this letter for my niece Marie-Thérèse. Though we have never met, I feel that I know you from all that she has told me about you and your beautiful child. Over the years she has worked for you she has felt herself to be a part of your wonderful family. And now that she cannot return and continue to work for you she finds it too difficult to write herself. When she came here three days ago, she was crying so hard that it was more than an hour before she could tell me what was wrong. Now you may say that Marie-Thérèse is a silly woman who believes in the devil and all kinds of bad magic. But she is not a foolish person. Where we come from we learn that not all the real things can be seen or touched. Evil has a shape and a voice and we know how to see it and hear it. Marie-Thérèse loves all of you and is afraid for you. She also fears for herself and cannot return until you move from this place. She doesn't know what will happen, but she knows it will be bad. She sends her love and says to be careful and watchful of your child.

Sincerely,
Hélène Poincaré (Mrs.)

P.S. If it isn't too much trouble could you send Marie-Thérèse's cat, Matelot, and her other things on Tuesday's

Trailways bus. It leaves Northampton 8:20 A.M., arrives Port Authority 12:35. The cat carrier is in the basement behind the green wheelbarrow. Thank you. (I've enclosed a money order for $25 to cover the cost.)

41

Now where the hell was the asparagus? Hal was in the green quadrant of the canned-veg section, so he knew he must be close. All he could see though were peas, petit and otherwise, and beans, French cut and regular. Not a can of asparagus in sight, let alone the kind Judy had specified. Extra-long, jumbo spears, Jolly Green Giant. Judy's shopping lists carried enough detail to qualify for inclusion in a time capsule on late-twentieth-century domesticity. She assumed Hal would make mistakes if left to his own devices. He had done beautifully until now. He had stuffed his cart with enough Alpo to keep Percy fit for weeks to come and, just a few minutes ago, had hit the jackpot with a special on Judy's favorite brand of Italian-style tomatoes.

They were here together on their bimonthly spend-like-crazy, tomorrow-will-be-worse grocery run. Judy was concentrating on cleaning products and dry goods. Next Hal would case coffees, teas, and condiments. They would rendezvous at the cash register, load the Jeep, and then shoot down to Northampton. A few days earlier a woman had called from Smith and asked Judy to exhibit in the faculty art show that began next week. With Hal throwing in his two cents' worth, Judy finally had settled on three canvases. The one she had just finished that Hal was so crazy about and two she had completed in California. One of these was so big they had to strap it to the roof.

Hal had about decided that either the store's color coding was out of whack or he was suffering from premature cataracts when he heard a child speak his name. He turned and there was Erin Simmons.

"Where's Annie?" she asked.

He was explaining that Annie was at Gwen Prescott's when

he noticed a large bandage wrapped around Erin's right hand.

"What happened to you?" he asked.

"Oh, just a little accident," said Erin vaguely. Her eyes wandered off. Clearly she wasn't that crazy about passing the time of day with her friend's father when her friend wasn't there. "Well, I'll be seeing you."

Hal watched Erin drift down the aisle and out of sight, then maneuvered his cart around to take the veg shelves from the top again. Just then Claire wheeled around the corner.

"Hey, there," said Hal. "What're you doing here?"

"Speak for yourself," she replied amiably.

"Well, you got to admit it beats Hilliard and Co. for action. But tell me, what happened to Erin? I just saw her. She said she had a little accident."

"Little! I thought I was going to have a heart attack. It happened yesterday. Tracy slammed the car door on her hand. Her forefinger was smashed. It was awful. There was just nothing the doctors could do. She lost the tip of the finger, to the bottom of her nail. She was amazing though. A real trooper. I don't know where she gets her pain threshold, but it isn't from my side of the family. Even the doctors couldn't believe it."

"Jesus, that kid's really accident prone, isn't she?"

"Right. My daughter, the daredevil. She thinks she's one of the Flying Wallendas. First the encounter with the pail of tar. Then the glass doors. Now this. Still"—Claire paused and lowered her voice, her tone conspiratorial—"I'm not going to say Tracy did it on purpose, but it was strange the way it happened. We weren't getting out of the car or anything like that. Lisa and I were standing in the parking lot talking and the girls were fooling around when, bingo, I looked up just in time to see Erin catch it on the hand. They hadn't even been anywhere near the car a moment earlier."

"Oh, boy. Poor Erin."

"You're right. I suppose she's lucky though. It could have been much worse. Well, I've got to run."

Yeah, lucky Erin, thought Hal. What was one fingertip more or less. It was all push-button this and push-button that these days anyway.

As soon as Claire had disappeared, he resumed his search for the asparagus. To no avail. He looked up in frustration and saw Judy heading down the aisle toward him. Her shopping cart was full.

"What's holding you up?" asked Judy.

"I was being polite listening to another sob story from Claire about Erin. This time she's hurt her hand somehow. Now where are those damned asparagus?"

"You're looking right at them," said Judy, smiling and pointing to the shelf.

And there the asparagus were. Exactly where they were supposed to be. Stage center in green.

42

Before she was halfway up the path to the house, Judy heard the sound of rock from Annie's room. But that was no surprise. Vicky Leland was baby-sitting. Where Vicky went, her records went. Judy hadn't objected because she didn't want to be a stick-in-the-mud, but she was beginning to have second thoughts. She hollered a hello upstairs, not sure she could compete, but Vicky materialized at once at the top of the landing. No, the girl said, there were no phone messages, and, yes, she could stay at least another hour.

As she unpacked the fruit and vegetables that she'd bought from a farmer's stand on the far side of town, Judy thought again how pleased she was with Vicky, musical tastes aside. She wasn't much use in the kitchen—Annie complained that even her peanut-butter sandwiches weren't "right"—and it felt odd to have someone new in the house after so many years with Mimi, but for now Vicky was more than fine. Judy could call at the last minute, and Vicky would pedal over from the Hilliards', the orange flag at the rear of her bike bobbing over her head like a marker buoy. And Annie liked her. She braided and combed Annie's hair, let her experiment with her makeup, and helped her with her knitting, which Annie had just discovered was fun now that she was old enough to really do it.

Of course Judy missed Mimi tremendously. She wished she could have stopped her from leaving. But it had been scary seeing such irrationality. Now at least she didn't have to concern herself about what Mimi's superstitions might be doing to Annie. And Annie really had outgrown Mimi. When school began in a few days, Judy wouldn't need Vicky's help that much either.

Judy lay down in the hammock on the porch to write her mother a long-overdue letter. Before she had finished the first paragraph, she had fallen asleep. When she woke up, almost an hour had passed. Time to fix dinner!

She was rinsing lettuce for a salad when Annie pushed through the swinging door into the kitchen. She kissed her mother and announced that she was starved. As Judy opened the refrigerator to get out some apple juice, she noticed the doll Annie was carrying. She had never seen it before. It looked Victorian. It had a dreamy, prettified expression, a mass of golden hair under a dark-green velvet hat, and a long velvet cape to match.

"Where did you get that?" she asked.

"Oh, she belongs to Aunt Laurie," said Annie, reaching for a glass. "She's adorable, don't you think?"

"Belongs to *whom?*"

"Aunt Laurie. I mean *Vicky's* Aunt Laurie. Vicky said I could borrow her for a week."

When Judy made no comment, Annie continued.

"Aunt Margaret thinks she's beautiful too. She said she has some miniature old-fashioned dishes she'll lend me for her."

"When did you see Aunt Margaret?"

"This afternoon. When she was here."

Judy turned off the tap, wiped her hands on the dish towel she had tucked over her skirt, and strode quickly to the bottom of the staircase. Why the devil hadn't Vicky told her? When she confronted Vicky, the girl looked as if she might cry.

"I'm sorry," she said wretchedly. "You asked if anybody called. Miss Love didn't *call*. She stopped by. I didn't think—"

"Don't be so literal," said Judy snappishly. "Of course I would want to know if a friend was here. Did she leave a message?"

"No, just that you should call her," said Vicky meekly.

On the kitchen phone Judy dialed Margaret's number. She heard the asthmatic whir that signaled the answering machine.

"Hello. This is Margaret Love," began her friend's voice. "I know I sound like the Road Runner, but please don't hang up. I'm never out for long, and I promise to call you back promptly. Promise! Just leave a fairly coherent message and you'll hear from me. And to all you Till Evlenspiegel fans, let us not forget that tomorrow marks the thirty-second anniversary of the death of Richard Strauss. And composing tone poems must be good for something, because he lived to the age of eighty-five.

"If any of you are trying to reach Harvey, remember he won't be back until Friday. I have an early dinner date tonight and will be going out at five. Judy, if I don't hear from you before then, can you come by my place tomorrow at eight for breakfast? It's important. I remember you said you had to stop off at the faculty exhibit later in the morning. 'Bye."

Judy glanced at her watch. It was twenty to six. She had missed Margaret. Well, tomorrow would be soon enough. She thought again of Vicky. She really shouldn't have been so angry with her. Poor Annie had taken the reprimand just as hard as Vicky had. And after all, anyone could forget a message.

43

As Judy waited for Margaret to open the front door, she noticed a recently planted line of dogwoods neatly fencing off the driveway from the tabletop lawn. Margaret gardened with a painter's eye, Judy thought admiringly. She rang the bell again. Annoyed at the delay, she tried the door. The knob turned easily. A well-oiled click and the door swung soundlessly inward.

"Margaret. Margaret. Your fellow conspirator and acolyte is here," Judy shouted into the house from the doorstep. She was sure that the neighbors next door heard her. Nothing.

The front-hall floor was slate. The stillness of the house made Judy's footsteps resound like wooden shoes. It was silly, but Judy was suddenly scared. She stood for a moment at the entrance to the living room. She finally walked in, pulled forward with the force of a strong tide. The night they found Brad pushed itself into her consciousness insistently. A rush of dark, closeted memories washed over her as if she were standing under a waterfall. Okay. That's enough. Things like that don't happen twice. Margaret's fine. Just relax. But it would be nice if Hal were here. Stop it! You're as jumpy as Annie without a night light.

The kitchen was empty save for Hodge, Margaret's cat, who was curled asleep in an empty breadbasket like a fur soufflé. He raised his head for a moment, showing Judy a look of exquisite boredom, then burrowed back under his tail. Judy moved into the dining room. The morning sun poured like a floodlight through an immense window that wrapped around one corner, underlining the silence of the room. Judy moved down the hall-way that she knew led to Margaret's bedroom. She kept calling Margaret's name. She was afraid to stop. As she entered Margaret's bedroom she heard something. What was it? Before she could identify the sound it abruptly stopped. And just as suddenly the bathroom door opened and there, stepping out of a rolling bank of steam like a magician at the start of his act, was Margaret. Her face was the pale pink of a tea rose and she was wrapped in a fluffy, sparkling-white terry-cloth robe. She didn't seem at all surprised to see Judy standing there.

"I just love this robe. Harvey stole it for me from the Hotel Negresco in Nice. Of course they just added it to his bill. Are you intending to take root or would you like to be useful? There's a Melitta just like yours on the kitchen table. The coffee is in a glass jar labeled, strangely enough, coffee. In the fridge. See you in a minute."

Judy was pouring boiling water over the coffee when Margaret walked into the kitchen. She wore a one-piece yellow cotton warm-up suit that looked more like a pair of Dr. Denton's than anything else.

"I don't want to hear any baby jokes, Judy. I get enough from Harvey. *I* think it's cute. And besides, it was on sale. And what's happened to your vision? Didn't you see the wild strawberries in the box? I built up an impressive set of knee calluses looking for the little buggers. They'd fetch a fortune at Fauchon's. A work-intensive crop, an economist friend of Harvey's calls them."

They marched the coffee and strawberries and appropriate crockery out to the table set by the side of the pool. The breeze had picked up, rippling the water. Margaret ducked back inside and came out with a catalog. She plopped it newsboy-style onto Judy's lap.

"It's from the auction that included the painting of the children. Mentions it a bit. Nothing we don't know, however. Give it a look while I finish my morning set."

Margaret began a series of stretching exercises. Judy scarcely looked at the catalog as she marveled at Margaret's amazing suppleness.

"It's called the Pilates Method. I've been doing it for years. I'll follow this up with twenty laps at granny speed followed by a nice ten-minute soak in the Jacuzzi and then, Brooke Shields, watch out. People find it hard to believe someone as scatterbrained as I am can be so regimented. But they forget I'm living with a man ten years younger than myself."

Lying on her stomach, Margaret simultaneously threw back her head and grabbed each of her legs at the ankle. She then proceeded to imitate a hobbyhorse.

"This is called rocking."

"I'm sure the Russians have another name for it. I'd confess first."

"Very funny. But it's marvelous for the tummy."

Margaret quickly proceeded to the cobra, the teaser, then the boomerang.

"You remember that umbrella I couldn't find?" she asked. "The rose-and-gray number?"

"Sure. Why?"

"Well, look, there it is," said Margaret, pointing to an umbrella leaning against a wall near the door. "Can you believe it? I must have been walking past that thing for two weeks and I never noticed it. And I just sent a check off to Vassar for another one. At least it's a good cause. Now tell me, are you still going by the exhibit this morning?"

"Thinking of contributing?"

"No repartee. It's too early. No tragedy if you're five or ten minutes later than you planned?"

"Where are you leading?"

"To Worthington. It's about twenty miles from here. Nice

little hill town. The store there has a marvelous cheddar. We must remember to buy some."

"Quite a hike for cheese. Even for us mice."

"That's only a side benefit," said Margaret, casting Judy a mysterious smile.

"You're becoming a terrible tease, Auntie Margaret," Judy replied, laughing. "Why am I here?"

"Patience. I've got something to show you, but there's time. Let's just say for now that the ride to Worthington might be productive. You know, I've had a funny feeling all morning. I just know I've forgotten something. That usually doesn't happen to me until *after* I've left the house. Well, it'll give me something to think about while I do my laps. What a trade-off! A firm bod for boredom."

Margaret shed her warm-up suit to reveal a figure that would do a woman of Judy's age proud. Her one-piece black Lycra tank suit made her look as sleek as a seal. After putting on a bathing cap she dived into the pool. With a smooth, regular stroke that neatly sliced through the water she easily swam lap after lap.

As Margaret slowly made her way back and forth, Judy looked through the catalog. Most of the photos were devoted to a collection of Shaker furniture. The pieces had an efficient and spare elegance that made them look strangely contemporary. The listing for *The Ripton Falls Children* could have been written for the Yellow Pages:

Painting (oil) of seven children, c. 1688.
Unsigned. Lot No. 237.

Spooky antecedents must not be very marketable. She searched the index for further information but found none. No wonder people were surprised at the sale price.

Margaret finished her laps and climbed out of the pool. She wasn't even breathing hard.

"This is the only thing I really miss in the winter. But the pool is heated. I use it into late October. Harvey always complains that he needs de-icer to get close to me at night."

"This catalog tells me less than I already know, Margaret."

"There's a nugget in it, Judy. Small, but a nugget. Flip to the page after the listing for the children's painting. See the photo? The name in the right-hand corner? N. Smithson. That's who we're going to see today. But I'll tell you more on the way. How about joining me for a nice soak? I have a suit inside that'll fit you."

"No thanks. I'm a slow starter in the morning. A few minutes in that would send me back to bed."

"Next time then," said Margaret as she took off her bathing cap and set it down on a chair next to the Jacuzzi, which was painted black, like the swimming pool. A heated mist was coming off its glass surface like steam from a hot cup of tea. Margaret bent down and turned a dial at the side of the tub. A swirl of bubbles, as if in a glass of champagne, rose to the top. As Margaret moved to get into the tub, Judy noticed an electric cord that led to the other side and dropped straight into the tub like a fishing line. She was about to ask what it was when Margaret screamed. A scream so full of surprise and terror that Judy couldn't move. A scream that seemed to be squeezed out of a place so deep within Margaret that there could be nothing more left after it stopped. Margaret shook like a pennant in a gale, her eyes wide and as white as a blank page. She was looking at Judy, but Judy knew that she didn't see anything. Then Margaret's hands reached out, the fingers rigid as drumsticks. Judy sprang from her chair and almost grabbed Margaret before she realized what was happening. She couldn't touch her. Mustn't. Then the same would happen to her. The cord! Judy raced around the tub and tugged on it. Hard. Breaking the surface like a fish trying to shake a hook, a small hedge clipper flipped out of the water onto the duckboard mat that circled the tub. Its blades chattering feverishly, the clipper grotesquely chewed at the air. Like a marionette with its strings cut, Margaret toppled out of the water. Judy pulled Margaret to a chaise. As she ran into the house to call the emergency number, she could still hear the hedge clipper snapping its teeth. But Margaret was quiet. Quiet as a grave.

44

Yesternight the Sun went hence,
And yet is here today . . .

Judy remembered that and one other couplet:

But think that we
Are but turned aside to sleep . . .

Donne. What else did she remember? The fragile blue eyes
of Margaret's sons as they stood beside Harvey. How small
Harvey seemed. As if an unseen tap had been opened somewhere deep within him. Of Margaret's death, Judy mercifully
remembered very little. The town ambulance arrived within
minutes and though the crew went through the resuscitation
procedures with speed and determination, Judy knew instinctively that it was all too late.

Margaret, why were you so forgetful? thought Judy. It had
seemed such a funny trait. A pair of panty hose in your glove
compartment just in case you left the house without them. "It
takes a mighty cold breeze sometimes to tell me that I'm inde-
cent," you told me once. Books coming from book clubs because you forgot to return the cards saying you didn't want
them. But that charming forgetfulness killed you. What was it
you said about something bothering you? I remember. That it
was the kind of feeling you usually got *after* you left the house.
It was that infernal hedge clipper that was nagging at you.
Why, oh, why, couldn't you remember that you left the damn
thing *on?* Did our latter-day Bobbsey Twins adventure with
that goddamn painting distract you? Or was it simply the
phone? That must have been it. The phone rang, and you put
the clipper down so you could get to the phone before it
stopped ringing. But you left that damned thing balanced with
the steadiness of a dime on its edge. Damn that phone! Damn
everything!

She had to stop this, Judy told herself. It wouldn't bring Margaret back. Nothing would. Nothing.

The service was simple, direct, and warm. Like Margaret. Margaret, ever the realist, had written down the way she wanted it to be years before. The poetry to be read. Her body to be cremated. The flowers to come from her garden, if possible. And no lilies, please! A minimum of the dark side and as little fuss as possible.

Judy's mother came up from Hilton Head for the service. For her sake, Judy knew. They hugged each other for only a moment though, they were both crying so hard.

The week following Margaret's death, Judy sleepwalked through the days. She tried to keep to her schedule, but at the end of the day she had no idea what she had been doing. Thank God for Hal. He took over. He helped Harvey with all the arrangements. He watched over the house and Annie. It was Hal's idea to have Harvey over for dinner that night. He needed them, Hal said simply.

Harvey showed up on time, his eyes red from lack of sleep. His face was tight and pale. His voice seemed lower, as if he didn't want to hear what he was saying. Annie came downstairs and gave Harvey a kiss. Judy had told her about Margaret's death the day after it happened. She had read a book which gave advice to parents on how to handle things like that. The approach seemed sensible and logical. The only problem was that Judy broke down while telling Annie. When Judy pulled herself together she realized that Annie was gently patting her back and saying, "It's all right, Mommy. Auntie Margaret is with the angels. She's happy and I know she wants us to be happy too. That's what Daddy told me when Mr. Peters died. That's right, isn't it?"

Annie also gave Harvey a picture she had done. A beach-ball-size sun with a smile drawn on it shone down on a garden of giant daisies. She instructed Harvey to tape it to his mirror. It was a happy picture and it would help make him happy every time he looked at it. She then went upstairs to watch *The Incredible Hulk.*

Dinner was filled with conversation about how terrible the TV programs for children were, the way every shopping mall looked like every other shopping mall, the weather, the new rise in gasoline prices. Torrents of words trying to fill a void that couldn't be filled. They were all afraid of silence. A silence that had the steady roar of surf on a gray, angry day.

It was while they were having espresso that Harvey handed Judy a small box clumsily wrapped in Christmas paper.

"It was all I could find around the house. I know it doesn't look very good, but I haven't had a lot of experience."

Judy quickly tore open the wrapping. Inside was a tight, square bundle of tissue paper. Carefully, Judy unfolded the paper. There, cradled inside a hollow, like an egg, was a sculpted silver pin of the head of Athena with a black pearl, like a dark beacon, set in her crown.

"I know she would have wanted you to have it. She didn't know you very long, Judy, but she loved you very much. I think she looked upon you as the daughter she never had. She was a woman who had a lot of love in her. God, how I miss her."

And then Harvey began to sob. The sound was so full of desolation that Judy instinctively moved toward him as she would to a child. She hugged him close. And then Judy started to cry. Tears from a vast reservoir of loss ran down her cheeks, so copious and dense with despair that their taste was strange. And now it was Harvey's turn to comfort her. Like one of those ridiculous children's huggy toys, they stood there, swaying slightly, sharing a sadness that made them see everything around them as if from the wrong end of a telescope.

Hal, his face drawn as taut as an archer's bow, came around from his side of the table and put his arms around both of them. How long they huddled there, Judy had no idea. The next thing she remembered was being put to bed by Hal.

"Hold me close, darling. I need you. I need you so much."

"I'm here, Jude. I'll always be here. It's okay. Cry. Margaret was worth a lot of tears."

"I don't know if I have any left. Poor Margaret. Poor Harvey."

"It's going to be all right, babe. I swear to you." Hal didn't know what else to say, so he held Judy tight. So tight that it was hard to tell where his body stopped and hers began.

Later, when they were both in bed and the room was as dark as a moonless night, Judy turned and clung to Hal again.

"Oh, Hal. I feel so bad. I keep thinking that Margaret would still be alive if it weren't for me."

"That's ridiculous. What are you talking about?"

"After Brad died Margaret thought there was some connection with the Hilliards. And I sort of encouraged her. Maybe if I hadn't she wouldn't have gotten so involved in trying to be a detective."

"Stop it, Jude. Remember what I told you already? It would have happened if you'd never met Margaret. It wasn't your fault. It wasn't anyone's fault."

"But if it weren't for me, she wouldn't have been distracted by all those crazy schemes. *Our* crazy schemes. She wouldn't have forgotten that she left the clippers by the tub."

"Judy, darling, be fair to yourself. Margaret was absent-minded. Very, and always had been. It was a freak accident. That's all."

And then Judy confessed to Hal, for the first time, about the map and the two sets of graves. About their finding the painting of the children. About everything. It felt so good to talk about it. To get it all out. All their secrets. The things that she had shared with Margaret. And it felt even better to hear Hal explain it all. Everything made sense the way Hal went through it. The graves without inscriptions? To say they were those of the coven children was just a wild guess. Were she and Margaret really so sure there were no names on the stones? Wind and rain would erode anything. And the other graves, the ones with the same dates? They had to belong to the victims of one of those raging diseases that used to decimate whole towns. Children always were the first to go. If she and Margaret had looked longer they probably would have found ten, twelve, fifteen such graves. Sad, but not an unlikely number of deaths in a place the size of Ripton Falls, no small town for those days. The painting? Well, obviously, the one they had seen in the Hilliard house was not the original. Not the one sold at the auction. It had to be a copy. Copies of paintings were not unusual. If it had been the original, it wouldn't have been knocking around inside a closet, and the Hilliards would never have let any kids near it. Who else but mischievous kids would slash up a painting that way?

"Really, you gals should have been writing Gothics," said

Hal chidingly. "Nothing would have stood between you and bestsellerdom."

Thank God for Hal. Of course he was right. It wasn't her fault. Of course not. It was good to feel the sleep seeping through her body. And even better to be held by Hal. The soft cat's tongue of fatigue lapped at her eyes and Judy soon floated on a calm sea of dreamless sleep.

45

Judy pushed through the heavy doors into the hush of the college museum, registering, but only just, the transition from outdoors to in. The professor from the art department who had put together the faculty show in a small, temporary exhibit area near the main entrance had called and asked her to stop by. Judy felt some curiosity about why, but not a lot. She hadn't picked up her brushes since the day Margaret had died. She could not shake herself free of the loop that played and replayed in her mind, even as it was doing now, with the maddening persistence of a top-ten chartbuster.

Everything was right in her life, and nothing was right. She loved her husband, her child, her work, her house. Both her parents were alive and sound as oaks. She had never lost *anyone* close to her. No high-school friend had been wrapped around a telephone pole in an auto crash. Vietnam was a tragedy she had viewed through a TV set. Her two miscarriages had been depressing, but she was able to get over them. Then, whammo. In less than two months, two new friends had died. Suddenly. And bizarrely. And one of them was as dear to her as . . . Oh, shit. Stop it!

And then Judy saw the red dots. Beautiful, shiny red dots. Dots the size of a goldfish's eye. Mandarin red. And there was one of them stuck onto the frame of each of the three paintings she had entered in the faculty show.

I've sold three paintings, she thought with astonishment.

She quickly ascertained that only one other painting in the entire show had been sold. Move aside, Jasper Johns, she whispered to herself giddily. She caught a flutter of movement by a door at the end of the gallery. It was the professor who had called. Mary Barnes. She strode toward Judy, beaming. She was an intense, homely woman in her late forties, with narrow eyes placed too close together and a chest as flat as rolled-out dough.

"Congratulations, my dear. Many's the year I've thought the faculty art show was a quaint tradition that should have gone out with ten o'clock curfews and beanies, but this makes it all worthwhile."

Judy reached out to shake hands before she realized Mrs. Barnes was holding up something for her. It was a check for $2,300. The handwriting on the check was as clear as the instructions on a form letter. It was signed by Jason Hawkins. She thought she recognized the name.

"That's right. *The* Jason Hawkins," said Mary Barnes, bending to pick up a small white card that had dropped to the floor. "And look at this."

It was Hawkins' business card. He owned and ran a gallery on Madison Avenue that Mary Barnes told her was, though considerably more conservative, on a par with Pace and Emmerich. He had scribbled a note on the back of the card that was short and flattering. He asked that Judy telephone him. At once.

Mary Barnes, who had been watching Judy with maternal attentiveness, spoke as soon as Judy looked up.

"Be our guest," she said, grinning. "Call him from here. This may be our only chance all year for a power call. And we'll take it."

Judy was put through quickly to Jason Hawkins himself. Dazed, she listened as he compared her to the pantheon of contemporary artists. She had the color sense of Stella. The instinct for surprise of Oldenburg. The strength of Frankenthaler. She should be among them. She would be among them. It was all in her.

"We have an opening for one more show in February," said Hawkins. "Late February. Do you have enough paintings available? We'd like at least ten. We could get by with eight."

"No . . . ," said Judy, hesitating for a fraction. She was too honest not to be frank. "But yes," she went on. "I could do it."

"You won't be putting yourself under too much stress? Your work won't suffer?"

"Don't worry," said Judy. "I'm as unblocked as Mount St. Helens."

They both laughed, and then Judy continued, more seriously, "Take my word for it. I'm ready."

And I need this, she added to herself. Then I won't have time to think. About anything.

"All right," said Hawkins, after making her stand on tiptoe only a few seconds, "you're on. I'm delighted. Truly delighted."

They made arrangements to speak again in two weeks' time, and just as their conversation was ending, Judy said, as an afterthought, "I'm puzzled about one thing though. From what I understand, your gallery specializes in more traditional painting. The old masters. The Impressionists. *Maybe* Ben Shahn. Why me?"

"You're right, Judy. I hope you don't mind me calling you that, but I feel I know you already. You've very neatly described the way we used to be. We've decided recently, however, that we need new people. Young and up-and-coming artists for the eighties. Artists like yourself."

46

"Love–forty," Sy Goldin announced sheepishly, though it was doubtful anyone was having difficulty keeping track of the score.

Sy and Lisa had spent a week at a new tennis camp in Vermont that they had read about in *New York* magazine. The teaching technique was a combination of Zen and ballet. It made the *Inner Game of Tennis* look as if it had been devised by Knute Rockne. When they returned, they challenged Hal and Judy to a mixed doubles match. They looked as though they were on the Grand Prix tennis tour as they walked onto the court. Their outfits and equipment were the latest and the most expensive: Prince graphite rackets, Fila whites, Diodora shoes, Teddy Tinling headbands and sweatbands. But it all fell

apart as they started to play. Before their tennis set, they had
been aggressive, energetic players, low on style but with determination to spare in running down each point. Now they were
frozen. Each stroke was a perfect still life. If the game had been
played without a ball they would have been Davis Cup material.

Hal and Judy had a hard time throwing them even one game
in the first set, and the second set was fast going the same
route. But what the hell, thought Hal. Judy was enjoying herself, and that was what counted. Margaret's death had really
upset her. Who could blame her? And to also be the witness of
such a tragedy. It took all his strength not to let it get to him
the same way. But that was what a relationship was all about.
One of the two had to put on a Cagney mask and tough it out.

Sy tossed the ball in the air, drew back his racket in a long,
graceful arc, and piddled the ball into the net. The next serve
made it over—just—but Judy polished it off with a short smash.
One more game, which took all of a minute and a half, and the
match was over.

Sy bounded over the net in a way that suggested all was not
lost for him athletically and shook hands with Judy and Hal.

"Losers' treat," he said good-naturedly. "You must stop by
our place and have a drink. If only to see our new sauna. We
had it installed last week. It went up as easily as a set of Lincoln Logs."

"I don't know," said Judy, checking her watch. "It's quarter
to seven and we were supposed to pick up Annie at Erin's
fifteen minutes ago."

"Come on, sport," said Hal. "Claire can wing it with the
girls."

It was only a short drive to the Goldins'. At first Hal had
been puzzled by why the Goldins had bought the house they
did when they had all of Ripton Falls to choose from. It had a
charming setting on a stream at the edge of town, but it was a
ranch house stamped out from a cookie cutter. But then, in record time, the Goldins began to remodel. They replaced asbestos
siding with shingles. They constructed a sensational master bedroom above the garage, so light and airy that it seemed almost
to float over the stream below. They stripped away an awkward
entrance and put up a sleek new one. Before the sauna had

come a billiard room. Sy promised a swimming pool by next summer. A tennis court would follow.

They turned into the Goldins' street. The house was coming up on the right when suddenly a buff-colored blur streaked across the lawn directly into the path of the car. Sy slammed down on the brakes and swerved, but there was no way to avoid hitting the dog. There was a nightmarish thud, a sound like no other, and then a string of piercing yelps.

They jumped from the car. The dog, which Hal saw immediately was the Goldins' spaniel, lay by the side of the road. As the dog tried to pull itself up by its hindquarters, Judy closed her eyes and turned away. Sy lifted the dog, but it struggled in his arms, its eyes vivid with fear.

"Hi," said a small, clear voice, dropped into their midst like a silver coin.

It was Tracy. At first, for Hal anyway, it was difficult to comprehend why the girl was there. Then Hal noticed the dog's leash dragging on the ground behind Tracy.

So did Lisa. She grabbed Tracy by the shoulders and shook her so roughly that for a moment Hal thought she might throw the girl to the ground as if she were smashing a plate.

"How many times have I told you never, never to let Ginger off her leash?"

Tracy gazed at her mother with unblinking eyes.

"Don't you understand? Look at poor Ginger!"

The girl stared at the dog in her father's arms. It was whimpering now, its body still shuddering in spasms. The girl made no response. Did not flinch. Did not move a muscle. Sy bent his head over the dog and held it tightly to his chest. Only a tiny blot of red on the shoulder of his shirt hinted at the violence of what had occurred.

Without a word, as if nothing had happened, Tracy turned and walked toward the house.

•   •

After Sy dropped off the dog at the vet's—she was going to be all right, thank God—he drove the Richardsons to Erin's to pick up Annie. No one spoke until the Simmonses' house came into view, and then all of Sy's anguish came pouring out.

"We're worried sick," Sy began without a preamble. "We've

taken Tracy to three different neurologists and they've tested the hell out of her. You remember the weekend we supposedly went to D.C.? Well, we went to Mass General. For CAT scans. She passed those tests. She passes them all. The doctors say not to worry, that sometimes it takes months for trauma to work its way out. And, you know, we want to believe them. So then we relax. Think of other things. Then something like this happens. You saw her. She has an emotional register between zero and one. It's—"

Sy broke off, almost gagging, and then he continued in a thin voice that was almost a whisper.

"It's hard to say this about my own daughter, but I don't think she gave a damn about what happened to Ginger. Not a good goddamn."

47

As Judy ironed Hal's shirt, she thought about steamrollers. As a kid, she had loved to watch them press strips of tar into seamless ribbons of road as flat as a leather belt. What a feeling of power and accomplishment to sit above that huge, wet roller that turned material as lumpy as oatmeal into a surface that was icy smooth. Occasionally, she and her friends were brazen enough to toss a penny in front of the roller. Few ever saw daylight again. When they did, only a bit of Lincoln's face would peek out like a fossil waiting for time to free it.

The chopstick sound of Annie knitting, like the chatter of a novice telegrapher, came from the bedroom next door. Annie only recently had taken to knitting, and like all passions of children, this one was total. She traveled with her knitting the way a doctor carries his little black bag. Her product was consistent. Long, snaking sleeves of a pattern that resembled aerial photographs of the moon. To all who asked, Annie told them that it was a muffler. When it passed seven feet she stopped calling it that. Hal insisted that she was rehearsing for the role of Mme. Defarge.

Judy's painting was going almost too well to believe. She had finished two canvases in under three weeks. The hours slid by so fast she had to use a clock alarm or she'd never stop. Her concentration was now absolute. If she said she would do something else after finishing work, she would forget about her promise by the time the moment rolled around. Was it only the motivation of a New York gallery show that was causing this? You could bet Jeff's Ferrari it was, she thought with a satisfied smile. But who cared where it came from? The work was good. She knew it. Positively. Felt it stronger than ever before. Her lack of uncertainty was new and a little scary, but Judy realized it was justified.

Ironing was a wonderful form of therapy. What had Hal said about that last weekend? It was while he was washing the car. It was something about both the ritual and the satisfaction of performing manual tasks. The kind you couldn't hire people to do anymore. Hal's other household therapy was periodically rearranging their books under new and, by definition, always better subject headings. Her father's was splitting wood. Her mother's was both weird and masochistic: washing the kitchen floor. But the best was ironing. No two ways about it.

Judy finished the toughest part of her laundry basket: the accordion pleats on Annie's jumper. It was all downhill from here. She pulled out the last of Hal's short-sleeved shirts. She had found it in a heap at the bottom of his closet. There were only a dozen of Hal's handkerchiefs left after this. She'd be finished in a few minutes.

At first Judy thought it was another Japanese beetle. Ugh! Annie had gone through a manic month during the summer as a budding naturalist. Fireflies, tadpoles, and, most of all, Japanese beetles suddenly were inhabiting all of Judy's available bottles. And Annie also had developed a habit of putting the beetles in her pockets. And if she was pocketless then Mommy's or Daddy's pockets had to do. And, of course, sometimes these little critters were forgotten. Only the crackling sound of their remains under the iron served as a reminder of their last journey.

Judy slipped her hand into the pocket, all set to sweep out the final, dusty pieces. But out came a photo. It was from a Polaroid. It *looked* as if it had been washed and ironed. Judy could still recognize the figures. The photo was of all the kids

who had been at the Luccis' picnic. The children were arranged
by height, like a banister heading to the second floor. An assortment of smiles and smirks looked back at Judy. Who took
this picture? Hal didn't have a camera. She'd ask him tonight.
Judy carried the photo to the window to inspect it more closely.
Tracy Goldin's smile, as ear to ear as a jack-o'-lantern's, underlined all that had happened since that day. So little time had
gone by but so much had happened. Oh, Brad. And Margaret.
Poor, dear Margaret. God, she missed her so much. And where
had that lovely smile of Tracy's gone? She carefully smoothed
the wrinkles on the photo with her palm and only stopped crying when she heard Annie walk into the room.

48

The riding helmet, like a fuzzy brown mushroom,
sat uncertainly on Annie's head. She examined herself in the
hall mirror with a look of happiness that edged toward delir-
ium. Her eyes moved down to her gray jodhpurs, the baggy
sides sticking out like elephant's ears. Her smile rose toward
her temples.

"Do I really look like a rider, Mom?"

"For someone who is going for her first lesson you look like
you were born in the saddle."

"Are you making fun of me, Mom?"

"Of course not, Annie. It's just that if you keep admiring
yourself we'll be late. It's a fifteen-minute drive to the stables
and we really have to move it."

"Do you think when I really learn how to ride I can get a
crop like Erin's? Do you, Mom?"

If Judy heard Erin's name one more time in connection with
riding she would scream. Erin had been riding for more than a
month, three times a week no less, and all during that time she
had been after Annie to join her. The problem was with Judy.
Except for Saturdays she didn't have the time to take Annie.
But that wasn't Claire's problem. For she had "Aunt" Laurie to
call upon.

"She's Mother of the Year material, Judy," Claire had said to her the other day. "If she's not taking Erin to the stables, she's driving Tracy Goldin to the zoo in Springfield. Or taking the two of them *and* T.C. Junior to the greenhouse at Smith. I've never seen any unmarried person so taken with kids. When she finally does marry I hope she has lots of kids. She certainly has enough love and patience in her."

Laurie had never struck Judy that way, but Claire's accolades made Judy doubt her feelings. She must be underestimating that side of Laurie.

Clark's Riding Academy was a collection of rickety barns and outbuildings with horses whose backs were shaped like mattresses in cheap hotels. Oliver and Lynn Clark were transplanted New Yorkers who had taken to the country with a vengeance. In addition to instructing their small riding clientele, they sold maple syrup in the spring and fruits and vegetables in the summer.

Lynn placed Annie on a scrawny pony named Mr. Rogers. Annie, displaying a concentration that would have amazed her teachers, diligently followed her instructions and by the end of the lesson was beginning to get the idea of posting.

"She's born to it," said a voice behind Judy. "I can tell. It's the way they sit. You know the first time they get up."

Judy turned to find Laurie Hilliard standing there. Erin was at Laurie's side. Both were dressed for riding. An air-brushing of dust on their boots showed that they had been out already.

"When Annie starts really getting the hang of it she can go out with us. There are some marvelous trails and old logging roads nearby. I keep a horse here, you know."

"Annie did very well, Mrs. Richardson. She really likes Mr. Rogers and I know that he liked her," said Lynn as she brought Annie over to Judy.

"Did you see me, Erin?" asked Annie.

"Just at the end. You didn't look like it was your first lesson. You'll be able to ride with me soon."

"How was your ride, Laurie?" asked Lynn.

"Marvelous. Except for Erin always wanting to gallop."

"Mrs. Richardson, may I take Annie into the barns? She's never been here before and I'd like to show her around," said Erin.

She looked directly at Judy, her riding crop striking a metronome rhythm against her thigh.

"Please, Mom."

Before Judy could answer, the two were running toward the stables.

"You're going to see a big change in Annie if she keeps up with this," said Laurie. "I've seen it in Erin. It gives them a marvelous sense of confidence and maturity. I'm not against ballet or learning an instrument, but riding goes way beyond them for life preparation. I know I'm prejudiced since I've been riding all my life, but I really believe it."

For a moment they both watched Lynn lead Mr. Rogers off to a barn.

"Would you like some?"

"What?"

"I asked if you might like some coffee. I have a thermos in my car. Fresh ground this morning."

The morning was chilly and the contrail of Judy's breath seemed to underline the waiting warmth of the coffee.

"That doesn't sound like a *good* idea. *Great* would be more fitting."

They were just a few steps from the car when Judy heard the sound. A bang as sharp as a rifle report. She heard it again. And again. And in between, a high, terrified scream. *Annie!*

Judy rushed toward the stables. The terrible noise continued, punctuated by Annie's desperate cries. It was almost deafening as she entered the barn. Now she could see the horse, flecks of whiteness spattered on its muzzle, rearing up in an almost mechanized frenzy. Erin stood outside the stall. She looked up at Judy, her face as emotionless as pie dough.

Judy stood anchored outside the stall door. She felt helpless. Annie crouched in a corner like a small trapped animal, the horse's kicks striking a corona around her head. Judy wanted to rush to her, but all she could do was call feebly to the crazed animal. And then Lynn brushed past her into the stall. She grabbed the horse's bridle, all the time intoning its name, like a litany, over and over again.

"Good Montana. Easy, boy. Easy, Montana. Good horse. That's it, Montana."

With her free hand, Lynn motioned Judy toward Annie.

Judy slipped inside and pulled Annie out. Within a minute Lynn had calmed Montana down. She eased herself out of the stall.

"Dammit, Erin, you know better than that," said Lynn as she latched the stall door. "I've told you half a dozen times that Montana's dangerous. That's why he's going to be gelded. Why in heaven's name did you let Annie go in there?"

"I'm sorry, Mrs. Clark. He seemed so quiet today. And Annie wanted to pet him. I thought it would be all right."

"That wasn't very smart, Erin. Lynn is right," Laurie said to the child as she stood behind her, hands gently bookending her shoulders.

"I really didn't mean it, Mrs. Clark. Really. I guess I was just stupid."

A small tear rolled out of the corner of Erin's left eye. As straight as a plumb line it sledded down her cheek. The rest of her face was as immobile as a mannequin's.

Judy held Annie close, her body still trembling. But Judy couldn't take her eyes away from Erin, who was now looking up at Laurie. A smile, like a cupped match on a windy day, flickered at the corners of her mouth.

49

Hal had stared at it so long that he now had a dull ache behind his eyes. A concentrated ball of pain the size of a marble throbbed with the regularity of a lawn sprinkler. He looked away for a moment and rubbed his eyes with the meaty edge of his palms. He looked back after a few seconds. Something was wrong, he thought. It looked right, but he knew that a piece didn't fit. What the hell was it?

The storyboard for the thirty-second spot—Hilliard's first: in fact, the company's first venture into nonprint advertising since the advent of the crystal set—was propped at a roller-coaster angle against Hal's coffee cup. Hal had been mesmerized by it for the past hour. His desk was covered with memos, ad rates, and media plans studding its surface like bales of hay in a field.

Only two weeks earlier the desk had been tundra sparse save for a small, neat pile of make-work in the right-hand corner.

The telephone rang with the shock of thunder on a sunny day. How long had he been gazing at the damn storyboard, Hal wondered, picking up the phone to strangle its second ring. He had the advertising equivalent of white-line fever.

"Hal?"

"Judy. I was just thinking about you."

"Bull pucky. You've probably got your nose in some ad schedule."

"Does my emotional Richter detect a tremor of petulance?"

"You're close. It starts with a *p*. But pissed off is closer to the mark."

"What's up?"

"Not up. Down. My soufflé. Flat as a carrier deck. It's almost seven-thirty. You're now an hour and a half late."

"It can't be."

"You said the same thing when I called you forty-five minutes ago."

"Okay. Message received. I'll wrap this up right now. Be home in ten minutes."

"You said that last time too."

"I mean it. Hear the shuffling of papers? I'm straightening my desk. I've got one foot out the door already."

"I'm ready to become a believer. See you in ten."

Hal went back to the storyboard again. Maybe the beginning was too soft. The fade from the tintype of the old factory was more than a little PBS. Whoa! The damn board was Alice and the Looking-Glass. A few more seconds and he'd be gone for another hour. He could figure it out tomorrow. Anyway, it wasn't scheduled to be shot for two weeks.

God, was it great to be busy. And challenged! And getting things done! It used to be that every proposal he had offered was tabled, endlessly budgeted and rebudgeted, or put into a merry-go-round "holding pattern." Now, all at once, every campaign and project were given an immediate green light. In a one-hundred-and-eighty-degree flip-flop, he suddenly had become the boy wonder of Hilliard and Company. The simple act of proposing something was tantamount to having it approved.

Budgets were given the scrutiny of a tab at McDonald's for two
Big Macs. Amazing! Maybe it was due to Laurie joining the
marketing meetings? No. She helped, but she didn't make the
difference. It was old man Hilliard. Now he trusted Hal and
personally encouraged him. Hal even got to see him every day.
It was almost scary, the kinds of changes that had come about.

Now that he had the power to put into action all the ideas he
had bottled up all these years, what if he didn't have it? Maybe
he wasn't as good as he thought. No. He wouldn't play that
head game. Hal knew he was good. It was like finally getting
the keys to the family car. He wouldn't bang it up. He could
handle it. And old man Hilliard knew it. Only once during this
heady time had he turned down one of Hal's proposals. What
was it? Of course. That space that had opened up in *The New
Yorker*. The type for the ad already had been set. But the old
man wanted to hold off everything until the spring, when they
could start their advertising assault with both feet. He was
probably right. And Hal had taken his cue from him. He didn't
want to, but he could wait. God, it would be great to see on TV
ads that he had created. To hear them on the radio. He even
had reserved some space in *Playboy*. Watch out, L. L. Bean.
En garde, Eddie Bauer. Here comes Hilliard's. He wouldn't
have to wait long. Spring wasn't that far away. As he tried to
cram the storyboard into his briefcase, he smiled. It was like
Christmas when he was a kid. It always seemed so far away.
But it always came around. And it was always worth the wait.

50

The drive from Boston to Ripton Falls generally
took Hal two and a half hours. But a hard rain added almost an
hour more. He felt a cold coming on, and the thought of heading straight home to Judy, Annie, and four fingers of bourbon
was very appealing. He had a few details to take care of at the
office, though, so he stopped there first.

He quickly leafed through his calls and then dialed home. He told Judy about his incipient cold and she promised lentil soup and vitamin C. Then he prowled the halls to see who was still around. Since it was almost six-thirty he really didn't expect to find anyone. He was right until he got to Reid Prescott's office.

"Howdy, workaholic."

"No such thing, Mr. Producer. Just ducking a school tea Peggy's throwing at our house. Should be over, but I'm playing it safe. Can I offer you a little sustenance? The liquid variety, of course."

Reid fished a bottle of Chivas and two tumblers from the lower drawer of his desk.

"Proper drinking should really be done with dirty motel bathroom glasses. But when in Ripton . . . ," said Reid as he poured an inch of Scotch into each glass.

"To a very gracious host and colleague," said Hal, clicking his glass against Reid's.

"Fun and good health."

"Everything okay with you? My opinion of myself is so strong that I wonder that the place is still standing when I come back."

"Your opinion is shared by others. I mean your family, of course. Don't want to see you get too big a head."

They drank in silence for a few moments. Hal found himself staring at the photograph on Reid's desk of his daughter, Gwen. She was incredibly freckled. He didn't know when he had seen so many freckles on one small face.

"To tell you the truth," said Reid, "I do have a problem."

Reid took another swallow and held the amber contents of his glass up to the light.

"Looks so nice. Can't understand why my liver doesn't embrace it the way I do."

"You were saying," said Hal.

"Yes, I was. Doesn't take much for my tongue to become friction-free. It's Peggy's father. He's pretty sick."

"Very?"

"It would not be serious if he were your age. Unfortunately, he's almost eighty. My problem is that he wants me to move to Augusta and take over the business."

"I don't want to give you advice, but you're a big boy."

"You're absolutely correct. But Peggy wants me to do it also. She'd love to live there again. And there's her mother. *And* the old family house."

"And the business?" asked Hal.

"Lucrative. Very lucrative. And boring as hell. Plumbing fixtures. Commodes. Elbow joints. Et cetera, et cetera. Employs two hundred people and it just makes money."

Reid tossed another splash of Scotch into his glass and raised the bottle inquiringly to Hal. Hal shook his head and capped his glass with his palm.

"I know I don't have to say it, Hal, but that's between you and old me. No one here knows. But enough of this. Let me show you something that's really important."

He reached into the top drawer of his desk and pulled out what looked like a large rubber band. He turned his back to Hal and seconds later spun around in his chair wearing swim goggles, the type that Mark Spitz had made famous.

"Well?"

"You look . . . committable."

"Here, yes. But not in Bermuda."

"Well, I agree. You do need a vacation."

"Thank you. I do. And so do you. We're all getting a vacation. Compliments of Cameron Hilliard. The first annual management seminar. A three-day weekend, all expenses paid, for the executive staff of Hilliard and Company, plus wives, at the Southampton Princess in Bermuda. The weather is always a little dicey there, but freeloaders shouldn't complain."

"When did all this happen?"

"Today. I guess you haven't waded through your mail yet. Laurie's organized the whole thing. Guest lecturers. The works. And we don't have to worry about the kids. They'll stay home with baby-sitters provided by the company. Laurie's planned a zillion activities for them, starting with a hayride the first night. The kids will have a ball."

"My cold feels better already. I was planning to take Judy and Annie down to Barbados in March. After Annie's operation. This'll give me a chance to lay down a primer coat for my tan."

When Hal got back to his office, he found the invitation. It was on heavy stock, elegantly engraved. This promised to be a very nice trip. He checked the calendar on his desk. Five weeks off. Great. He wouldn't have to miss his night of raccoon hunting with Aldo. That was in three weeks. On the second full moon of the fall, the hunter's moon.

51

The Ripton Falls Country Fair was held every year on the first weekend in October. It was such a popular event that it bankrolled its co-sponsors, the Ladies Benevolent Society and the Volunteer Fire Department, for the balance of the year. It always took place on the football field behind the regional high school. The school's football coach invariably beefed about the disruption this caused his team. Once, several years earlier, he even had taken the floor at Town Meeting and insisted the team had lost the northeastern championship because of it. He'd had to be ushered from the meeting hall when he became abusive to the head selectman. He was lucky not to have lost his job and, of course, he hadn't a prayer anyway of changing the site.

The fair was partly traditional, with sheep and cattle judging, ox pulls, and canning competitions. But mostly it was pure carnival: games of chance, stomach-turning food, and plenty of rides for the kids.

The evening it began, Hal and Judy had a date to meet Harvey in Northampton for dinner. A new Chinese restaurant had opened that was supposed to be "as good as New York." On Saturday Judy and Annie would go to the fair together and spend the whole day there if Annie was so inclined. Annie, however, immediately began lobbying to go the first night as well. She was such a pest about it that when Judy discovered Vicky Leland was taking the Lucci boys and Erin Simmons and could easily include Annie, Judy almost said no on principle. But, softy that she was, she relented. She worked it out with Vicky that after dinner she and Hal would swing by and pick up Annie.

• •

A man decked out in a straw boater with a wide ribbon sash

across his chest waved them on with a flashlight to a spot in the parking lot behind the bleachers. As Hal swung the car around, the headlights caught and illuminated the words on the sash: "Ripton Falls, the Fairest Fair of All."

The fair was going flat out, and if there were any people who were not enjoying themselves they were faking it pretty well. Judy had no idea there would be so many—several counties' worth, or so it seemed. Volunteers, beribboned and hatted, manned the booths. Slowly Hal and Judy worked their way into the heart of the fair, stopping to chat with Minna Gannon at the Ping-Pong toss, trying their luck with the Midas Muffler man's skeet shoot, spending fifty cents here and a dollar there, all in the name of good neighborliness.

They found Vicky and the kids waiting in line for the Ferris wheel. Even before Judy saw Annie, she spotted the two Lucci boys, their summer-bleached hair like flecks of gold. Behind them were Annie and Erin. Arguing.

"You're just afraid," Erin was saying.

"No, I'm not. I don't like this dumb old ride, that's all."

"Ah, come on," said Vicky. "Don't be a baby. Everyone else is going on it."

"I'm not a baby!" shouted Annie, glaring at Vicky. "I just don't like Ferris wheels. They're stupid. I want to go back and see if I can win the big stuffed bear we saw."

"The one at the ring toss?" said Vicky. "Fine. We'll go there next."

"But I won't have any money left if I spend it on this old thing," wailed Annie, now close to tears.

As the line began to move forward, Judy decided the time had come to run a little motherly interference.

"Look, Vicky," she said, "if Annie doesn't want to go for a ride, she doesn't have to. It's her money to spend as she likes."

"What if I get on with you, Annie?" said Vicky, making one last try, her voice extra-sweet.

"No!"

Vicky's group was at the head of the line now.

"Have your tickets ready, boys and girls," the ticket collector called out cheerily.

The Luccis climbed into the waiting car. Annie hung back

stubbornly. A pair of high-school kids in orange hockey jerseys standing behind her were growing impatient.

"Make up your mind, kid," said one. "We want to get on too."

"Everybody's making too much of this," said Hal, stepping up. He gently led Annie from the line. "What do you say we chase down that bear?"

"Oh, yes, Daddy," said Annie, clapping her hands.

Vicky and Erin reluctantly dropped out of the line with Annie. The high-school boys settled themselves in the car behind the Luccis. Then, its complement full, the wheel began to move, at first creakily slow and then with gathering speed.

Judy watched the lights on the Ferris wheel spin like a giant whirling sparkler against the night sky, then turned and followed the others. The girls were chattering happily now. Annie seemed to have forgotten the stuffed bear. Instead she and Erin were promoting a visit to the cotton-candy concession.

Judy had just caught up with them when suddenly there was the sharp, piercing sound of something snapping. The Ferris wheel! Judy spun around toward it just in time to see a shape hurtle off it through the night air. The screech of metal silenced the crowd. Then the wheel shuddered to a stop and the screaming began. As it swelled around them, Judy and Hal could see two figures hanging from the open car at its uppermost point, at least four stories high. Their feet bicycled in the air. It was the high-school boys. Judy looked for the flashing gold hair of the Lucci twins. Instead, where they had been, there was an empty car, tipped open like a huge mechanical mouth shrieking into the night.

52

Hal found the note attached by a rubber band to the sun visor of the Jeep. At first he thought it was one of Judy's lists. Judy was a major-league list maker. Hal generally found them, like unlucky pari-mutuel tickets, scattered on the floor of the car. They always had headings: "Things to Buy,"

"People to Call," and once, "Words *Not* to Say Around Annie." Then he remembered that Judy hadn't used the Jeep in at least a week. He slipped the note out and opened it. It was from Cameron Hilliard. On his personal note paper. The handwriting was as spidery and fine as the engraving on a dollar bill.

CAMERON HILLIARD

Hal:

I must see you tomorrow morning.

The Tannery Falls Road leads into Bluff St. Go for approximately one mile until you see an old sugarhouse on your left. It's about one hundred feet off the road. The dirt road leading to it contains a few wicked rocks and chuckholes. So, drive slowly. I'll be waiting in my car.

Please forgive an old man for all this secrecy, but trust me that it's important. I must see you *alone and out of the office.* Therefore I'd appreciate it if you didn't mention this meeting to Judy, or anyone else for that matter, until *after* our meeting.

I expect that eight A.M. is not too early.

Thank you,
Cameron

Why did he feel guilty not telling Judy about the meeting? It was stupid, but he did. Twice that morning while they were talking over coffee about the Lucci boys' miraculous luck—their fall had been broken by the awning on the ticket booth, and they were not seriously injured—Hal almost blurted out where he was going. Why? He'd be able to replay it chapter and verse after the meeting. But he had never kept a secret from her before. That was it. He wondered again why old Cameron was being so cloak-and-dagger. Well, he thought as he kissed Judy goodbye, he'd find out soon enough.

Town rumor had it that Bluff Street was paved because of Ed Pleshette. He lived in a rambling farmhouse that sported half a dozen gutted trucks in the front yard, all with their hoods up, like gaping patients at a dental clinic—and he was a selectman. His was the only dwelling on the road before the sugarhouse. Small towns were no different from big ones: it was just easier to see where the money went and who directed it there.

Cameron hadn't been kidding about the road to the sugarhouse. It looked as if it had been constructed by German sappers fleeing the Kursk salient. Hal pulled up behind Cameron's Chrysler Imperial. Though it appeared showroom fresh, the old boat had to be a 1965 model at least. No conspicuous consumption here! A fragile breath of vapor drifted from the car's exhaust.

"Morning," said Cameron as Hal got in. The heater was way up and the windows were as foggy as a bathroom mirror after a shower.

"Good morning, sir," answered Hal as he settled himself into the roomy seat.

"Bouillon?" asked Cameron, offering Hal a thermos with one hand, a plastic mug with the other.

"No, thanks. I just had coffee."

Cameron carefully placed the mug back on the dashboard.

"When I was young, Hal, I could never understand my grandfather sitting on the porch in the dog days of summer wearing a sweater. Unfortunately, I understand now. Old blood gets thin. I wake up cold and I go to sleep cold. Everything I drink these days is hot. Doesn't help much, though. The steam coming off the top of the cup warms me as much as the contents."

He filled his mug again and sipped the drink delicately. The blue veins on his hands were as clear as lines in a child's notebook. Against the whiteness of his skin they stood out like rivers on a map.

"I'm dying, Hal."

Suddenly the sound of the fan on the heater seemed to roar like a jet. Cameron stared straight ahead. Hal couldn't look at the old man. He followed his gaze. The outside world swam in a sea of milk, as if viewed through cataracts.

"I don't mean 'dying' in the sense that I'm old and death is just a few local stops down the track. I mean I've got six months. At the outside. I was thinking the other day that when I was your age it didn't seem that many people died of cancer. But I think that was because most people viewed it a lot like syphilis. Something you didn't talk about. Of course, people died then of so many things that today would require just a shot and a few days in bed. I lost a sister to mastoids. Another to scarlet fever."

Hal loosened his collar. His shirt stuck to his back like tape.

"People beat it all the time, Mr. Hilliard," he said after what seemed like a long time.

"Thanks, Hal. I believe in optimism. But not this time. I didn't ask you to come here to talk about dying, though. I'm only interested in life. The life of Ripton Falls. And that of Hilliard and Company."

He stopped and took another sip of bouillon. With each swallow he made a wet sound like a footstep on a rainy pavement.

"You weren't followed, were you, Hal?"

The question startled Hal. It took him a moment to answer.

"I don't think so. No. I'm sure I wasn't."

"Good. I didn't think you would be. That's why I left the note. The telephone isn't safe, even if you call someone in the same room. Know who I wanted to keep in the dark about our meeting?"

Cameron held up his hand to stop Hal from answering. He coughed softly into his handkerchief. With each cough the gull-shaped mole above his eye seemed to dance.

"My family. They mustn't know yet that I want you to run Hilliard and Company after my death."

Hal turned and faced Cameron. His mouth was suddenly dry. He tried to swallow and all he got was a clicking sound as sharp as a coin hitting the sidewalk.

"You heard me right. I've already changed my will. They know I'm dying, but they don't know about the will. I'm doing this because I love them. But I also love the company. And Ripton Falls. I know this makes me sound like a booster out of *Babbitt,* but I really love this town."

A small tear, cloudy as smoke, formed in the corner of the old man's eye.

"Ten days after our weekend together, you will be named chairman and chief executive officer. My son, Elliott, will be designated president. Laurie and Howard will remain executive vice-presidents. All three will, of course, report to you. I've established an outside board of directors who will help you run things and fully support you. They know my wishes and have sworn to uphold them. My family will still control the ownership of the company, though upon my death fifteen percent of the company will be passed on to you, Hal. Your salary will be raised to a hundred and fifty thousand a year. You will sign a five-year contract that will give you twenty percent increments annually. I've established a profit-sharing incentive program that will use this year as a bench mark. It could effectively double your salary every third year."

"Mr. Hilliard," Hal almost shouted, "you're going too fast for me."

"I doubt it, Hal. What I've said might be surprising to you. Perhaps even shocking. But not too fast. If it were, I'd be talking to the wrong man. I didn't recruit you and the others to help us take the company public. On the contrary, it's vital that Hilliard's remain a private company. What I was really doing was gathering an unusual executive talent pool to find both the person to run the company after I die and people to aid him in it. Now you're probably asking yourself why, after more than a century and a half, I'm putting the company into the hands of an outsider. But, frankly, to do anything else would be willfully stupid and show no true feeling for the company. My son is a good man but totally incapable of running Hilliard's in the eighties and beyond. My grandson, though as loyal as a guide dog, couldn't run a bathtub unless the operation of it was shown to him on a regular basis. Perhaps that's unfair and cruel, but so be it. My granddaughter, on the other hand, has more than enough intelligence to run our company. Why, then, am I passing her over for you? It would be easy to blame it on the old-fashioned idea that a woman, no matter how competent, still isn't as tough as an equally able man. But the larger reason is that I want Laurie to have a normal life. A husband and family. She's wonderful with children, you know. I want her to have her own. If she were running the company, *it* would be her husband and family."

Cameron Hilliard gripped the steering wheel tightly. His hands were so thin the knuckles resembled irregular cubes of sugar.

"Would you please open the glove compartment, Hal? There's an envelope in there that contains a draft of your new contract, the various papers pertaining to the incorporation changes of the company, and the transfer of stock to you. I'm sure you'll want to have a lawyer look them over."

"I can't give you a quick answer on this, sir. I have to give it . . . a lot of thought. I have to talk to Judy about it. I have—"

"Of course. I understand completely. That's why I won't make the announcement until ten days after the trip."

"As incredible as all that you've said is, sir, and as flattered and stunned as I am, I don't know if I'll be able to accept. To be honest, Mr. Hilliard, Judy hasn't been very happy here lately. Things have happened."

"What things?"

Hal hesitated, wondering where to begin and what and how much to say. He suspected Judy would resent his saying anything to Cameron. He shouldn't have brought it up. But before he could speak, Cameron continued.

"Actually, I think I know a little bit about it, Hal. In small towns like this, you get to know a lot of things. I'm sure you didn't know half the names of the families on your street when you lived in Los Angeles. Tragedy that struck at the end of the street was as unknown to you as if it happened in Kansas. But small towns are not that way. The town is a fabric, and a tear anywhere affects the whole cloth. Your wife doesn't realize this. She's never lived this way before. It's up to you to support and guide her. She's also an artist. They're very different people. As you well know. What they imagine is very real to them. Sometimes more real than reality."

Cameron Hilliard looked over at Hal. His gaze was as steady as a surgical light. Why did old man Hilliard's voicing of Hal's dreams scare him so? He knew he could handle the job. And God, how he wanted it. *That's* what scared him! He put his hand on the car door handle.

"I'd advise you to go home first before driving to the office. It wouldn't look right if you arrived from the wrong direction. Might get someone thinking. I love my family, Hal. But it will take them a while to understand that what I'm doing is for their benefit too. Have a good day."

Hal opened the door and a wave of frosty air hit him with the same effect as if he had been leaving a sauna. He started to close the door when Cameron called to him.

"Hal."

Hal bent over and peered in.

"The glove compartment."

"What?"

"Your future. It's in the glove compartment."

For the first time, Cameron Hilliard laughed and Hal started laughing too.

53

Judy was in a hurry. She was already ten minutes late, and the walk to The Beanery, where Tina Stein was waiting for her, would take at least another five. And Tina did not wait well. At thirty, a high-strung painter with two ex-husbands, she split teaching a life-study class at the college with Judy. She had taken it over from an instructor on maternity leave. Added to an already full schedule of classwork, this had been too much for her, though she badly needed the money. She was a serious painter whose heart was bounded by the dimensions of SoHo and whose soul was found at the uptown galleries that started on Fifty-seventh Street. She had a direct line to what was happening in the New York art scene ("the *only* place for art in the *world*") and Judy loved to gossip with her about it. What show bombed, who was up and coming, who was sleeping with whom, and, most important, who was switching galleries. It took Judy a while to realize and accept that *she* had a gallery. Tina was the first new friend she had made since Margaret's death and being with her to talk shop, shop, and more shop was a joy. Hal didn't share Judy's enthusiasm for Tina: "All she does is talk about painters I've never heard of and smoke like a chimney. It's like being back in L.A. when she's here. In fact, I think the air was better there."

Teaching two classes each week took a small but precious chunk from Judy's days, but it was more than made up for by her being able to use studio space in the art building again. The light was fantastic, the phone didn't ring, and there were no silly chores around the house to distract her. With Annie tucked safely away in school, her time was completely her own.

Judy was about to go out the front door of the art building when she remembered her mailbox. She hadn't cleared it out in more than a week. It would take no time. Well, no more than a minute.

She said hello to Mrs. Beckmann, the department secretary, and headed straight for the box. Though half again as large as an ordinary mailbox in a post office, it was crammed full. It took some effort to dislodge the wad of envelopes and notices from the tight space. Judy knew she should shove all of it into her bag and keep on moving, but she couldn't resist leafing through the accumulation.

A bill from The Quill. That must be for that outrageously expensive book of Klimt drawings. Another bill. This one from the nursery where she'd bought those redwood tubs. Had they been delivered yet? Then there were two notices for faculty teas. She'd toss those after she left the building. Wouldn't want to hurt anyone's feelings. There was a large brochure in four colors describing the fun and exhilaration of cross-country ski weekends at a nearby resort. How did mailing lists work? she wondered. Where did they get her name? Next stop, waste-basket. And then she came to a large envelope with a note stapled to the front. It was from Harvey. The envelope wasn't stamped. He must have dropped it off himself.

FROM THE DESK OF HARVEY STERN

Judy dear—

The enclosed came about a month ago. Took me a little while to get at it. Somehow I remember that you and M. were interested in this painting. The note/bill that accompanies this has been already paid for by yours truly. So don't go paying it again. M. used to do that all the time. We were the only household in Northampton getting refund checks from the butcher and the cleaners. Not to mention many others! I'm leaving tomorrow for Vancouver for yet another meeting and will ring you on my return. Next dinner is on me. Best to Hal and a big kiss to Annie.

Love,
Harvey

Judy quickly opened the envelope. She pulled from it a stiff photographic print. Covering the front of it was a letter typed

on plain white bond paper. It was dated September 8, the day
Margaret died.

Dear Miss Love,

I guess something came up that kept you from making it out
to my neck of the woods today. That's not surprising. Though
the trip is pleasant, lots of my friends find the drive too much.
(But not my Preston. He's a country boy at heart and
wouldn't think of living anywhere else. Do you know, I haven't
seen a movie in more than six months?)

I'm enclosing the blowup of the photo we talked about that
I took at the Springfield sale. I'm afraid the definition of the
figures leaves a lot to be desired. It is not, I assure you, a good
example of my work. As I told you, I was photographing the
painting hanging *next* to it. It was just a piece of luck that I
caught the one you asked about in one of my shots. Since
you're a friend of Betty Collier's (we went to school together) there is no charge for the use of the picture. I did,
however, incur an expense of $14.85 in having the attached
color enlargement made. Please make the check out to The
Antique Snapper, Inc. (My new stationery hasn't arrived
yet.)

Best,
Nancy Smithson (Mrs.)

Judy fumbled for the photograph of the painting and rushed
back up the stairs to her studio. She took the photo over to the
window for a close look, then managed to move over to the one
chair in the room and slowly lowered herself. Her hands had
started to shake. That Tina Stein was waiting for her in a restaurant was now as far from her mind as her high-school gradu-
ation. It took all her will power to look again at the photograph.

The figures were lined up in the same way as in the Polaroid
snapshot taken on the day of the Luccis' picnic. There was a
girl at one end who was a ringer for Erin. With short hair. And
next to her two identical faces capped by blond curls. The
Lucci twins. Then T.C. Junior in profile. Though this figure was
slightly out of focus, Judy was positive she could make out the
scar on his cheek—a faint, brittle line of pigment. What Alan
Glicksman had thought was a strong cheekbone. The other

children's faces became progressively less distinct, as if she were looking at them underwater. But there at the far end was a figure that was achingly familiar. A small girl whose hair was red. No amount of poor focus could hide that. And though the photo showed it as only a shadow, Judy knew that if the lens had been turned just a bit, a birthmark as bright as flame would be jumping out at her. Annie!

54

"Hi, babes," said Hal, bending down to kiss Judy. It was already dark outside. Judy could see that Hal was still on a work high. His eyes were glittering, and he radiated energy. He sailed his briefcase onto the front-hall chair and tilted his head up toward the head of the stairs.

"Annie! I'm home," he hollered cheerfully. Then, after a moment of silence, he looked quizzically at Judy. "Where's the other half of my reception committee?"

"At Tina Stein's. She's spending the night there."

"On a school night? Way down in Northampton?"

"Don't worry. I'll see she gets to school on time tomorrow. It's just that Tina could take her on short notice, and I thought we had better have some time to ourselves tonight."

"Always a good idea," said Hal, leering playfully at Judy.

Judy started up the staircase, two steps at a time. "Wait there," she said over her shoulder. "I want to show you something." She reappeared almost at once with the photograph of the painting. "This was in my mailbox at Smith," she said, thrusting the photograph into Hal's hand, too upset to say any more.

"Oh, is this that painting again that you and Margaret were all steamed up about? I see someone knew where the original was."

Judy nodded grimly.

"Look at it carefully. What do you see?"

"What am I supposed to see? I'm having a hard time making out anything. It's fuzzy as hell."

"Look at the girl at the end."

"Right. I'm looking."

"It's Annie! Red hair. Same smile. The right age. And I'm positive that's her birthmark. There, under her chin."

"Hey, wait a second. That's not Annie."

"Oh, yes it is. And look at this kid," said Judy, stabbing her finger toward another small face. "It's Tracy Goldin. And that one's Erin. And these two with the blond hair are the Luccis. And this boy, this *Indian* boy, for God's sake, is T.C. Junior. And there's Gwen Prescott."

"I'm sorry, Judy. This picture's awful. You're reading too much into it. And what's your point anyway?"

"My point is, these children"—Judy shook the photograph at Hal—"are the children from the coven. *Not* our kids. This was painted three hundred years ago. Why do Annie and the others look just like these children? Exactly like them! What's the connection? I know there is one."

"If you know all the answers, you tell me."

"Okay, for one thing, they've all had accidents."

"Annie hasn't," said Hal quickly. Then he put his arm around Judy's shoulders. "What do you want me to say?" He glanced at the photograph. "For instance, these two towheads remind me of the Lucci twins? Maybe. A lot of these kids have been in accidents? Sure. But nothing's come of them. Kids get hurt all the time. And nothing has happened to Annie!"

"You call nearly being kicked to death by a mad horse nothing?"

"Oh, Jude," sighed Hal, "we're getting nowhere fast."

"I'll say!" said Judy fiercely. "You and I are out in left field. We don't know what's going on in this town. You're working at Hilliard's now fourteen hours a day, and I'm busy painting. We're preoccupied. Hell, consumed. We can't see what's going on right under our noses."

"That's just not true, Jude. It's the other way around. In small towns like this, *everyone* knows what's going on. Back in L.A., we didn't know half the families on our street. If something happened to someone down at the other end, it might as well have happened in Kansas, for God's sake. But places like

Ripton Falls aren't that way. A little tear in the fabric of the town, and everyone's affected. Believe me, darling, there's nothing going on here that we don't know about."

"I wish I could believe you," said Judy with a sudden, sharp sense of desolation. And confusion. Were her fears, which she couldn't even name, only a sick fantasy?

"I've been thinking," said Hal after a moment, "maybe we're really not cut out for small-town life. Maybe we should look for a house in Northampton where I could still commute. We could buy one of those comfortable old Victorians near the college. We'd have more of a choice of schools for Annie. And lots more to do ourselves."

"We'd still be within their reach."

"What're you talking about?"

"The *Hilliards*. They brought us to Tipton Falls because of Annie. I know it. I don't understand why, but the reasons for everything are in this painting."

"What reasons? I still don't understand what you're talking about. I wish I did, because then I could help you."

He paused and looked at Judy tenderly. When she didn't speak, he went on.

"All right. There are some resemblances between the children in this painting and Annie and the others. But so what? It's just coincidence. I know for a fact that they resemble other kids just as much as ours. Kids this age all look alike. Cute and pretty. It's only when they're older that they begin to look really different. Besides, this painting's a primitive! The faces are flat. There's no depth. No dimension. It's about as realistic as Grandma Moses. I hate to say it, Judy, but you're letting your imagination run away with you."

"I know this isn't a perfect photo, but can't you see the similarity?"

"No, I can't. You see it because you want to. You could see it on a box of Cheerios. Remember what you said yourself, that you and Margaret started this whole coven thing as a game. You're taking it too seriously now."

"You think I'm crazy, don't you?"

"Not for one moment, but, as I said, Jude, if you're frightened we can leave. We *will* leave. But I'll be honest. I want to say yes to Cameron. I want to sign that contract."

"Don't. *Please* don't."

"If I don't, I walk away from my future. From *our* future."

Hal's tone had grown short, and, as he leaned down to pick up his briefcase, Judy knew she had lost him. For now. It scared her that they were so apart.

"Call a couple of real-estate agents in Northampton," he said as he walked to the study, "and let's talk tomorrow. Right now, I've got a shit load of work to do. Oh, and hon, bring me a glass of wine, will you? And have one yourself. It might make you feel better."

As Judy walked to the kitchen, the clamor in her head was deafening. She was alone and she was near panic. Hal hadn't *really* heard a word she was saying. She had to talk to someone who would listen. The other husbands, she knew, wouldn't believe her any more than Hal had. It was the mothers she had to talk to. They would understand.

55

"Lisa!" Judy called out sharply, at the same time beeping her horn.

A woman pushing a stroller looked up, but not Lisa Goldin. Judy had tried to reach her by phone the day before as well as this morning. Now, by chance, here they both were in the middle of Northampton, and it seemed as if Judy was going to miss her again. She concentrated for a moment on the traffic around her, then picked out Lisa walking further along the sidewalk just past the bank.

"Lisa! It's Judy," she shouted. "Wait."

Judy looked hurriedly back to the road. This time she was headed straight for a panel truck in the other lane. She braked hard and swerved, just missing it. Her tires complained loudly. Chagrined, she maneuvered back into the right lane, waving apologetically to the other driver. Out of the corner of her eye, she saw that her sidewalk-audience rating was high. She could swear she saw Lisa staring at her with the others. But then Lisa turned and continued down the street. Damn!

She drove on, more irritated than embarrassed. Then she saw an empty parking spot by the bank. Quickly she pulled into it. She might still be able to catch Lisa on foot before she disappeared into one of the stores.

She was in luck. She parked and then as she ran down the sidewalk, dodging shoppers, she saw Lisa turn into a side street.

"I thought I was going to miss you," she said when she caught up with her. "I've got to talk with you. Can we have coffee together?"

Lisa was shaking her head before Judy finished.

"I can't, Judy. I have a hundred things to do."

"It'll only take ten minutes. It's very important. There's something going on that you've got to know about."

"I just don't have time now . . ."

"Lisa, I'm not kidding. This is important. You've got to—"

"Judy," interrupted Lisa, suddenly cold, "I know what you want to talk to me about, and I'm not interested."

"What!"

"I've been waiting for you to contact me," she said, her voice flat and controlled, as if she had memorized what she was going to say. "Both Claire and Terry called me. They warned me that you would try to talk to me too. About our kids. But, Judy, don't you understand? What's wrong with Tracy is a *medical* problem. It's neurological. We're worried half to death—"

Lisa gulped and took a breath, but her resolve broke. She couldn't go on. She bent her head and quietly began to cry. Judy instinctively reached out her arm to comfort her, but Lisa abruptly stepped away. She struggled with herself for a few moments, and then looked up again. There was no mistaking her anger and bitterness.

"Don't you see?" she said. "You're just making things worse with these crazy theories of yours. You and your . . . *artistic sensibility*. If I believed you— Oh, God! We'll find out what's wrong with Tracy. We have to! But by talking to doctors, not to painters. Just leave us alone, will you? We're not the ones who need help, Judy. It's *you* who needs help."

56

"So you've finally taken my advice. You're leaving him for me."

After being put on hold for several minutes by one of Jeff Fields's secretaries, Judy almost dropped the phone at the suddenness of his voice, but she couldn't help laughing.

"I'm really sorry they kept you on hold, Judy. I don't know how many times I've said to them: family or friends, especially friends, put right through. But what can I do? One of my secretaries just left Scientology to get into body-building and the other split from a rock drummer to move in with the guy's sister. I think it's the sun. It's only good for avocados. But you know all that. You and Hal are graduates. Survivors. So what's up?"

"Are you still serious about giving Hal a job?"

"Of course I am. I'm going to discuss it with him when I visit you next month."

"That's the problem. Next month is too late."

"What do you mean? Too late for what?"

"Cameron Hilliard has just offered him the moon. Chairman of the company. Twice the salary. A piece of the business."

"Wow. I can't match an offer like that. It sounds fantastic. He should jump for it."

"But I don't want him to. I can't explain now, but we have to leave this town. It's too complicated to go into, but you have to believe me. It's vitally important that we move. And if you can offer Hal the job that you talked about, I still think I can persuade him to take it. But old man Hilliard is drawing up papers. And I know Hal. Once he signs, nothing I say or do will get him to leave. Nothing. Until it's too late."

"Okay. I get the picture. I think. You just take it easy for a second. I have to make a couple of fast calls. I'm going to put you back on hold."

The soft hiss of the static line took on a rhythm and a voice like the wheels of a train. *Please, Jeff, say you'll come. Please, Jeff, say you'll come. Please, Jeff—*

"Make up my bed. And make it a double. Jenny'll be with me. You'll love her. We'll be arriving on Friday. We'll leave here at eight in the morning from Burbank. And we'll arrive about four o'clock your time."

"Wait a second, I want to write that down."

Judy placed the phone on the countertop and rummaged through several drawers in the kitchen in search of a pencil. No luck. The shelf in the pantry yielded one the size of an index finger. Without a point.

"Come on, I know you're in there somewhere," she said aloud as she ransacked another drawer.

"There's one over there. By the cutting board," said Vicky as she walked into the kitchen.

"Thanks, Vicky," said Judy, picking it up. "I thought you and Annie were outside."

"Got back ten minutes ago. Well, I've got to get back to Annie. We're in the middle of another game of concentration. And you can guess who's winning."

Judy heard Vicky's steps as she picked up the phone again. "You still there?"

"For you I'd hang by the thumbs."

"Now you said you'd arrive around four?"

"Right. And where's the airport?"

"Greenfield, I think."

"Well, I hope it can handle a corporate jet. I was able to snag the plane. The rest of the honchos are in London hand-holding with our latest wunderkind director. The kid is only twelve million over budget, but he's getting the 'values' he's searching for. What a business!"

"Oh, thank you, Jeff. Now I have to give the good news to Hal. Jeff?"

"What, Judy?"

"I love you."

•   •

An hour after she had spoken to Jeff, Hal came home. She told him all about her call. How never before in her life had she wanted anything this much. They had to leave Ripton Falls. And this was the only way.

"Just promise me you'll listen to Jeff. Please."

"Oh, Judy, you know I will," said Hal. He pulled her close and kissed her softly on each eye. "I'll give him all the time in the world. I'll let him talk my ear off. And I promise I'll be as receptive as I can be to what he has to offer. But, darling, I can't give you any guarantees."

57

"Leaving early for a little fishing?" asked Aldo Lucci as Hal got into his car in the parking lot behind the office. Aldo was overseeing two workmen busy painting the white lines that marked the parking spaces. Hal could have sworn that that had been done only a few months before.

"No such luck, Aldo. Just picking up some friends who're coming in from L.A. They're due at the Greenfield airport at four."

"All you hear about these days is L.A. Even my in-laws are looking to buy a condo there. And just a couple of days ago one of my guys had to drive Howard Hilliard to the airport in Boston. I think he was going to L.A. too. God knows why. What's it about the place that everybody wants to go there? It can't be just the water. People aren't birds. Is it because they make it look so good on TV? You lived there, Hal. What the hell is it?"

"Living there isn't the answer, Aldo. That's why I'm here. But this discussion will have to wait. I'm running late."

Hal was making good time until he got behind a new Saab whose owner was intent on getting the maximum m.p.g. that the little book indicated was possible. He maintained thirty-five with precision. Hal could stand it for only five minutes. Then, his frustration tipping him over into sheer stupidity, he passed the guy on a double yellow line—going *up* a hill.

Hal had made up most of the time before he turned off Route 20 onto the narrow road that coiled up the mountain.

The airport sat between two rises on a flattened slope that resembled a carrier deck. He was within a half mile of it when he was forced to stop. Ahead a line of stalled cars was strung out as far as he could see. It must be an accident, he thought. He took a copy of *Advertising Age* from his briefcase. Nothing else to do but wait. There was no other route to the airport except in the opposite direction. And that would take at least twenty minutes.

Within ten minutes, three fire engines, their sirens screaming, rushed up the hill. They used the oncoming lane. Hal realized that traffic had been stopped in both directions.

Exactly when his sense of foreboding began, Hal couldn't say. Maybe it was all those fire engines. Too many for just a car accident. But he knew he couldn't simply sit there. He had to see what had happened. He pulled his car off the road. He didn't bother to lock it. He just walked quickly up the road, following the line of cars.

As Hal rounded a bend he saw a state trooper's car at the head of the roadblock. Two troopers stood in front of the car.

"Excuse me, officer. Could you tell me what's going on?"

"We were told that there's been a plane crash, sir," answered the taller of the two.

"Jesus," said Hal, his heart beginning to pound wildly. "Do you know what kind of plane it was? Were people hurt?"

"I'm sorry. That's all we know."

"You see, I'm supposed to meet some friends. They were arriving by private jet."

"Phil," said the taller trooper to the other, "I better take this gentleman to the airport manager. Be back in a minute."

The airport swarmed with police and firemen. Hal saw four fire trucks at the end of the runway, their spinning red lights swirling out of the smoke that surrounded them like lighthouse beacons on a foggy day. A small rainbow from the spray of the hoses hung incongruously above the maelstrom.

"Mr. Marsh," the trooper called to a balding man who was talking to a fireman. The man finished with the fireman and came over to them.

"This gentleman was expecting to meet some people here. Said they were coming in by private jet."

"Your party arriving in a Gulf Stream II?"

"I don't know the make of the plane."

"Was their point of departure Burbank, California?"

"Maybe. They were coming from L.A."

"Was the plane owned by York Pictures?"

"Oh, no," said Hal. "Jesus, no," and it was more of a cry than words. "How bad is it?" he was finally able to ask.

The airport manager looked at Hal for a long moment, then reached out and placed his hands on Hal's shoulders.

"Bad. Real bad. Let's go to my office, sir. It'll be easier to talk there."

Once inside the office, the airport manager poured an inch of bourbon into a paper cup and handed it to Hal. Then he told Hal what had happened.

"I didn't see the landing, but I'm told it appeared normal. We found a lot of brake fluid on the runway. A lot. That could mean the blowout plugs on the brakes may have melted. But maybe it was just pilot error. The runway here is short and slanted downward. It's happened before. We won't know for sure until there's been an investigation. Inspectors will be on the scene by tonight."

"And after it landed?"

"We have a drop of more than forty feet at the end of the runway. There was an immediate explosion after the overshoot."

"No survivors?" Hal barely got it out.

"I'm afraid not. We'll need dental records to establish positive identification," said the airport manager as he poured another shot into Hal's paper cup.

•   •

Three days later Hal and Judy made the trip into New York for Jeff's funeral service. Thank God, Hal thought, that everything had moved so quickly. With so much to do so fast, there was less time to think. And *not* thinking was the only thing that had gotten Hal through the agony of telephoning Jeff's parents to tell them what had happened.

Jeff had been Hal's oldest good friend. They had first met at Cornell, but it was only when they both went for M.B.A.'s at Wharton that they became truly close. They ended up sharing a three-room dump on Society Hill, when living there was pioneering. It was Jeff who had introduced Hal to Judy. Jeff had infiltrated the ranks of the college set on the Main Line. Judy, he declared, was the pick of the lot. How right he had been.

These memories of Jeff were too distant and too familiar to trigger anything but affection. But if Hal lowered his guard for a moment and slipped into the present, he was overwhelmed with grief. Jeff was his first loss. And a deep one. It would take an act of will to come to terms with his absence. Who would he bounce his life off now?

And Judy. He knew she must be going through her own, very different kind of turmoil. He also wondered if Jeff's death made her again feel trapped in Ripton Falls. He hadn't the strength to face that question yet, but she hadn't asked him to. A moment of silent understanding had passed between them on the night of the accident that was so intense it was as if she had spoken out loud. The message was: I can handle being here. For now.

The service at Riverside Chapel was brief and moving. A large California contingent had flown in, and it looked as if most of the guys from Jeff's old Flatbush neighborhood had made it too. The graveside ceremony that followed was for family only, so after the service Hal and Judy drove north again.

When they arrived in Ripton Falls, Hal decided to stop and check the office for mail and phone messages. Judy waited in the car.

Hal emerged a short while later. There had been too many calls to deal with now, but there was one thing he wanted to tell Judy right away. He watched her closely as he spoke. "Reid Prescott did it. Gave his notice. Next Friday is his last day. I'm surprised. I didn't think Peggy could put that much pressure on him. You should feel relieved though. There goes a kid from the painting."

Judy looked back at him as if what he was saying wasn't registering. She seemed confused.

"Come on, Judy darling," he said gently, "I'm going to take you home now. We both need a good stiff drink."

58

"I'm not fooling you. The damn thing tipped over at twenty-two miles an hour. I almost phoned you right then. Jesus! You should have seen the mannequins that were supposed to be the driver and the passenger. Tossed out like rice at a wedding."

A few days before, on a rerun of an old *60 Minutes,* Sy had seen an exposé on the dangers of the Jeep. The exact model Hal owned! An insurance company contended it had the stability of a unicycle. Hal tried to tell Sy that everyone knew Jeeps were top-heavy and had to be driven with caution. And, Hal reminded him, he also was no slouch behind the wheel. But Sy insisted they use his car. He could just see those dummies bouncing out like dice on a crap table. No way would he get in Hal's Jeep again. And if it were up to him, Hal would trade it in tomorrow.

"Luckily I taped the show. When we get back from the wine run, you can take a look. Believe me, after seeing it, you'll want me to drive you home. Or you'll walk."

They were knocking off early to drive into Northampton to buy wine at a discount store called Red, White, and Bleu that had opened during the summer. Sy had discovered it when it advertised a free wine-tasting course. By the end of the second session, Sy had decided he had a wine palate. Hal loved to watch him hold his glass of wine to the light as if searching for a flaw in the Kohinoor diamond. Next he would insert his nose into the glass, breathe in as if he were using a nasal spray, and then take a tiny, slurpy sip. It was at this point that he would nod his head slightly and the others at the table would get a chance to drink while Sy discoursed on "fruitiness," "bottom," "aftertaste," and, sometimes, always said with a frown, "immaturity."

Sy, who had built a storage cellar for his wine alongside his new sauna, bought six cases. Hal, who improvised with a honeycomb of brick-red plumbing pipes stacked like Lego next to the laundry room, bought two.

As the clerk loaded the cases into Sy's wagon, Hal spotted Laurie Hilliard across the street. She was standing next to her car, looking away from Hal toward the front windows of Grimaldi's Travel Center. Just then the front door opened and her brother, Howard, walked out. He was holding a large envelope. But what Hal really noticed was that he was wearing white gloves again. Before he could call across to them, they were both in the car.

"It's sort of like gilding the lily, isn't it?" said Sy, who had been looking over Hal's shoulder in the same direction. "I mean, Howard's unusual enough looking already, but when he wears those gloves—Jesus! He'd stand out in Greenwich Village."

"I agree. I didn't know he was wearing them again."

"Just started the other day. When he got back from the coast. Laurie said he was overtired. She was trying to get him to go away. For a rest this time. Guess that's why he was at Grimaldi's."

"Where's he going?"

"Don't know. Someplace warm, I'd imagine, though it's hard to picture him nursing a rum concoction in a scooped-out coconut while talking up some number in a bikini."

They both laughed so hard they forgot to tip the clerk. Hal reminded himself to tell Judy Sy's line, but on the drive back to Ripton Falls, Sy returned to the subject of the Jeep so obsessively that when Hal finally got home all he could think of was to make sure Judy didn't use the Jeep again unless he was in the car too.

59

The Hunk. Or rather, the *latest* Hunk. Sounded like one of Annie's favorite TV shows. But no. This was Tina Stein's new flame. She had been talking about him constantly for the past two weeks, planning the dinners and activities they would partake of during his upcoming visit from New York as if she were in charge of arranging a five-power summit meeting. She secreted bowls of sachet around her apartment like so many olfactory limpet mines designed to both lure and stun. She tossed out frayed and droopy undies with the abandon of an heiress.

When Judy came to Tina's apartment on the gray, spritzy afternoon of his arrival to finally meet the Hunk over a little Lillet, she had all she could do to keep a straight face. The Hunk weighed perhaps one-twenty, and that would be after a crash course at Baskin-Robbins. He had seen forty when Reagan first started thinking about the Presidency. But this didn't stop Tina from looking at him as if John Travolta's body had been welded to John Ashbery's mind. Yes, the Hunk was an art critic. "An important voice," Tina said significantly. Of course, he taught too. N.Y.U. His name was Sebastian Rabinowitz.

What Sebastian lacked in male attractiveness, he more than made up for in one particular aspect: he thought Tina was immensely talented. In fact, that was how they met. Sebastian had singled out her work in a group show at UMass. He described the two paintings she had in the show as "magically polished gemlike visions in a sea of the familiar and the, thankfully, forgotten." Tina had this snippet blown up and framed. It appeared in no less than two places in her apartment. At least that was all that Judy had found so far.

Sebastian had commandeered the one comfortable chair in Tina's living room. The rest of the seating was made up of bright-colored modular units. Soft and low. Tina had arranged them around Sebastian's chair, in a style reminiscent of a royal levee. Though Sebastian was barely tall enough to look Woody Allen in the eye, from the angle Judy had to view him he could be a high draft pick for the New York Knicks.

"Tina tells me you have a show coming up," said Sebastian, between sips, his mouth so pursed it seemed ready to spit a seed.

"Yes. My first. That is, my first one-woman show."

"I'd love to see some of your work. Tina's very impressed with it. Sounds like new Al Held."

"I'd like to think of it as new Judy Richardson," she answered a bit testily.

"Where again are you showing?"

"The Hawkins Gallery. It's on Madison near—"

"Oh, I know the place. Haven't attended an opening there in I forget how long. They used to serve good booze and simply great hors d'oeuvres. I was quite surprised when Tina told me about their taking you on and about their purported change in direction. I thought the name change had been merely cosmetic, but I guess I was wrong."

"What name change?" Judy asked as she placed her drink on a small lacquered end table. She smiled. There was a third framed enlargement of Sebastian's review, this time coupled with a photo of the critic himself.

"Until four, maybe five years ago it was known as The Hawkins-Hilliard Gallery. Though who Hilliard was I have no idea. Probably the moneyman. Every gallery needs one. Or maybe Hilliard supplied the little old lady clientele. The kind who want expensive minor Impressionists to complement their Clarence House fabrics."

Sebastian laughed mightily, with Tina just an adoring beat behind.

60

"It's the Welcome Wagon lady. Do I look the part?"

Laurie Hilliard stood at the front door, a wide smile framing a row of snowy teeth that actually glinted in the morning sun. But all Judy could look at, drawn to it like a fly to a sugar cube, was the gull-shaped mole that danced above her eyebrow as she spoke.

"I'm doing the introduction number for the female half of our new executive family. Judy Richardson, meet Miki Braun."

For the first time, Judy noticed the tiny Japanese woman who stood slightly behind Laurie. She barely reached Laurie's shoulder and her hair was as black and shiny as a wet umbrella. She reached out a hand that was the size of Annie's.

"I'm very pleased to meet you, Mrs. Richardson."

"Call me Judy. And your name is Mickey?"

"Almost. M-I-K-I. I pronounce the first part *ME*."

"Doesn't she speak beautifully? Just five years ago when she met Walt, her husband, all she knew in English was Merry Christmas and Clint Eastwood."

Miki laughed, as soft and charming as a child. She fluttered a hand up like a fan to cover her mouth, and only the steeples of her smile peeked above it.

"Walt's the lawyer who's replacing Reid Prescott. He's top-notch. He was really our first choice if the truth be known. But Miki's family was in San Francisco and it took some doing for us to persuade them to come to Ripton Falls. But I've been telling Miki that she'll absolutely love it here. Isn't that right, Judy? Won't she?"

And then Judy heard a child cry. Quickly, Miki dashed down the front steps. She opened the back door of Laurie's car and emerged with a baby girl no more than a year old. With the speed of a light being turned off, the child stopped crying.

"This is Melissa. Say hello to Mrs. Richardson," said Miki.

The child was beautiful. She had cheeks as ruddy as strawberries and her eyes were a perfect blend of East and West, large but tipped slightly at the corners. Judy held her hands out and the little girl reached for her.

"She's very friendly," said Miki as Judy held Melissa, all the while making funny faces at the child who played the perfect audience by laughing uproariously.

"She's lovely. Is she always this happy?" asked Judy.

"Yes, but when Walt plays with her she's even happier."

"Is she your only child?" asked Judy.

"Yes, but we're hoping for more."

"God, what a terrible host I am. Here I've had the two of you standing on the front steps all this time. Come in, please. I'll make some coffee."

"We'd love to, but this is just our second stop. In addition to the welcomes, I'm taking Miki around to meet some of our shopkeepers."

"I hope to see you again soon," said Judy, handing Melissa back to Miki.

"Yes. Me too."

With the baby waving back toward Judy, Miki descended the steps and put the child back into her car seat.

Laurie started after her, then stopped.

"You know, I never congratulated you on your forthcoming show," she said, turning back to face Judy. "I'm getting terribly forgetful these days. First I was going to send you a bottle of champagne. Then a note. And, of course, I wound up doing nothing. But I'm terribly happy for you. And when I heard that you'll be showing at the gallery we used to have an interest in, you could have knocked me over. I know you'll have more luck there than we had. It wasn't the right thing for us. Grandfather just felt a need to diversify. He also had been thinking of selling prints through our mail-order list. Those were the days when all you heard was either diversification or synergy."

Judy watched as Laurie, pausing hardly at all where the driveway met the road, drove off, a small blizzard of gravel in her wake.

It was when Judy closed the door that she started to laugh. A laughter that swept out the terror from inside her like a window opened in a smoky room. It *had* been her imagination all the time! And thank God for little Eurasian Melissa Braun. A child you might find in a Gauguin, but never in an American primitive like *The Ripton Falls Children*. It was all so suddenly funny.

Annie, who was home sick from school, came down from her room and asked Judy why she was so happy. And all Judy could do was to hug her and just keep on laughing.

61

MEMO TO: Executive Staff
FROM: Laurie Hilliard

One more note from your neophyte tour director (I'll never take this job again!): the date for the first annual Hilliard and Company Executive R & R has been moved forward by two weeks. The new departure date is October 30, a week from today. All other particulars—flights, rooms, arrangements for children, etc.—stay the same. The reason for the change is that my grandfather is determined to make the trip with us. His health, however, seems to have different ideas. The doctors want Grandfather in the hospital for tests and, perhaps, exploratory surgery on our original departure date. Therefore the change. We will accompany Grandfather on his flight to join you the following day. So, lay in your supplies of Bain de Soleil a little earlier. Hopefully, this is the last memo you will be getting from me on this subject. Bon voyage, and don't forget to reserve a chaise poolside for me.

62

Judy couldn't believe it was so early. Only twenty to seven, and she was already awake. On weekends she had taken to sleeping as late as she could. Annie had standing orders to prepare her own breakfast—a decent one, please!—and to keep the TV turned low so as not to disturb old Mom. But this morning was different. And then Judy remembered. There was no longer any reason to bury herself in sleep. Everything was okay. *Everything.*

Ever since Laurie and Miki's visit three days ago, she had been giddy with relief. She found herself smiling at the oddest moments. Just as she was now, though there was no one to appreciate it, except Percy. From his vantage point at the foot of the bed, he thumped the floor tentatively with his tail, watching Judy debate whether to collapse back beside Hal or get up. Well, why not? She felt so good. In all ways.

By the time Judy heard Annie get out of bed and hit the TV, clicking her way around the dial like a frenzied safecracker, she already had made a big dent in her weekend chores and was treating herself to a second cup of coffee. After Annie watched a half hour of cartoons, Judy talked her into coming with her on the morning grocery run. The bribe was a pumpkin—a big one for the front doorstep. On the way to the car, Judy had another idea. They would have the car washed. They would make that stop number one. Fun for Annie, and Hal would be pleased too. He should be up by the time they returned. And later, at eleven, Vicky would take over Annie while Hal went to his office and Judy to the studio.

"Roll up your windows, Mom," commanded Annie when they pulled up at the car wash.

Judy got almost as big a kick as Annie out of the whole procedure: the roiling steam, the giant scrubbers, and, best of all, the curtain of dark wormy fabric streamers that wrapped around the car to soap it, like spaghetti around a spoon. From inside the car it was like being Alice in the teacup.

They popped outside, clean and shiny, to find a teenager waiting to dry the car. It looked so wonderful, sunshine ricocheting off the hood, that Judy decided to spring for the extra quarter to vacuum it as well. She had just finished the front seat and was about to tackle the rear as soon as Annie cleared the floor of bubble-gum wrappers when she heard her name called. From the high, thin lilt of the voice she knew it was Miki Braun.

With Annie trailing behind, she walked over to the other car to say hello. Beside Miki sat a man with a wide, friendly face and sandy lashes that were pale against dark-cobalt eyes. Walt, of course. Next to him, Miki looked almost as tiny as a doll.

Judy peered past them into the interior of the car, but the sunlight was too strong for her to see inside.

"Is Melissa with you?" she asked. "Annie adores babies. She'd love to meet Melissa."

Miki murmured something over her shoulder, and the back door of the car swung open. Clutching the squirming baby in her arms, a young girl, who seemed to be about Annie's age, carefully eased her way out of the car.

"Hi, I'm Karen Braun," she said, looking up from the baby for the first time.

Everything stopped when Judy saw the girl's face. She knew she was staring, but she couldn't help herself.

"Wow, look at your freckles!" chirped Annie. "You look exactly like a girl who used to live here. My friend Gwen."

Then, apparently not the least nonplussed by Karen Braun's startling resemblance to Gwen Prescott, Annie shifted her attention to Melissa. As Judy watched the girls, her eyes dead, transfixed by Karen's unsmiling freckled face, she finally realized that Walt was speaking to her. His words were faint, filtered through clouds of panic burgeoning inside her like sponges filling with water.

"You'll be seeing lots of Karen, I'm sure," Walt was saying sociably. "She spends summers with her mother, but she'll be here with us for the whole school year. She's very excited because she loves to ski." He lowered his voice so his older daughter would not hear him. "To tell you the truth, she's lucky she'll be able to get out on the slopes at all. She took a really bad fall a few weeks ago. I don't like to knock my ex-wife, but she's much too lax. A couple of the steps coming down from her deck are so rotten they'd collapse under the weight of a cat. Instead poor Karen caught it."

Walt suddenly stopped talking and looked closely at Judy. "Are you all right?" he asked.

Judy followed his gaze to her hands and saw she was gripping the side of the Brauns' car as if it were a lifeline, her knuckles white from the pressure. She shook her head to clear it and tried to speak, but her throat was so dry that at first nothing came out. She was finally able to pull herself together and persuade the Brauns that nothing was wrong.

"Are you all right, Mommy?" Annie asked when they were back in their car.

"I'm fine, darling."

"What about my pumpkin?" asked Annie plaintively when they turned down Quarry Road toward the house. "You promised."

"I'm sorry, Annie," said Judy, struggling to keep her voice even. "Daddy will take you instead."

She knew now that everything she had feared before was true. She had no idea how to fight back, or even if she could. But she knew what she had to do first. An hour later, when Vicky came up the front path, Judy was waiting for her. Waiting with money in her hand to pay Vicky for not baby-sitting. Their plans had changed and they wouldn't be needing her help that day after all.

Or ever again, she added to herself.

63

"Hello. Alan?"

"Speaking."

"This is Judy Richardson."

"Hi, Judy. Are you accepting?"

"What?"

"Our party. Didn't you get the invitation?"

"Oh, yes, we did. Just yesterday. And we are accepting. But I'm not calling about that."

"Great. Let me just write that down. Richardson, OK. Now what can I do for you? Not that children's painting again?"

"Well, yes. It *is* about that. I want to ask you a question. Did one of the girls have a distinguishing birthmark?"

"Damn it! Yes. That's it. I started thinking about that one girl after you left but couldn't for the life of me recall what it was that made her different. Of course. It was the birthmark. On her neck, I think."

"Do you remember what it looked like?"

"Well, there was something very strange about the shape of it . . ."

"Yes?" said Judy urgently.

"Ah, now I can see. It was shaped exactly like a leaf."

64

By that evening, Judy had begun to make terrible sense of what had been happening in Ripton Falls since all of them had arrived last May so full of hope and expectation. As she rinsed the dinner dishes, snapshots of their life here flashed through her mind. Thank goodness Hal was in the living room watching *Nova* and she could be alone. It had been difficult enough sitting through dinner without blurting out to him what was on her mind. Judy managed to nod and smile and contribute an occasional yes or no to the conversation, but whatever was said she immediately forgot. She could think of one thing only. The Hilliards.

From the flesh and blood of all their children—from her child, *from Annie!*—the Hilliards were bent on re-creating the coven. What else could it be but that? Now Judy understood why she and Margaret had not been able to find the seventh grave that day. It didn't exist. There had been seven in the coven, but only six had died. One had escaped burning with the others, and that one was a girl. A Hilliard girl, and through her the dark, demonic strain had continued. And prospered. Now at last, three hundred years later, the girl's descendants were acting as evil midwives to the birth of a new coven. They must have attempted it before and failed. They had been saved by technology. Jet planes. Computers. Only these had made it possible for them to search out exact physical duplicates of those first children, for this was what they demanded. The match between the new child and the original had to be perfect. If the match wasn't right, the Hilliards themselves completed the duplication. They scarred T.C. Junior's face. They shortened Erin's hair. And they prevented Annie's birthmark from being removed.

But they didn't stop there. In some deep, insidious way, they took over the children's minds. Through those awful "accidents," which weren't real accidents. They were engineered. The children recovered, and inside the net cast by the Hilliards, waited to do their bidding. It was only the greatest of luck that they hadn't claimed Annie yet. The Hilliards had intended her to go through the glass doors with Erin. To be nearly asphyxiated with T.C. Junior. Or, all else failing, to be kicked to pieces by that vicious horse. To join those other children who had been changed. Who had grown so serious. Who no longer laughed and seldom smiled. Who were matched to the children out of a distant, dark cauldron of time.

When Hal first told her the date for the executive weekend had been moved forward, she hadn't given it any thought. But now she saw there was a sinister logic to it. In Karen Braun the Hilliards had found a replacement for Gwen Prescott. A duplicate. And on that Friday night they would have something extra. A full moon. A hunter's moon. A moon that would shine full and clear and bright into only one building Judy knew of in Ripton Falls. The barn without a roof! The one that they had discovered on their picnic that day so long ago. That, Judy knew instinctively, was the place where the children of the first coven had died. The legend had been wrong. It hadn't burned to the ground. And that was the place where the new coven would spring to life. That was where they would take Annie. Without Annie the new coven was incomplete. For Annie was the seventh child. Only Judy stood between the Hilliards and Annie. Only she could save her. Hal would never understand until it was over. But could she blame him? Who could believe this nightmare from a time long forgotten?

Margaret had begun to understand, and for that she was murdered. And Brad's "suicide" was the reward he received for stumbling on town records the Hilliards wanted lost forever. And poor Jeff and Jenny. Judy had heard at the time that Howard had gone to California. Now she realized why. He had sabotaged Jeff's plane. Nothing and no one were beyond the Hilliards' bloody reach.

Least of all Judy herself. She had to move fast to save Annie. And the Hilliards would be waiting. Her only hope was to behave normally. Another smiling parent who didn't know what was happening. She must go about her business as usual.

And so, when she finished up in the kitchen, she forced herself to join Hal in the living room for the tag end of the television show. Outwardly calm but feverish with plans she couldn't speak of, she challenged Hal and Annie to a three-way game of Scrabble. Later she read Annie a chapter from *Treasure Island*. And then, just as Annie began to yawn mightily, Judy pretended to have a wonderful idea. Why didn't Annie bring her Snoopy sleeping bag into their room? A special treat. She could sleep there for the night. Annie was thrilled, and Hal, furious. He thought Judy was spoiling Annie. But Judy knew she could never sleep unless Annie was with them. Not down the hall, two doors away, but right there in the same room. For the one thing Judy knew, surest of all, was that she must never let Annie out of her sight. Not even for one brief moment.

65

Control. From now on. Every minute. She could never relax. If she did, then Annie would be lost. Forever. She had to be two people. A perfectly ordinary Judy on the outside. Someone comfortable to be with. Not a crazy with wild ideas about covens. But on the inside she could never let up. Not for an instant. She knew she was alone. She could only count on herself. No one else.

She pasted a smile, false as a puppet's, on her face. Though rubbing inside her was a pearl of fear and horror, she smiled at Hal over coffee. Lots of teeth. Careful! Don't overdo it. She told him to eat a light lunch because she was planning to cook a mega-batch of pasta for dinner. With broccoli. Hal's favorite. She could see how pleased he was with her happy state. Her normalcy. He probably thought that her "fixation" was over. Good old Judy had returned.

She kissed him full on the mouth, a long, deep kiss of court-ing, as he left for the office. His face softened. She could see all the seeds of worry that had recently drawn his face wire tight ease away and disappear like words written on an ocean beach. All the heartache of Jeff dying. And Brad. And Margaret. All terrible coincidences. It was easier to believe that. *That* was natural. But evil, true evil, was not.

Hal turned back to her just as he was getting into his car.

"Why hasn't Annie gone to meet the school bus? She's going to miss it."

"I promised I'd drive her in myself today. She's been good about cleaning her room lately. She's won the chauffeur treat-ment."

Lie. Actually, lie number two. Annie's room still ranked a close second to the Augean stables. And Annie wasn't going to school today. Nor tomorrow. Hal would be told later that she was sick. Something she picked up in school. They passed viruses around there the way college students threw Frisbees. Back and forth. Slight fever too. No, Annie would not, could not, ever be out of her sight. Not until they were free. She knew that she could win. She had to.

"Hey, Mom. We'd better hurry or I'll miss the bus. Where's my lunch?" said Annie, staring at her watch as she bounded down the stairs. She had just been given a Wonder Woman watch and used every opportunity to consult it. In the mornings, she timed herself brushing her teeth and eating breakfast.

"It's almost ready. You know your face looks a little flushed," said Judy, placing her fingers on Annie's brow. "You might have some fever."

"Yeah, I do feel hot. And my stomach hurts," Annie replied, always ready to forgo a day at school.

"I'll get the thermometer."

The thermometer registered 98.5, yet Judy shook her head.

"You're going to have to stay home today, young lady. Probably tomorrow too."

Judy, who generally doled out school day TV time in a miserly fashion, let Annie watch *Woody Woodpecker* and *Heckle and Jeckle*. When the shows were over, Judy and Annie went out to run some errands.

"Should I go out if I have a temperature?"

"Don't worry, it's not that high."

Judy drove to Stevensville, a small mill town twenty miles away. She stopped at a Gulf station. While she had the car greased and the tires rotated, neither of which was necessary, she placed three calls from a phone booth near the road. Two of them she paid for from a lump of change that puffed her jacket pocket as if she had her fist in it. The first was to Eastern Airlines. Using her American Express card, Judy booked two seats, one way, to Hilton Head via Atlanta and Columbia. They would leave Friday on the 11:30 A.M. flight from Bradley International Airport. Then Judy reserved a Hertz car, also at Bradley. She charged this to her Visa card. She would pick the car up the next day. She took a break to buy Annie a Coke, then headed back to the booth. Her next call was collect. Her father answered and, after a puzzled few seconds, accepted the call.

"My affluent son-in-law suddenly on welfare?" he said, laughing.

"Absolutely, Daddy. Food stamps too. Is Mother there?"

Judy told her mother she suddenly had decided to come with Annie for a visit. They'd be arriving that Friday afternoon. Though Judy knew her mother generally liked at least the amount of time it took to plan D Day before she felt ready for company, she greeted the announcement with surprising alacrity. After all, she said, she hadn't seen her only grandchild since Easter.

"Oh, and Mother," added Judy just before hanging up, "your doctor down there is a good man, isn't he? Could you ask him to line up a plastic surgeon, please? For Monday. It's very important. I'll explain later, but Annie's got to have her birthmark removed. Now."

On the way back to Ripton Falls, Judy stopped at a toy store to buy Boggle and Parcheesi and a new Simon to replace the one that had broken two weeks before. Annie was beginning to really like the idea of being sick.

In the afternoon, with Annie's help, Judy made both popcorn and caramel apples. When Hal came home shortly after seven, Annie was leading at Boggle, nine games to seven.

66

"Can you keep a secret, Annie?" asked Judy the next morning after Hal left for the office.

"Sure, Mom," Annie answered, her eyes not moving from the TV screen.

"Remember what I told you about looking at me when I talk to you?"

Annie swiveled her head a half-turn, the pull of *The Munsters* as strong as a magnetic pole.

"Turn all the way, Annie. Face me, please. That's better. Now this is a secret that you can't even tell Daddy."

"Why not Daddy?"

"Promise to keep it first, then I'll tell you."

"Okay. I promise."

"We're going to Hilton Head to visit Gram and Grandpop. Daddy's going to come too. But later. If we tell him we're going early, he'll want us to wait for him. So you mustn't mention it to him. Understand?"

"Sure. That's great. Will I be able to go with Grandpop on his boat?"

"Of course."

"Yippee. When are we going?"

"This Friday. And to make sure that your temperature is gone I think I'm going to keep you home from school until we leave."

"Double yippee."

•   •

Judy took the same route she had taken the day before. She drove slowly, constantly checking the rearview mirror to see that she was not being followed. No. Nothing. Annie sat in the back knitting. She had knitting stashed everywhere, including Hal's Jeep. She knitted with almost frantic determination now so that she could finish her "things" for Gram and Grandpop.

The drive to the airport took a half hour more than it normally would because Judy drove under the speed limit and doubled back once when she thought a car had been behind her for too long. When they finally arrived, Annie wanted to stay in the car and knit while Judy went into the rent-a-car office. But Judy insisted Annie come with her. She had never rented a car before and was pleased by how quick the procedure was. Fifteen minutes later, after parking their own car in the airport lot, they were heading to Springfield in the rental car.

Annie, still enmeshed in her knitting, didn't question Judy when she parked the car in a municipal garage in the downtown area and then took a cab back to the airport. Judy felt the need, though, to say something about why they were doing this. She couldn't tell Annie the truth—that she planned to throw the Hilliards off their trail by using an unfamiliar car. Instead, she explained they were leaving an extra car in Springfield for Daddy because the Jeep had to be fixed. Annie wasn't even listening—she had dropped a stitch.

The trip back to their house from the airport was uneventful. Judy felt herself relax a bit. Don't get overconfident, she told herself. But inside she knew that she was going to win. They would not get Annie.

•   •

The telephone calls started that afternoon. Right after
school. Luckily, Annie was watching TV so Judy took the calls.
First Erin. Then Tracy. The Lucci twins were next. Followed
by T.C. Junior and the Braun girl. All of them called. One after
the other. Could they come over and play with Annie? Or
maybe she'd like to go to their house? Was she all right? They
had missed her at school. She still would be going on the hayride and doing all the other great things they had planned
for that weekend, wouldn't she?

Yes, Judy told them, Annie would be joining them. But she
had a bit of temperature and it wouldn't really be a good idea
for them to play with her until it went away.

67

"Do you think it's smart to let her watch so much
TV?" asked Hal. "I know she's been sick, but in the last few
days she's seen more than she has in the last two months."

The sounds of *The Brady Bunch* seemed to be coming
straight at them even though the den was on the other side of
the house. Annie not only sat too close to the set, she raised the
volume to rock-concert level.

It was going to be a lovely day. The sky was scrubbed clean
of clouds, and the morning sun sparkled behind a line of ever-
greens. Hal and Judy sat at the small butcher-block table in the
kitchen. They were on their second cup of coffee.

"Should I carry the bags down now?" Hal asked as he stirred
his coffee.

"If you want to. Everything's packed. We'll have plenty of
time later."

"Maybe even time for . . ."

He reached under the table and ran his hand along the inside
of her calf.

"That would be nice. Very nice."

"What time are you taking Annie to the Luccis'? That's

where the kids are going to be picked up for the hayride, isn't it?"

"That's right. I'll drop her off at three. When will you be home?"

"No later than four-thirty. I just have this luncheon meeting in Hartford. The office is closed, so I probably won't even stop there on my way back."

"When are the others leaving?"

"About the same time we are, I guess. The Goldins are going with the Brauns. And the Luccis are taking Claire. T.C. and Emily are driving from Boston. Last night they drove down to see the new Neil Simon show that's trying out there. But we'll be alone. Which is exactly the way I want it to be. Even though we're going away with a group, I'm going to make sure the two of us get plenty of time together. Very private time."

Hal stood and gently pulled Judy up from her chair. He held her close and softly kissed her neck.

"If I were a small animal this is where I would burrow. It's warm, always, and it smells so good. So much like Judy. My Judy. Do you know how much I love you, baby?"

She tried but she couldn't hold back the tears. Before Judy could answer her cheeks were wet.

"Hey. Stop that. Everything's okay."

He held her so tightly she couldn't move. That helped. You've got to be strong, she told herself. If Hal thinks something's wrong, he won't go to Hartford. He'll stay. He'll make sure Annie goes to the Luccis' at three. Then we'll fly away and when we return Annie will be lost. Gone. Be strong, Judy!

"I love you too, Hal. I could never tell you how much. Ever. Always remember that."

"I will, don't worry. Tomorrow we'll be in the sun lying on a beach with sand as white as snow. And we'll be drinking dumb things like planter's punch. And we'll be laughing. Laughing a lot. At everything. All the bad stuff is behind us now. I'm sure of it. Absolutely."

Hal kissed her again and then stepped back. He traced the outline of her cheek with his finger.

"I know you've been through a lot, baby, but that's all in the past," he said. "But don't forget, for all the bad things that have happened, there've been good things too. Your painting.

My job. This house. And Annie. She's really blossoming. What happened to Brad and Margaret . . . shook me too. And Jeff. . . . But I remember my mom lost two of her best friends over one summer. Not counting her brother. Things like that happen. You can't let it get to you. Life goes on. But we're okay now, right?"

Judy nodded and they kissed again. She followed Hal into the den where he hugged Annie.

"You be a good girl. I'll see you soon."

"And you be a good boy."

This was their routine, and they both enjoyed it immensely. After they had rubbed noses and exchanged butterfly kisses with their eyelashes, Judy walked Hal to the front door.

"See you around four," Hal said as he walked down the stairs.

Judy stood squinting into the morning sun until Hal was out of sight.

"I love you, Hal," she said softly. And then she closed the door.

•   •

Though the note to Hal was short, it took Judy fifteen minutes to write it. Only the last few sentences came quickly:

Please believe me. I know it all sounds crazy, but it's not. By the time you read this, Annie and I will already be in Hilton Head. And she finally will be safe. There is a flight that leaves Bradley—Eastern 105—at 7:30 tonight. I've booked a seat in your name. I love you, darling. Always remember that.

"Mommy, will you be mad if I tell you something?" Annie asked from the back seat of the car. Judy glanced in the rearview mirror. Annie's head was down, but she wasn't knitting.

"Of course not, honey."

Everything had gone perfectly. The trip to the kennel to drop off Percy. The drive to Springfield. The exchange of cars. The roundabout approach to the airport along secondary roads. Now they were on a country road that bisected fields of recently harvested corn, row upon row of cut stalks no bigger than thumbs lined up as precisely as crosses in a military cemetery. In ten minutes they'd be at the airport. Away from Ripton Falls forever. Safe.

"You promise?"

"Promise what?"

Judy noticed a car come up fast behind her. Brown. A light flashed on its dashboard. Must be the police. An unmarked car. She automatically glanced down at the speedometer. Forty-two. Well, he wasn't after her.

"That you won't be mad at me?"

"I promise."

The brown car was less than a hundred feet away. Judy eased off the gas. Thirty. He'll probably want to pass me, she thought.

"I told someone we were going to visit Gram and Grandpop. But don't worry. I didn't tell Daddy."

"What?"

The brown car was right behind her now. There was a big man behind the wheel. His hand motioned Judy to pull over and stop. She started to brake.

"I called Erin this morning. While you and Daddy were having coffee. I just had to find out what had happened in school. And then I told her the secret. I'm sure she won't tell Daddy."

Judy had almost come to a full stop when she made out the features of the man behind the wheel of the brown car. Alien fingers of ice shimmied along her spine. Sweat as cold as hoarfrost licked its way down her back. It was Howard.

Judy slammed the gas pedal to the floor. For a second the car hesitated, then with a cough of exhaust, it shot forward. Howard was taken by surprise but within a half mile was again on Judy's bumper. They were approaching a settled area. Houses began to slide by with the speed of an amusement-park ride. Howard hit his horn and held it, like an enraged animal.

"Mommy! Why are we going so fast? You're scaring me."

Judy could not keep her eyes from the rearview mirror. She wasn't going to let Howard catch them. Ever. And then, in a finger snap of time, Howard was no longer right behind her. He had slipped back. But not so far back that Judy couldn't see his face, and the expression on it. Of horror. And surprise. Something was happening that he hadn't planned on. At the moment she looked ahead she saw what Howard had seen seconds before. A green van was pulling out onto the road. Before Judy smashed down on the brake, she knew it was too late. There was a metallic scream that splintered her senses. A swirl of glass like so many diamonds scattered by an invisible hand. And then nothing.

68

Hal's lunch was with a printer who had a large plant outside Hartford. Hal got a tour of the plant, a lousy lunch, and, the redeeming feature, a huge martini in a glass big enough to hold a baseball. The printer, clad totally in double-knit except, maybe, for his shoes, was a rabid Hartford booster. His conversation ranged from the Hartford Civic Center to the Hartford Whalers and on to the Hartford Light Opera Company. To top it off, his prices were sky-high. Hal mixed tact and celerity in an uneven blend that had him finished with the lunch before two. He was back in Ripton Falls by three-thirty. Since he was running early he decided to stop by the office to check his mail.

He knew the office was closed, but he had expected to find at least one of the Hilliards there. But he quickly saw from a large bundle of mail trussed with twine in the entranceway that no one had shown up all day. He carried the mail inside and dropped it on the receptionist's desk. He was about to leave when he heard a phone ring. He followed the sound to his own office. It was a very persistent caller since he couldn't get to the phone until what must have been the twelfth ring.

"Harold?"

Only his mother-in-law called him that.

"Hello, Hester. How are you?"

"Confused, Harold. And a little worried. I'm here at the airport. Judith and Ann didn't get off the plane they were supposed to be on. There isn't another plane until late this evening. Will they be on that?"

What plane? What the hell was going on? Come on, Hal.

Scramble. Show you're on top of it. If you don't, the old girl will really get scared. Maybe as scared as you are.

"Maybe Judy's car broke down. She's been having trouble with it. Electrical system. Let me get on the phone and see if I can find out what the problem is. I'm sure it's nothing serious."

"Thank you, Harold. I feel better already. It was just a little shocking to see all those people get off and not to see Judith or Ann. Luckily, Dad is with me. I tried calling your house but there was no answer. But Dad said to keep trying you at the office. Thank God I reached you."

"Everything's all right, Hester. Don't worry. I'll call you back as soon as I can."

Hal didn't stop to put out the light in his office. He was too scared to think. He just ran. He remembered Sy Goldin's fear scenario about the Jeep overturning, but that didn't stop him from keeping the pedal to the floor.

Judy's car was gone. There were no lights on anywhere in the house. Hal heard the phone ring inside, but it stopped before he could get his key in the lock. As he opened the front door a piece of paper fluttered down like a leaf. He flipped on the hall light and reached to pick it up. It was a note from Judy. He started to read it.

"Jesus," he said out loud.

He felt Judy's terror etched in every word. The fears inside her rolled off the page like thunderheads racing to smother the sun.

The phone rang with a suddenness that made him drop the note. He raced into the living room and picked up the receiver.

"Hello. Could I speak to Mr. Harold Richardson, please."

It was a woman's voice.

"Speaking. Who is this?"

"Thank heavens I've finally gotten you. I've been trying since eleven this morning. My name is Mrs. Horn. I'm a nurse here at East Springfield Hospital. Now don't get worried, but your wife and daughter were admitted this morning. They were in a car accident. A van from a side crossing pulled out in front of them without warning."

"My God."

"Your wife's been hurt, but your daughter's fine. A few contusions, a small cut that we had to suture above her eyebrow.

The doctor says it won't show when she gets older. She's going down to X-ray shortly. Her wrist. The doctor is almost positive that it's a bad sprain, but he wanted to make sure."

"But my wife?"

"Fortunately she had her seat belt on. Her condition is stable. She broke her left arm and three ribs. She's sleeping now, but she was lucid when she came in. There is a chance that she might have a blood clot near her left temporal lobe. The doctor feels that this would be no problem to remove if he has to. That's why we need you here immediately. We need authorization to operate if necessary. But don't worry. Doctor feels that an operation probably won't be needed."

Nurse Horn quickly gave Hal directions on how to get to the hospital.

"Oh, one more thing, Mr. Richardson."

"Yes."

"Don't forget to bring proof of medical coverage."

69

"It's me, baby, Hal. Everything's going to be all right."

A bruise, gray as cigar ash, circled one of Judy's eyes. Her lips were thick as rope and still had flecks of blood in the corners. She stirred again.

"Judy, I'm here. It's okay. You're going to be fine. Annie just got bumped around. I'll be able to take her home tonight. You'll be out by Tuesday. At the latest. Do you hear me?"

"Annie. Annie, honey."

Her eyes were still closed.

"Annie's not hurt. Just a few scratches."

Judy's eyes snapped open with the speed of a camera shutter.

"Hal! Where's Annie? You must get Annie. Oh, please. Get Annie."

"Take it easy, Judy. Annie's fine. I saw her fifteen minutes ago. She just got back from X-ray. Negative. She's scratched up. That's all. Just scratches."

"No, Hal. No. Stay with Annie. Don't leave her alone or they'll take her away. They'll change her. Like they changed the other children. They never laugh now."

Judy screamed, her voice a strangled cry corded with fear.

"Relax. I told you she's okay."

"She's not. They'll get her. Howard almost did. Only the car crash stopped him. That wasn't part of their plan. They'll take Annie to that barn. The one without the roof. Please listen to me. It's Annie they want. They need her. Don't you understand?"

Her cries brought the nurse into the room. She motioned Hal to leave. He bent over to kiss Judy.

"I'm not crazy, Hal. Go to Annie. Now. Please. I beg you."

A knot of people waited for the elevator so Hal took the stairs. It was only two floors. The door to Annie's room was closed. He edged it open.

The bed was empty.

"Excuse me," Hal said to the on-duty nurse sitting behind the floor desk. "I just went to see my daughter in five-seventeen, and she wasn't there. Do you know where she is?"

"Name?"

"Richardson. Ann. She's nine."

The nurse flipped a page on a clipboard.

"Your brother is checking her out."

"My brother?"

"Well, maybe your wife's brother. He took her down to the cashier's office. Just a few minutes ago."

Hal turned and started to run down the corridor to the stairs. He stopped and called back to the nurse.

"Was he a big man?"

"Does Reagan dye his hair?" she said, laughing.

Hal took each flight of stairs in two bounds. He couldn't grasp what Judy's voice kept repeating in his head. It's just a mix-up. That's all. Nothing more. But something else, as cold as the earth in winter and as dark as the inside of a fist, kept saying that there was something terribly wrong. But it was easier to just run than to think it through.

"I'm looking for my daughter, Ann Richardson. She's nine. Did she just check out?" Hal shouted to the startled clerk at the cashier's office.

"Richardson? Little girl with red hair?"

"Yes. Yes."

"Her uncle just paid the bill."

"Her uncle?"

"That's right. Just a few minutes ago. I couldn't forget. It's been many years since someone around here paid in cash."

70

A fury as strong as a winter sea twisted through Hal. And a fear. Fear of losing Annie. That was part of it. But the other part was fear of the unknown. An unknown that was the wellspring for all fears.

Hal had thought he knew evil. It was that faceless road company that played nightly on the TV evening news. But if Judy was right, then the evil that was trying to take Annie came from a place beyond this world. And Hal now knew that Judy was right. She had been all along. They and the others had been lured by the Hilliards to Ripton Falls like geese enticed over a blind by a wooden whistle. But the Hilliards didn't want them. They wanted their children. Why hadn't he believed Judy? Instead, he had been logical. But evil, true evil, had no logic.

The barn. Judy had said they would take Annie to the barn. That strange, roofless building which Percy had been afraid to enter. Where burned planks were stitched to new ones. That was where the Hilliards' coven must have ended three hundred years ago.

He pushed the Jeep as hard as he could. A month ago Hal had gone bird-watching with Reid Prescott. They had taken Hal's Jeep and ridden the logging trails and old roads that spider-webbed the hills ringing the towns. And they had passed the clearing near the barn. He recognized the screen of trees at its far edge that hid the barn from the road. But this time they had come at it from the direction of Northampton. He had been amazed at how close by it had been. And that was the way, the only way, he could beat Howard there now. For if he didn't get there first, then he would be too late. For Annie and for all the children. No, he couldn't even think about that. He had to get there first.

Hal was sure Howard would not go above the speed limit. He wouldn't risk being stopped. Since Howard's lead was only ten minutes, maybe less, Hal had a good chance of reaching the barn ahead of him. But he couldn't be sure of that, he told himself, as he drove the Jeep flat out, the emergency flasher silently screaming out at the cars he passed.

The turnoff he wanted was on the other side of Northampton. He remembered that it was the first right immediately after a diner. He was moving so fast that when he spotted the turn he couldn't stop soon enough to make it. He backed up and just missed hitting an oil truck that was coming onto the main road. The trucker leaned furiously on his air horns. Hal was down the road almost a half mile before the angry echo was swallowed into the night.

The road up into the hills was narrow and its blacktop surface was pocked like a child's sandbox. The steering wheel bounced in and out of Hal's hands as if it were on a spring. Within a few miles the houses started to thin out. In between houses the Jeep plunged through a dreamy darkness where the only light came from the cold, dead glow of the full moon, a moon that seemed suspended in front of Hal like a sinister balloon.

And then he realized he hadn't passed a house in some time. Suddenly the road pinched in and became dirt. Hal struggled with the wheel to stay on the road, then slowed the car to a stop. He switched off the flasher and killed the headlights. He sat there for a minute, his eyes adjusting to the milky light of the moon.

You're not taking my kid, you bastards, he thought to himself. I'm coming, Annie. Don't worry.

He began slowly to inch the Jeep forward, acutely aware of time passing. He couldn't turn his headlights on though. No. They must not know he was coming. They had found out what Judy had been planning to do with Annie and they had tried to stop her. If it weren't for the dumb luck of a real accident— thank God for that van!—they would have Annie now. And Judy? Judy, he knew in his heart, would be dead. Like Mar-

garet . . . Brad . . . Jeff . . . A chill ran through Hal, a sinu-
ous ripple of terror.

Stop it. Now. Don't be scared. Kick it out the window. No
room for that here.

And Hal's rage, a storm of hatred, cooled his fear like a pail
of water on a campfire.

The road came to a fork. Which way? Come on! Remember.
Left or right? He closed his eyes and tried to recall that day
with Reid Prescott which now seemed years away. Left. That
was it. But the road ran quickly into a rutted path choked with
saplings and brush. He pounded the wheel. No. No time for
that. Back this thing out of here. It's simple. It's the other road.

After two miles the road to the right began to drop in a long,
gentle downward slope. He cut the engine. The Jeep rolled
silently down the decline, the hungry crunch of dirt under the
wheels and the immense hollow hush of the surrounding woods
the only sounds Hal heard. Then he saw what he was looking
for: the clearing with the screen of trees at its edge that hid the
barn from view.

Before he reached the bottom of the hill, he pulled hard to
the right and eased the Jeep into a clump of blackberry bushes
off the road. He got out and just caught himself before slamming the door shut. Watch it. No sound. Nothing.

Crouching low, Hal broke out of the cover of the pines by
the road and raced hard across the expanse of the clearing. He
felt as exposed as a soldier in a rice paddy. On the far side, he
pushed his way into the woods, through the brush, and out the
other side. And there it was. The barn. Sitting at the end of a
second, smaller field, the moon tilted down on it from overhead
like a spotlight.

Hal moved forward, his feet lightly touching the ground, as if
probing for shards of glass. He heard a voice as he neared the
barn. He stopped. It was Cameron. Hal lowered himself to the
ground and crawled on his stomach the last twenty yards over
the wet grass.

He raised himself on a bale of hay that rested against the
base of the barn. And then he saw that the entire side of the
barn was banked with bales set neatly together like a row of
dominoes. As Hal leaned over the hay searching for an opening
to look through, the smell reached him. He rubbed his hand

along the top of the hay and brought it up to his face. Gasoline. The bales were soaked through with it. Primed at the drop of a match to become a funeral pyre. Once they had used the children for what they wished, was this how they planned to cover their tracks? Hal shuddered at the thought of it.

He pushed his eye against a chink in a board the size of a poker chip and looked inside. There, circled by a ring of moonlight, were the Hilliards. Cameron. Elliott. Laurie. They were dressed completely in black and Hal realized they wore clothing he had never seen before. Nor had anyone else for three hundred years.

"When will Vicky be here?" asked Cameron.

Though Cameron had his back to him, Hal saw that he stood ruler straight. His voice was clear and strong.

"She's on schedule, Grandfather," answered Laurie, kneeling before something that Hal couldn't make out. She reached toward it. What was she doing? Hal canted his head to the side, but the angle was blocked by a thick post. It stood perhaps five feet high, and then he saw there were others, arranged in a semicircle. Of course! The hole he had tripped over so long ago was a socket. Made for, waiting for, one of these posts. What were they for? Silently he counted them. Seven.

"Remember, Vicky has to take the village children home from the hayride first before bringing the others here, Father," said Elliott. "Anything else might raise suspicions. I know she'll have them here on time."

"But why is Howard taking so long?" Cameron said angrily.

"Don't be fearful, Grandfather," said Laurie, still busy, her back turned toward Hal. "You know nothing will stop him. He just has to wait at the hospital for the right moment. He'll have her with us when we need her."

"We must not fail now," the old man said, almost to himself. "They've waited such a long time. Oh, it will be wonderful for all of us. To see it. And taste it. Savor our revenge, like a dog gnawing on a bone."

The old man's words, ripe with passion, caused Hal to recoil. Revenge? What did Cameron mean by that? Instinctively, Hal looked toward Laurie. He had to get a better view of her. He carefully backed away from the barn and moved around to the

other side. The smell of gasoline-drenched hay followed him
with its harsh fiery promise.

Hal found a crack as wide as his thumb. Here, too, bales of
hay stretched out in a perfect line against the barn. And then he
saw what had preoccupied Laurie. It was one of those large
dolls they had seen at the Hilliards' during the house tour. In
that air-conditioned room. His "children," Cameron Hilliard
had called them.

As it had then, the doll sat on a small chair. And there were
the others. Seated alongside the first in an arc that faced the
posts. Laurie and Elliott stood silently behind them, like atten-
dants. Again Hal couldn't keep from looking at the dolls' eyes.
They glinted fiercely under the steady shine of the moon. They
almost seemed to move. But that couldn't be.

"Now," said Cameron, breaking the stillness of the tableau.
"We must ready our children now for the witnessing of what
we have hungered for since they were betrayed."

"Yes, Father," said Elliott, with an excitement that Hal had
never seen in him before. "For so long it's seemed a distant
dream. But now it's going to happen. The blood of the others
will be as warm as sand."

"And their screams will be a chorus to our laughter," answered Cameron, roaring mightily. "Now we must prepare our
children. Vicky and Howard soon will arrive." He paused and
turned searchingly toward his granddaughter. "Laurie?"

"Yes, Grandfather," she said. "I will begin."

She walked to the first doll and knelt again in front of it. She
paused, looking at it the way a parent gazes at a newborn. Then
she reached down to the doll's face, twisted something at its
edge, and gently, tenderly removed the wax face. Hal almost
gasped out loud. For there, beneath what he now could see had
been a mask, was the shriveled, parchment skin of a mummy.
Shriveled except for the eyes, flaring even now with cruel ani-
mation in the ghostly light.

Laurie went to the second doll. Again she lovingly peeled the
waxen guard from its face, and there was the mummy of a girl.
Clinging to its shrunken skull was short, pale hair that looked
as white as cotton in the sheen from the moon. As Laurie
moved inexorably toward the next doll in the arc of chairs, Hal
staggered blindly away from the barn.

A nauseating brew of loathing and terror swirled through him. He pushed his face against the cold ground to keep from screaming. The shock of seeing, almost touching, a partnership of such penetrating horror between the living and the long dead locked his legs in a paralytic rigidity. Who were those dolls? He knew, but he couldn't deal with it yet. He pushed the question from his mind.

Move. Come on. Move, damn it. They didn't have Annie yet. Nor the other children. There was still time. But he had to reach her, and the others too, before they entered the barn.

Hal snaked back the way he had come. The wetness of the grass soaked through his shirt. It felt good. Real. But what he had just seen in the barn was real too. A sickening nightmare that there was no waking from.

When he no longer heard the voices from the barn, he rose and ran back to where he had hidden the Jeep. Howard would be coming soon. He had to stop him. Without thinking he scrambled into the thicket on the side of the road. His hands grasped a fallen tree limb. He quickly threw it aside. Too small. Then he found what he was looking for. A branch as wide as his thigh and long enough to stretch across the road. He felt blood oozing from cuts where bracken flayed him as he struggled to pull the branch onto the road. And then it was done. The branch rested squarely in the middle. Nobody could pass without first moving it aside. He ripped his shirt off and gingerly brushed away the marks his shoes had left in the road. Though it was cold enough for him to see his breath, the night air felt warm against his body.

Hal had moved back into the thicket looking for another branch when he saw the lights of the car. His hands searched blindly until they rested on another dead branch. His fingers circled it easily, too easily, but it would have to do. He moved farther away from the road. His back touched the Jeep. He took a deep breath and waited.

The car stopped ten feet short of the branch in the road. The engine's throaty moan sounded like the quiet growl of a large animal. The car door opened and Howard got out. For a moment he stared at the obstacle. Then, as if it were kindling, he lifted the limb and moved it to the side of the road. Right to where Hal was crouched.

Hal wanted to yell, to send a sound into the night that the whole world would hear, but the only noise he made was an asthmatic grunt as he swung the branch in his hand with all his might against Howard's temple. The limb snapped in half. Howard fell to one knee, his fingers raking blood from his hair, and then, almost in one motion, he sprang at Hal. He slammed Hal's head back against the side of the Jeep. Hal staggered up and opened the car door, why he didn't really know. And then Howard grabbed him. Fingers of reptilian strength laced around Hal's neck and shoved him into the car across the front seat. Hal lay on his back as helpless as an overturned insect. He looked up at Howard's horrible eyes, as emotionless as stone, and knew he was going to die. He tried to claw at the giant's face, but Howard just leaned away from him and smiled. Hal closed his eyes. He heard a gurgling sound, like a partially opened tap, and realized it was coming from him. He tried to scratch at Howard's eyes again and just met air. His right hand fell back between the seats. He felt something. Soft. Then hard. Long. Thin. Metallic. Annie's knitting needles! With his last bit of will he grabbed a needle and thrust it wildly above him. As if he had skewered a ripe melon, he felt the needle enter Howard. The big man's fingers suddenly flew off his throat. Hal opened his eyes to see the button of the knitting needle sticking out of Howard's eye, like a pen in an inkwell. Soundlessly, Howard toppled backward. His hands started to move for the needle, trying vainly to pull it out. Then his legs jerked as if he were at the end of a huge whip. That was all. Nothing more. Then he was quiet.

Hal didn't know how long he lay there on the car seat. He tried to swallow. It felt as if a rusty pipe had been inserted down his throat. He sat up. He coughed and spat. He could taste the blood. He got out and limped over to Howard's car. There on the back seat was Annie, curled catlike, asleep. He reached into the car and shut off the engine. Then he turned off the lights.

When he opened the back door a sweet astringent smell swept over him. Ether. He saw a costume, as old as the ones worn by the Hilliards, folded neatly on the seat beside Annie.

"Honey. Wake up. It's me. Daddy. Please, baby. Wake up."

Hal rubbed Annie's cheeks. Her eyes cracked open. Then

shut. Then they opened fully. She stared at Hal. Not the slightest trace of recognition crossed her eyes. No! Had Howard somehow gotten to her on the drive here? Was she theirs? He remembered what Judy had said. Afterward the children don't laugh.

"Annie, baby. Do you hear me?"

She nodded, confusion struggling with sleepiness.

"Listen, Annie. Knock, knock."

She looked blankly at Hal.

"I said, 'Knock, knock.' "

"Who's there?" said Annie finally, in a tiny voice that Hal hadn't heard from her in years.

"Pencil."

She rubbed her eyes.

"I said, 'Pencil.' "

"Pencil who?" she asked.

"Pencil fall down if you don't wear a belt."

Annie stared at Hal for what seemed like minutes. And then came a smile. And right after that she laughed.

"You're silly, Daddy," she said groggily.

Hal grabbed her tightly and hungrily kissed her face. Thank God. They hadn't reached her yet. She still belonged to Judy and him.

"Stop, Daddy. Your beard is itchy."

He held her in front of him for a moment and then placed her back down on the seat.

"You're very tired, baby. Just rest here. Don't leave the car. I'll be right back. Understand?"

"Yes, Daddy. I'm very sleepy. Where's Mommy? We had an accident. Is Mommy . . ."

Exhaustion silenced her. Hal watched her until he was sure she was sleeping soundly. He knew now what he had to do. He went back to the Jeep, stumbling in the darkness over Howard's body, and reached into the glove compartment for a book of matches. He lighted one. It flared with a hiss. He put out the fire with two fingers.

He ran back to the barn and slid along the wall until he found one of the holes he had looked through before. He jammed his eye against it. He could see all the dolls now. The masks made of wax had been stripped away from them. He forced himself to look at them closely. He knew who they were. They were the remains of the coven children, preserved all these years through some hideous Hilliard alchemy. Bracing himself, he studied their features, grisly with rot but still distinctive. One had a small, nastily bent nose like the barb at the end of a fishhook. Another's lips were so full they seemed ready to burst. The doll at the end, a girl with bangs, had a long, crooked scar. But unlike T.C. Junior's, this one wound like a dangerous road from the corner of her mouth clear across her jaw. He searched for the resemblance between these . . . *things* and their own children, but there was none. None at all.

And then he understood.

Of course. Judy had been right, but also wrong. Very wrong. Their children were duplicates, but not of the evil children. Their children were carbon copies of the good children. The children the coven believed had betrayed them and whom then they had sacrificed. That meant the painting also was of the good children. Of course. A commemorative for the grieving parents. Something for them to remember their poor children by. No wonder the faces in that painting had been slashed to bits. The Hilliards could not tolerate the sight of them. They were the objects of three hundred years of hatred.

"I think I hear them now," said Elliott, breaking into Hal's feverish train of thought.

Yes. Hal heard something too. Far off. It was the children. They were singing.

"See, Grandfather, here they come," said Laurie. "Hannah wouldn't let us down."

Hal saw the old man smile. He reached out toward his granddaughter, and the two embraced. Then as they turned back toward the dolls, Hal saw for the first time a table that had been set up on a circular platform of polished stones. On it, gleaming wickedly, was an array of lethal instruments from Elliott's collection. Scalpels, razors, shears. Not barbering instruments. *Surgical* instruments! And now Hal knew what was going to happen. Unless he could stop it.

Their look-alike children—his Annie!—had been brought to Ripton Falls for one reason. So that they could be killed. Killed in a ritual re-enactment of that first killing. That was the revenge Cameron had spoken of. What had been done to the good children of that time long ago, the Hilliards, the conservators of the coven, would do again to these good children. They would rope the children to the posts. They would slaughter them like animals. They would carve their hearts from them. All in the name of revenge. A revenge that had festered within them and their ancestors for hundreds of years.

Hal gagged at the ferocity of such evil. But then the high, thin sounds of singing washed over him again. The voices were as haunting as the cry of a loon.

> *"Who'll fly at night*
> *When the moon is bright*
> *And the children rush to dream?"*

They were getting closer. Hal had to act now. The accidents had brought the children under the Hilliards' control, but there was still time to break that hold. He must succeed.

Hal lighted the first match as Cameron laughed triumphantly. Laurie and Elliott joined the old man. The sound was as chilling and final as death.

Hal didn't stay to watch the match ignite the hay at the back of the barn. He ran to the front. The door hung open. He could not fail now. He swung the door closed, snapping the latch down with a hard click. He dropped another match on the hay that girdled the front. Now he could hear the roar of the fire at the back of the barn. He ran to the far side but he didn't have to touch a match there—the fire was already racing along the wall like a river at flood tide.

The heat drove Hal back with the force of the wash from a propeller. A board exploded out and he could see the whole interior. The Hilliards were crowded in the center of the barn, their clothes smoldering. They were screaming, their cries soaring above the roar of the flames.

Hal turned and plunged back through the brush and across the clearing to where he knew the wagon would be by now. It was only a hundred feet down the road. He saw a slender figure slip off and run into the woods. He thought for a moment of pursuit. But when he reached the wagon the idea vanished, dispelled by the fixed, empty faces of the children. They too were dressed in clothes hundreds of years old. But they neither moved nor spoke. Their eyes homed in on to the twisting fire that rushed up into the night sky. They were so still, so silent, Hal wondered if they comprehended anything of what they saw.

The old horse that pulled the wagon nervously shifted from side to side. Before the horse could panic, Hal grabbed the bridle and ran with the horse and wagon down the road. As they neared the barn, the screams of the Hilliards echoed out at the night. The children leaned away from the sound like a line of reeds in a storm. Then the screaming stopped. Silence. Silence except for the hungry howl of the fire.

Ahead was Howard's car. And Annie. Hal reined in the horse tightly, trying to steady it to a standstill. He couldn't drop the reins. What would happen to the children? And then he realized something. The children were giggling. No. They were laughing. Really laughing. He was astonished. Laughing and joking? Now? He strained to make out their words.

"Do raisins have fur coats?" T.C. Junior asked Erin.

"Of course not," she answered between giggles, still laughing at something else.

"Then I just sat on a caterpillar!"

This set off another wave of laughter. They laughed so hard tears slid down their cheeks.

And then Hal understood. The Hilliards were dead, and the dark bonds that had held the children had been released.

"Let's wake up Annie!" he shouted at them, exhilarated. He pointed to Howard's car. "She's in there."

Whooping and shouting, the children tumbled out of the wagon and rushed to Annie. Hal tied the horse to a tree and followed them. As soon as Annie was awake, he herded the children into the Jeep. It was a tight fit, which they loved. When he reached his house, he switched on the TV. *Dallas.* Then he called the hospital. The head nurse on Judy's floor started to give him the runaround about it being too late to talk to the patients, but then she lowered her voice and said, "I'll put her on for one moment." Hal had just enough time to tell Judy that Annie was safe. That all the children were safe.

The next call he made was to their neighbors, the Malleys, who lived down the road. Would they watch the children? He wished he could stay with them, but he knew he had to go back. As soon as the Malleys arrived, Hal drove again up through the hills. The smoke from the fire did not reach down into the valley. As the night wore on, no one came to join him.

Hal stood there alone until only ragged fingers of smoke curled from the ashes. By then a line of light traced the horizon. He took a few tentative steps into what had been the barn.

There in the center were the remains of the Hilliards. Three forms now barely discernible as having once been human. He could still tell which had been Laurie. The skull was smaller, more delicate.

He walked to where the arc of chairs had been, then stared at the ground in astonishment. The dolls! The Hilliards' witnesses. Where were they? He kicked at the smoldering ashes. What had happened to the dolls? There had to be something left of them. Clouds of ash like sepulchral parachutes hung in the air. He kicked at the ashes again and again. He knelt in the gray powder and searched maniacally. His hands burned from the heat. There was nothing there. But they had to be here. Some fragments. Something! Where were they? Where were the dolls? Where were the dolls?

The young man looked up at the main departure board in the terminal. Logan International Airport was quiet since it was after eleven on a weekday night. The board flipped its metallic semaphore again, and the young man smiled. That's better, he thought. We finally got a gate number. He checked his watch. Takeoff time was almost an hour away. Time for a brew.

Though he was two years out of college, Jerry Butler had to show his I.D. more often than not when he drank at a bar. It didn't really bother him except when he was with a date. Then, with the girl next to him trying to pretend that *this* was not going on, he would search awkwardly through his wallet for the damned driver's license. Two out of three times he dropped the wallet like a kid magician doing his act in the school auditorium. But the bartender at the upper-level lounge didn't question him. There was only one old guy down at the other end of the bar, and the bartender was trying to get his register receipts straight so he could close down early. He probably would have served Snoopy. The idea of Snoopy sitting at the bar nursing a Bud made Jerry smile.

He sipped his beer slowly. He had just enough money for a cab to his apartment when he got to Chicago. If his dad knew that he had missed his original flight because of sitting through the Kurosawa movie a second time, it would confirm once again his often spoken opinion of his youngest son: "Jerry doesn't march to a different drummer. He crawls to it."

He was thinking about how nice it would be to have another beer when the girl sat down. Though there were at least four empty stools on either side of him, she plopped down right next to him. She was nineteen or twenty and looked great. She carried a huge suitcase. The bartender served her without a word and went back to his work. A screwdriver. I'd love to clone this guy, Jerry thought. He looked straight ahead and saw the girl in the mirror that ran along the back of the bar. The girl's hair was long and the kind of dark brown that picks up whatever light is around and spins it off like one of those mirrored globes that turn above dance floors. Even in the dim light of the bar he could see there was something different about the color of her eyes. Probably gray, but soft, like cat's fur.

"It's only eighty percent correct."

It took Jerry a moment to realize the girl was talking to him. He turned toward her. She was looking at him with the concentration one reserves for an eye chart. She was smiling.

"Because of refraction, I think. At least that's what they said in Physics."

"What?" said Jerry, unable to say much else. Her eyes were beautiful. Looking at them was like stepping into a fogbank.

"What a mirror reveals. Only about eighty percent of what we can see directly. We never see ourselves as clearly as others do."

"That's a real sad thing. Because you're missing a lot," said Jerry, returning her look.

"That's nice. Very nice. I'm flattered. Really. And I'll remember that."

He bought them both another drink. Fuck it, I'll take a bus, he thought.

"I saw you on line checking in. I couldn't help overhearing you. I missed my flight too. This is the first time I've been to Chicago."

As Jerry moved closer to her, he noticed the bandages. Gauze like a spider's web cocooned her hands, barely hiding the redness beneath.

"Campbell's," said the girl, a slight grin playing at the corners of her mouth.

"What?"

"Soup. Vegetarian vegetable. All over both hands. As Julia Child says, 'Never toke while cooking.'" They both laughed hard enough for the bartender to stop his totaling and look over at them.

They exchanged thumbnail biographies. Vicky Leland told Jerry that her name was Vivian Laidlaw and about all the kidding she got when she was growing up about the first part of her last name. Some of the jokes were really funny and they both laughed.

The call came for their flight. Jerry overtipped the bartender out of gratitude. He couldn't get over it. This was a first. A definite first. This knockout had just picked *him* up. He reached over to help her with her suitcase, but she quickly pulled it away from him.

"Come on," he said. "I want to be a gentleman."

"No, that's all right. I always carry my own bags."

He laughed.

"What have you got in there? The family jewels?"

She looked at him, startled for a moment. Then she smiled.

He stood behind her as they waited to board the plane. She absently reached back, pushed her hair aside, and scratched her neck. Her neck was the color of eggshell and curved slightly, like the base of a rainbow. And below her ear was a small mole. Jerry generally never noticed things like that. But this mark was different. It was shaped like a gull and seemed to hang in space above the whiteness of her neck. She removed her hand and the curtain of hair silently slid back.

On the plane they had another drink. First, Jerry toasted his luck at having met Vivian. Then she clicked her plastic glass against Jerry's again. To her first friend in Chicago.

She looked out the small window and watched the lights of a city, like birthday candles set against a black sea, slip by below. She thought of the suitcase riding silently in the baggage compartment. It seemed so ordinary. Just another girl traveling with too many clothes. She smiled. The red blisters and scorched skin that were hidden by the gauze bandages didn't bother her a bit. The fulfillment of her hatred, a fulfillment she knew she would find someday back in Ripton Falls, cooled her hands like ice in a tall glass. She would have to wait. A long time. But eventually she would return to Ripton Falls. *They* would return. For she felt the power of Cameron and Laurie, of Elliott and Howard too, of all the Hilliards who had gone before, burning malignantly inside her. Stronger than ever before.

And the next time, nothing would stop them.

The city was gone now. Only the darkness of the night, black as death, remained. She loved the night. For it was there that someday at last they would be avenged.

ABOUT THE AUTHOR

Brooks Stanwood is Howard and Susan Kaminsky. Their first novel, *The Glow,* published here in 1979, was also translated into eight languages and sold to the movies. Howard, who wrote screenplays before embarking on a novelist's career with his wife, is the president and publisher of Warner Books. Susan was a fiction editor at the *Saturday Evening Post* and a senior editor at E.P. Dutton before leaving to devote herself full time to writing. They live with their eight-year-old daughter in a landmark building in Manhattan and spend the weekends in a two-hundred-year-old house in a small town in the Berkshires that has neither village green nor evil doings.